The Mystery of Mr. Bernard Brown

The Mystery of Mr. Bernard Brown

E. Phillips Oppenheim

MINT EDITIONS

The Mystery of Mr. Bernard Brown was first published in 1896.

This edition published by Mint Editions 2021.

ISBN 9781513281209 | E-ISBN 9781513286228

Published by Mint Editions®

MINT
EDITIONS

minteditionbooks.com

Publishing Director: Jennifer Newens
Design & Production: Rachel Lopez Metzger
Project Manager: Micaela Clark
Typesetting: Westchester Publishing Services

Contents

I

Falcon's Nest

Thurwell Court, by Thurwell-on-the-Sea, lay bathed in the quiet freshness of an early morning. The dewdrops were still sparkling upon the terraced lawns like little globules of flashing silver, and the tumult of noisy songsters from the thick shrubberies alone broke the sweet silence. The peacocks strutting about the grey stone balcony and perched upon the worn balustrade were in deshabille, not being accustomed to display their splendors to an empty paradise, and the few fat blackbirds who were hopping about on the lawn did so in a desultory manner, as though they were only half awake and had turned out under protest. Stillness reigned everywhere, but it was the sweet hush of slowly awakening day rather than the drowsy, languorous quiet of exhausted afternoon. With one's eyes shut one could tell that the pulse of day was only just beginning to beat. The pure atmosphere was buoyant with the vigorous promise of morning, and gently laden with the mingled perfumes of slowly opening flowers. There was life in the breathless air.

The sunlight was everywhere. In the distance it lay upon the dark hillside, played upon the deep yellow gorse and purple heather of the moorland, and, further away still, flashed upon a long silver streak of the German Ocean. In the old-fashioned gardens of the court it shone upon luscious peaches hanging on the time-mellowed red-brick walls; lit up the face and gleamed upon the hands of the stable clock, and warmed the ancient heart of the stooping, grey-haired old gardener's help who, with blinking eyes and hands tucked in his trousers pockets, was smoking a matutinal pipe, seated on the wheelbarrow outside the tool shed.

Around the mansion itself it was very busy, casting a thousand sunbeams upon its long line of oriel windows, and many quaint shadows of its begabled roof upon the lawns and bright flower-beds below. On one of the terraces a breakfast-table was laid for two, and here its splendour was absolutely dazzling. It gleamed upon the sparkling silver, and the snow-white tablecloth; shone with a delicate softness upon the freshly-gathered fruit and brilliant flowers, and seemed to hover with a gentle burnished light upon the ruddy golden hair of a girl who sat there waiting, with her arm resting lightly upon the stone balustrade, and her eyes straying over the quaint well-kept gardens to the open moorland and dark patches of wooded country beyond.

"Good morning, Helen! First, as usual."

She turned round with a somewhat languid greeting. A tall, well-made man, a little past middle-age, in gaiters and light tweed coat, had stepped out on to the balcony from one of the open windows. In his right hand he was swinging carelessly backwards and forwards by a long strap a well-worn letter-bag.

"Is breakfast ready?" he inquired.

"Waiting for you, father," she answered, touching a small handbell by her side. "Try one of those peaches. Burdett says they are the finest he ever raised."

He stretched out his hand for one, and sinking into a low basket chair, commenced lazily to peel it, with his eyes wandering over the sunny landscape. A footman brought out the tea equipage and some silver-covered dishes, and, after silently arranging them upon the table, withdrew.

"What an exquisite morning!" Mr. Thurwell remarked, looking up at the blue cloudless sky, and pulling his cap a little closer over his eyes to protect them from the sun. "We might be in Italy again."

"Indeed we might," she answered. "I am going to imagine that we are, and make my breakfast of peaches and cream and chocolate! Shall I give you some?"

He shook his head, with a little grimace.

"No, thanks. I'm Philistine enough to prefer devilled kidneys and tea. I wonder if there is anything in the letters."

He drew a key from his waistcoat pocket, and, unlocking the bag, shook its contents upon the tablecloth. His daughter looked at the pile with a faint show of interest. There were one or two invitations, which he tossed over to her, a few business letters, which he put on one side for more leisurely perusal later on, and a little packet from his agent which he opened at once, and the contents of which brought a slight frown into his handsome face.

Helen Thurwell glanced through her share without finding anything interesting. Tennis parties, archery meetings, a bazaar fête; absolutely nothing fresh. She was so tired of all that sort of thing—tired of eternally meeting the same little set of people, and joining in the same round of so-called amusements. There was nothing in Northshire society which attracted her. It was all very stupid, and she was very much bored.

"Some news here that will interest you, Helen," her father remarked suddenly. "Who do you think is coming home?"

She shook her head. She was not in the least curious.

"I don't remember any one going away lately," she remarked. "How warm it is!"

"Sir Geoffrey Kynaston is coming back."

After all, she was a little interested. She looked away from the sunny gardens and into her father's face.

"Really!"

"It is a fact!" he declared. "Douglas says that he will be here to-day or to-morrow. Let me see, it must be nearly fifteen years since he was in England. Time he settled down, if he means to at all."

"Was he very wild, then?" she asked.

The squire nodded.

"Rather!" he answered dryly. "I dare say people will have forgotten all about it by now, though. Forty thousand a year covers a multitude of sins, especially in a tenth baronet!"

She asked no more questions, but leaned back in her chair, and looked thoughtfully across the open country towards the grey turrets of Kynaston Towers, from which a flag was flying. Mr. Thurwell re-read his agent's letter with a slight frown upon his forehead.

"I don't know what to do here," he remarked.

"What is it?" she asked absently. She was watching the flag slowly unfurling itself in the breeze, and fluttering languidly above the tree-tops. It was odd to think that a master was coming to rule there.

"It's about Falcon's Nest. I wish I'd never thought of letting it!"

"Why? It would be a great deal better occupied, surely!"

"If I could let it to a decent tenant, of course it would. But, you know that fellow Chapman, of Mallory? He wants it!"

She looked up at him quickly.

"You surely would not let it to a man like that?"

"Certainly not. But, on the other hand, I don't want to offend him. If I were to decide to stand for the county at the next election, he would be my most useful man in Mallory, or my worst enemy. He's just the sort of fellow to take offence—quickly, too."

"Can't you tell him it's let?"

"Not unless I do let it to some one. Of course not!"

"But are there no other applications?"

"Yes, there is one other," he answered; "but the most awkward part of it is that it's from a complete stranger. Fellow who calls himself 'Brown.'"

"Let me see the letter," she said.

He passed it over the table to her. It was written on plain notepaper, in a peculiar, cramped handwriting.

London, May 30

Dear Sir,

I understand, from an advertisement in this week's *Field*, that you are willing to let "Falcon's Nest," situated on your estate. I shall be happy to take it at the rent you quote, if not already disposed of. My solicitors are Messrs. Cuthbert, of Lincoln's Inn; and my bankers, Gregsons. I may add that I am a bachelor, living alone. The favor of your immediate reply will much oblige,

Yours faithfully,
Bernard Brown

She folded the letter up, and returned it to her father without remark.

"You see," Mr. Thurwell said, "my only chance of escaping from Chapman, without offending him, is to say that it is already let, and to accept this fellow's offer straight off. But it's an awful risk. How do I know that Brown isn't a retired tallow-chandler or something of that sort?"

"Why not telegraph to his solicitors?" she suggested; "they would know who he was, I suppose."

"That's not a bad idea!" he declared. "Morton shall ride over to Mallory at once. I'm glad you thought of it, Helen."

Having come to this decision, Mr. Thurwell turned round and made an excellent breakfast, after which he and his daughter spent the day very much in the same manner as any other English country gentleman and young lady are in the habit of doing. He made a pretense of writing some letters and arranging some business affairs with his agent in the library for an hour, and, later on in the morning, he drove over to Mallory, and took his seat on the magistrates' bench during the hearing of a poaching case. After lunch, he rode to an outlying farm to inspect a new system of drainage, and when he returned, about an hour before dinner-time, he considered that he had done a good day's work.

Helen spent the early part of the morning in the garden, and arranging freshly cut flowers about the house. Then she practised for an hour, solely out of a sense of duty, for she was no musician. Directly the time was up, she closed the piano with a sigh of relief, and spent the rest of the time before two o'clock reading a rather stupid novel. After luncheon she made a call several miles off, driving herself in a light-brown cart, and played several sets of tennis, having for her partner a very mild and brainless young curate. At dinner-time she and her father met again, and when he entered the room he had two slips of orange-colored paper in his hand.

"Well, what news?" she inquired.

He handed the telegrams to her without a word, and she glanced them through. The first was from the bankers.

To Guy Davenant Thurwell, Esq.,
Thurwell Court, Northshire

"We consider Mr. Brown a desirable tenant for you from a pecuniary point of view. We know nothing of his family."

The other one was from his lawyers.

To Guy D. Thurwell, Esq.,
Thurwell Court, Northshire

"Mr. Brown is a gentleman of means, and quite in a position to rent 'Falcon's Nest.' We are not at liberty to say anything as to his antecedents or family."

"What am I to do?" asked Mr. Thurwell, undecidedly. "I don't like the end of this last telegram. A solicitor ought to be able to say a little more about a client than that."

Helen considered for a moment. She was so little interested in the matter that she found it difficult to make up her mind either way. Afterwards she scarcely dared think of that moment's indecision.

"Perhaps so," she said. "All the same, I detest Mr. Chapman. I should vote for Mr. Brown."

"Mr. Brown it shall be, then!" he answered. "Douglas shall write him to-morrow."

A fortnight later Mr. Bernard Brown took up his quarters at Falcon's Nest.

II

The Murder near the Falcon's Nest

I call it perfectly dreadful of those men!" Helen Thurwell exclaimed suddenly. "They're more than an hour late, and I'm desperately hungry!"

"It is rank ingratitude!" Rachel Kynaston sighed. "I positively cannot sit still and look at that luncheon any longer. Groves, give me a biscuit."

They were both seated on low folding-chairs out on the open moorland, only a few yards away from the edge of the rugged line of cliffs against which, many hundreds of feet below, the sea was breaking with a low monotonous murmur. Close behind them, on a level stretch of springy turf, a roughly improvised table, covered with a cloth of dazzling whiteness, was laden with deep bowls of lobster salad, *pâtes de foie gras*, chickens, truffled turkeys, piles of hothouse fruit, and many other delicacies peculiarly appreciated at *al fresco* symposia; and, a little further away still, under the shade of a huge yellow gorse bush, were several ice-pails, in which were reposing many rows of gold-foiled bottles. The warm sun was just sufficiently tempered by a mild heather-scented breeze, and though it flashed gayly upon the glass and silver, and danced across the bosom of the blue water below, its heat was more pleasant than oppressive. The two women who sat there looked delightfully cool. Helen Thurwell especially, in her white holland gown, with a great bunch of heather stuck in her belt, and a faint healthy glow in her cheeks, looked as only an English country girl of good birth can look—the very personification of dainty freshness.

"There go the guns again!" she exclaimed. "Listen to the echoes. They can't be far away now."

There was a little murmur of satisfaction. Every allowance is to be made for such a keen sportsman as Mr. Thurwell on the glorious twelfth, but the time fixed for the rendezvous had been exceeded by more than an hour.

"I have reached the limit of my endurance!" Rachel Kynaston declared, getting up from her seat. "I must either lunch or faint! As a matter of choice, I prefer the former."

"They will be here directly, miss," Groves remarked, as he completed the finishing touches which he had been putting to the table, and stepped back a little to view the effect. So far as he was concerned they might come any time now. For once his subordinates had not failed him. Nothing had been forgotten; and, on the whole, he felt that he had reason to be proud of his handiwork.

He glanced away inland again, shading his eyes with his hand.

"They'll be coming round the Black Copse in five minutes," he said, half to himself. "James, get the other chairs out of the wagon."

Rachel Kynaston was still standing up looking around her. Suddenly her eyes fell upon a quaintly built cottage, perched upon the edge of the cliff about a mile away.

"I meant to ask you before, Helen," she exclaimed. "Who lives in that extraordinary-looking building—Falcon's Nest, I think you call it?"

She moved her parasol in its direction, and looked at it curiously. A strange-looking abode it certainly was; built of yellow stone, with a background of stunted fir trees which stretched half way down the cliff side.

Helen Thurwell looked across at it indifferently.

"I can tell you his name, and that is all," she answered. "He calls himself Mr. Brown—Mr. Bernard Brown."

"Well, who is he? What does he do?"

Helen shook her head.

"Really, I haven't the least idea," she declared. "I do not even know what he is like. He has been there for two months, and we haven't seen him yet. Papa called upon him, but he was out. He has not returned the call! He—oh, bother Mr. Brown, here they come! I'm so glad!"

They both got up and looked. Rounding the corner of a long plantation, about half a mile away, were several men in broken line, with their guns under their arms; and a little way behind came three keepers, carrying bags.

Rachel Kynaston looked at them fixedly.

"One, two, three, four, five," she counted. "One short. I don't see Geoffrey."

Helen moved to her side, and shaded her eyes with her hand. On the fourth finger a half hoop of diamonds, which had not been there three months ago, was flashing in the sunlight.

"Neither do I," she said. "I wonder where he is."

Her tone was a little indifferent, considering that it was her *fiancé* who was missing. But no one ever looked for much display of feeling from Helen Thurwell, not even the man who called himself her lover. Indeed, her unresponsiveness to his advances—a sort of delicate composure which he was powerless in any way to break through—had been her strongest attraction to Sir Geoffrey Kynaston, who was quite unused to anything of the sort.

The men quickened their pace, and emptying their guns into the air, soon came within hailing distance. On that particular day of the year there was only one possible greeting, and Helen and her companion contented themselves with a monosyllable.

"Well?"

Mr. Thurwell was in the front rank, and evidently in the best of spirits. It was he who answered them.

"Capital sport!" he declared heartily. "Birds a little wild, but strong, and plenty of them. We've made a big bag for only three guns. Sir Geoffrey was in capital form. Groves, open a bottle of Heidseck."

"Where is Geoffrey?" asked Rachel—his sister.

Mr. Thurwell looked round and discovered his absence for the first time.

"I really don't know," he answered, a little bewildered; "He was with us a few minutes ago. What's become of Sir Geoffrey Kynaston, Heggs?" he asked, turning round to one of the gamekeepers.

"He left us at the top of the Black Copse, sir," the man answered. "He was coming round by the other side—shot a woodcock there once, sir," he said.

They glanced across the moor toward Falcon's Nest. There was no one in sight.

"He's had plenty of time to get round," remarked Lord Lathon, throwing down his gun. "Perhaps he's resting."

Mr. Thurwell shook his head.

"No; he wouldn't do that," he said. "He was as keen about getting here as any of us. Hark! what was that?"

A faint sound was borne across the moor on the lazily stirring breeze. Helen, whose hearing was very keen, started, and the little party exchanged uneasy glances.

"It must have been a sea-gull," remarked Lord Lathon, who wanted his luncheon very badly indeed. "We'd better not wait for him. He'll turn up all right; Geoffrey always does. Come—"

He broke off suddenly in his speech and listened. There was another sound, and this time there was no mistake about it. It was the low, prolonged howl of a spaniel—a mournful sound which struck a strange note in the afternoon stillness. There was breathless silence for a moment amongst the little group, and the becoming glow died out of Helen's cheek.

Rachel Kynaston was the first to recover herself.

"Had Sir Geoffrey a dog with him, Heggs?" she asked quickly.

"Yes, miss," the man answered. "His favorite spaniel had got unchained somehow, and found us on the moor. I saw her at heel when he left us. She was very quiet, and Sir Geoffrey wouldn't have her sent back."

"Then something has happened to him!" she cried. "That was Fido's howl."

"Has anyone heard his gun?" Mr. Thurwell asked.

There was no one left to answer him. They had all started across the moor toward the black patch of spinneys around which Sir Geoffrey should have come. Mr. Thurwell, forgetting his fatigue, hurried after them; and Helen, after a moment's hesitation, followed too, some distance behind.

She ran swiftly, but her dress caught often in the prickly gorse, and she had to pause each time to release herself. Soon she found herself alone, for the others had all turned the corner of the plantation before she reached it. There was a strong, sickly sense of coming disaster swelling in her heart, and her knees were tottering. Still she held on her way bravely. A few yards before she reached the corner of the plantation, she almost ran into the arms of Lord Lathon, who was hurrying back to meet her. There was a ghastly shade in his pale face, and his voice trembled.

"Miss Thurwell," he exclaimed in an agitated tone, "you must not come! Let me take you back. Something—has happened! I am going to Rachel. Come with me."

She drew away from him, and threw off his restraining arm.

"No; I must see for myself. Let me pass, please—at once."

He tried again to prevent her, but she eluded him. A few rapid steps and she had gained the corner. There they all were in a little group scarcely a dozen yards away. A mist floated before her eyes, but she would see; she was determined that she would see this thing for herself. She struggled on a few steps nearer. There was something lying on the grass around which they were all gathered; something very much like a human shape. Ah! she could see more plainly now. It was Sir Geoffrey—

Sir Geoffrey Kynaston. He was lying half on the grass and half in the dry ditch. His white face was upturned to the cloudless sky; by his side, and discoloring his brown tweed shooting coat, was a dark wet stain. In the midst of it something bright was flashing in the sunlight.

She stood still, rooted to the spot with a great horror. Her pulses had ceased to beat. The warm summer day seemed suddenly to have closed in around her. There was a singing in her ears, and she found herself battling hard with a deadly faintness. Yet she found words.

"Has he—shot himself?" she cried. "Is it an accident?"

Her father turned round with a little cry, and hastened to her side.

"Helen!" he gasped. "You should not be here! Come away, child! I sent Lathon—"

"I will know—what it is. Is it an accident? Is he—dead?"

He shook his head. The healthy sunburnt tan had left his face, and he was white to the lips.

"He has been murdered!" he faltered. "Foully, brutally murdered!"

III

Mr. Bernard Brown

Murder is generally associated in one's mind with darkness, the still hours of night, and bestiality. It is the outcome of the fierce animal lust for blood, provoked by low passions working in low minds. De Quincey's brilliant attempt to elevate it to a place among the fine arts has only enriched its horrors as an abstract idea. Even detached from its usual environment of darkness, and ignorance, and vice, it is an ugly thing.

But here was something quite different. Such a tragedy as this which had just occurred was possessed of a peculiar hideousness of its own. It seemed to have completely laid hold of the little group of men gathered round the body of Sir Geoffrey Kynaston; to have bereft them of all reasoning power and thought, to have numbed even their limbs and physical instincts. It was only a few minutes ago since they had left him, careless and debonair, with his thoughts intent upon the business, or rather the sport, of the hour. His laugh had been the loudest, his enjoyment the keenest, and his gun the most deadly of them all. But now he lay there cold and lifeless, with his heart's blood staining the green turf, and his sightless eyes dull and glazed. It was an awful thing!

Physically, he had been the very model of an English country gentleman, tall and powerful, with great broad shoulders, and strikingly upright carriage, full of vigorous animal life, with the slight restlessness of the constant traveler banished by his sudden passion for the girl who had so lately promised to be his wife.

She drew a little nearer—they were all too much overcome by the shock of this thing to prevent her—and stood with glazed eyes looking down upon him. Everything, even the minutest article of his dress, seemed to appeal to her with a strange vividness. She found herself even studying the large check of his shooting-coat and the stockings which she had once laughingly admired, and which he had ever since worn. Her eyes rested upon the sprig of heliotrope which, with her own fingers, she had arranged in his button hole, as they had strolled down the garden together just before the start; and the faint perfume which reached her where she stood, helped her to realize that she was in the thrall of no nightmare, but that this thing had really happened. She had never loved him, she had never even pretended to love him, and it was less any sense of personal loss than the hideous sin of it which swept in upon her as she stood there looking down upon him. She recognized, as she could never have done had he been personally dear to her, the ethical horror of the thing. The faintness which had almost numbed her senses passed away. In that swift battle of many sensations it was anger which survived.

Her voice first broke the deep, awed stillness.

"Who has done this?" she cried, pointing downward.

Her words were like a sudden awakening to them all. They had been standing like figures in a silent tableau, stricken dumb and motionless. Now there was a stir. The fire in her tone had dissolved their torpor. She was standing on rising ground a little above the rest of them, and her attitude, together with the gesture by which she enforced her words, was full of intense dramatic force. The slim undulating beauty of her form was enhanced by the slight disorder of her dress, and her red-gold hair—she had lost her hat—shone and glistened in the sunlight till every thread was shining like burnished gold. They themselves were in the shade of the dark pine trees, and she standing upon the margin of the moor with the warm sunlight glowing around her, seemed like a being of another world. Afterwards when they recalled that scene—and there was no one there who ever forgot it—they could scarcely tell which seemed the most terrible part to them—the lifeless body of the murdered man with the terrible writing of death in his white face, or the tragic figure of Helen Thurwell, the squire's cold, graceful daughter, with her placid features and whole being suddenly transformed with this wave of passion.

Mr. Thurwell drew a few steps backward, and his keen gray eyes swept the open country round.

"There was no one in sight when we got here; but the blackguard can't be far away!" he said. "Heggs, and you, Smith, and you, Cook, go through the spinney as fast as you can, one in the middle and one on each side, mind! I will go up Falcon's Hill and look round. Jem, run to Mallory as fast as you can for Dr. Holmes, and on to the police station. Quick! all of you. There's not a moment to lose!"

The desire for action was as strong in them now as had been their former torpor. Mr. Thurwell and his daughter were alone in less than a minute.

E. PHILLIPS OPPENHEIM

"Helen, I forgot you!" he exclaimed. "I can't leave you alone, and some one must stay here. Where is Lathon?"

"He has gone on to take Rachel home," she answered. "I will stay here. I am not afraid. Quick! you can see for miles from the top of the hill and you have your field glass. Oh, do go. Go!"

He hesitated, but she was evidently very much in earnest.

"I will just climb the hill and hurry down again," he said. "I cannot leave you here for more than a few minutes. If only we had more men with us!"

He turned away, and walked swiftly across the moor toward the hill. For a minute or two she stood watching his departing figure. Then she turned round with a shudder and buried her face in her clasped hands. Her appearance was less hard now and more natural, for a sickly sense of horror at the sight of his body was commencing to assert itself over that first strange instinct of passionate anger. It was none the less dreadful to her because in a certain way his removal was a release. She had promised to marry this man, but there had been scarcely a moment since when she had not found herself regretting it. Now the sense of freedom, which she could not altogether evade, was like torture to her. She dropped on her knees by his side, and took his cold hand in hers. A few hours ago she dared not have done this, knowing very well that at the caressing touch of her fingers, she would have felt his strong arms around her in a passionate and distasteful embrace. But there was no fear of this now. She would never have to shrink away from him again. He was dead!

The warm sunlight was glancing among the thickly growing pine trees in the plantation by her side, casting quaint shadows on the cone-strewn ground, across the little piece of broken paling in the bottom of the dry ditch, and upon the mossy bank where his head was resting upon a sweet-smelling tuft of heather. Most of all it flashed and glittered upon the inch or two of steel which still lay buried in his side—a curiously shaped little dagger which, although she strove to keep her eyes away from it, seemed to have a sort of fascination for her. Every time her eyes fell upon it, she turned away quickly with a little shudder; but, nevertheless, she looked at it more than once—and she remembered it.

The deep stillness of the autumn afternoon presently became almost oppressive to her. There was the far-off, sweet low murmur of a placid sea rolling in upon the base of the cliffs, the constant chirping of ground insects, and the occasional scurrying of a rabbit through the undergrowth. Once a great lean rat stole up from the ditch, and—horrible—ran across his body; but at the sound of her startled movement it paused, sat for a moment quite still, with its wide-open black eyes blinking at her, and then to her inexpressible relief scampered away. She was used to the country, with its intense unbroken silence, but she had never felt it so hard to bear as on that afternoon. Time became purely relative to her. As a matter of fact, she knew afterwards that she could not have been alone more than five minutes. It was like an eternity. She listened in vain for any human sound, even for the far-off sweep of the scythe in the bracken, or the call of the laborer to his horses. The tension of those moments was horrible.

She plucked a handful of bay leaves from the ditch, and strove, by pressing them against her temple, to cool the fever in her blood. Then she took up once more her position by his side, for horrible though the sight of it was, his body seemed to have a sort of fascination for her, and she could not wander far away from it. Once or twice she had looked round, but there had been no human figure in sight, nor any sign of any. But as she knelt there on the short turf, pressing the cool leaves to her aching forehead, she was suddenly conscious of a new sensation. Without hearing or seeing anything, she knew that some one was approaching, and, stranger still, she was conscious of a distinct reluctance to turn her head and see who it was. She heard no footsteps; the soft stillness was broken by the sound of no human voice. She wished to turn round, and yet she shrank from it. Something fresh was going to happen—something was at hand to trouble her. She made a great effort, and rose to her feet. Then, breaking through her conscious reluctance, she turned round.

A single figure, at that moment on a slightly elevated ridge of the bare moor, stood out against the sky. He was walking swiftly toward her, and yet without any appearance of hurry; and from the direction in which he was coming, it was evident that he had just left Falcon's Nest. This fact and his being unknown to her sufficiently established his identity. It was her father's tenant, Mr. Bernard Brown.

IV

An Evil End to an Evil Life

They say that, as a rule, the most grotesquely unimportant trifles flash into the mind and engage the last thoughts of a drowning man. Regarding this in the light of an analogy, something of the same sort was now happening to Helen Thurwell.

With her mind steeped in the horror of the last few hours, she yet found that she was able afterwards to recall every slight particular with regard to this man's appearance, and even his dress. She remembered the firm evenness of his movements, swift, yet free from all ungraceful haste; the extreme shabbiness of his coat, his ill-arranged neck-tie, escaped from all restraint of collar and waistcoat, and flying loosely behind him; his trousers very much turned up, and very much frayed, and the almost singular height of his loose angular figure. His face, too—she remembered that better than anything—with its pale hollow cheeks and delicate outline, deep-set dark blue eyes, black eyebrows, and long, unkempt hair, which would have looked very much the better for a little trimming. A man utterly regardless of his appearance, untidy, almost slovenly in his attire, yet with something about him different from other men.

He was within a few yards of her when she saw a sudden change flash into his face as their eyes met. He hesitated and a faint color came into his cheeks, only to fade away again immediately, leaving them whiter than ever. There was something in his intense gaze which at that time she had no means of understanding. But it was over in a moment. He advanced rapidly, and stood by her side.

She still watched him. She could see that his whole frame was vibrating with strong internal emotion as he looked downward on the glazed eyes and motionless form of the murdered man. His lips were pallid, and his hands were tightly clasped together. There was one thing which seemed to her very strange. He had not started, or exhibited the least sign of surprise at the dreadful sight. It was almost as though he had known all about it.

"This is a terrible thing," she said in a low tone, breaking the silence between them for the first time. "You have heard of it, I suppose?"

He dropped down on one knee, and bent close over the dead man, feeling his heart and pulse. In that position his face was hidden from her.

"No; I knew nothing. He has been killed—like this?"

"Yes."

"Did anyone see it? Is the man caught?"

"We know nothing," she answered. "We found him like this. There was no one in sight."

He rose deliberately to his feet. Her heart was beating fast now, and she looked searchingly into his face. It told her little. He was grave, but perfectly composed.

"How is it that you are alone here?" he asked. "Does no one else know of this?"

She moved her head in assent.

"Yes; but they have all gone to hunt for the murderer. If only you had been looking from your window, you would have seen it all!"

He did not look as though he shared her regret. He was standing on the other side of the dead man, with his arms folded and his eyes fixed steadily upon the cold white face. He seemed to have forgotten her presence.

"An evil end to an evil life," he said slowly to himself, and then he added something which she did not hear.

"You knew him, then?"

He looked at her for a moment fixedly, and then down again into the dead man's face.

"I have heard of him abroad," he said. "Sir Geoffrey Kynaston was a man with a reputation."

"You will remember that he is dead," she said slowly, for the scorn in his words troubled her.

He bowed his head, and was silent. Watching him closely, she could see that he was far more deeply moved than appeared on the surface. His teeth were set together, and there was a curious faint flush of color in his livid cheeks. She followed his eyes, wondering. They were fixed, not upon the dead man's face, but on the dagger which lay buried in his heart, and the handle of which was still visible.

"That should be a clue," he remarked, breaking a short silence.

"Yes. I hope to God that they will find the wretch!" she answered passionately.

She looked up at him as she spoke. His eyes were traveling over the moor, and his hand was shading them.

"There is some one coming," he said. "We shall know very soon."

She followed his rapt gaze, and saw three men coming toward them. One was her father, another the underkeeper, and the third was a stranger.

V

The Inner Room at the Falcon's Nest

Together they watched the approaching figures. Helen, standing a little apart, had the better view.

"There is my father, and Heggs, and some one whom I do not know," she announced quietly. "I wonder if it is a doctor."

He did not answer her. She glanced toward him, wondering at his silence and rigid attitude. His eyes were still bent upon the three men, and there was a hard, strained look in his white face. While she was watching him she saw a spasm of what seemed almost like physical pain pass across his countenance. Certainly this was no unfeeling man. In his way he seemed as deeply moved as she herself was.

They were quite close now, and she had a good view of the stranger. He did not look, by any means, a person to be afraid of. In all her life she thought she had never seen such a handsome old gentleman—and gentleman he most assuredly was. His hair was quite white, and his beard—carefully trimmed and pointed after the fashion of one of Velasquez' pictures—was of the same color. Yet his walk was upright and vigorous, and he carried himself with dignity. His high forehead, and rather long, oval face, with its delicate, clearly cut features, had at once the stamp of intellect and benevolence, and, as though preserved by careful and refined living, had still much of the freshness of youth. He was dressed in a rough tweed walking-suit, with gaiters and thick boots, and carried under his arm a somewhat ponderous book, and a botanical specimen case. Helen felt a woman's instinctive liking for him before she had even heard him speak.

"Have you thought us long, Helen?" her father exclaimed anxiously. "We haven't seen anything of the scoundrel, but Heggs was fortunate enough to meet Sir Allan Beaumerville on the moor, and he very kindly offered to return."

Sir Allan was on his knees by the body before Mr. Thurwell had finished his sentence. They all watched his brief examination.

"Poor fellow! poor fellow!" he exclaimed in a shocked tone. "That wretched thing"—lightly touching the handle of the dagger—"is clean through his heart. It was a strong, cruel arm that drove that home.

Nothing can be done, of course. He must have died within a few seconds!" He rose from his knees and looked around. "What is to be done with the body?" he asked. "It must be removed somewhere. Sir Geoffrey Kynaston, did you say it was? Dear me! dear me! I knew his sister quite well."

"She is not far away," Mr. Thurwell said. "She and my daughter were awaiting luncheon for us on the cliffs yonder, when this horrible thing occurred. Lathon went back to look for her. We were afraid that she might follow us here. She was very fond of her brother, and he had only just returned home after many years' traveling."

"Poor fellow!" Sir Allan said softly. "But about moving him. Who lives in that queer-looking place yonder?"

Mr. Thurwell, who knew his tenant by sight, although they had never spoken, looked at him and hesitated. Sir Allan did the same.

"That is where I live," Mr. Brown said slowly. "If Mr. Thurwell thinks well, let him be taken there."

He spoke without looking round or addressing any one in particular. His back was turned upon the celebrated physician.

"The nearest place would be best, in a case like this," Sir Allan remarked. "Have you sent for any help?"

"Some of my men are coming across the moor there," Mr. Thurwell said, pointing them out. "They can take a gate off the hinges to carry him on."

A little troop of awed servants, whom Lord Lathon had sent down from the Court, together with some farm laborers whom they had picked up on the way, were soon on the spot.

Mr. Thurwell gave some brief directions, and in a few minutes the high five-barred gate, with "private" painted across it in white letters, was taken from its hinges, and the body carefully laid upon it. Then Mr. Thurwell turned resolutely to his daughter.

"Helen, you must go home now," he said firmly. "Jackson will take you. We can spare him easily."

She shook her head.

"I would rather stay," she said quietly. "I shall not faint, or do anything stupid, I promise you."

Sir Allan Beaumerville looked at her curiously. It was a strange thing to him, notwithstanding his wide experience, to find a girl of her years so little outwardly moved by so terrible a tragedy. Mr. Thurwell, too, was surprised. He knew that she had never loved Sir Geoffrey

Kynaston, but, nevertheless, he had expected her to show more emotion than this, if only for the horror of it all. And yet, looking at her more closely, he began to understand—to realize that her calmness was only attained by a strenuous repression of feeling, and that underneath it all was something very different. Though her voice was firm, her cheeks were deadly pale, and there was a peculiar tightening of the lips and light in her eyes which puzzled him. Her expression seemed to speak less of passive grief, than of some active determination—some strong desire. She had all the appearance of a woman who was bracing herself up for some ordeal, nerving herself with all the stimulus of a firm will to triumph over her natural feelings, and follow out a difficult purpose. Mr. Thurwell scarcely recognized his own daughter. She was no longer a somewhat languid, beautiful girl, looking out upon the world with a sort of petulant indifference—petulant, because, with all the high aspirations of a somewhat romantic disposition, she could see nothing in it to interest her. All that had passed away. The warm breath of some awakening force in her nature seemed to have swept before it all her languor, and all her petulance. They were gone, and in their place was a certain air of reserve and thoughtful strength which seems always to cling to those men and women who face the world with a definite purpose before them. Mr. Thurwell knitted his brows, and had nothing to say.

A sad little procession was formed, and started slowly for the cottage on the cliff side, the four stalwart men stooping beneath their heavy burden, and somehow falling into the measured steady tramp common to corpse bearers. None of them ever forgot that walk. Slowly they wound their way around many brilliant patches of deep yellow gorse and purple heather, and the warm sunlight glancing across the moor and glittering away over the water threw a strange glow upon the still, cold face of their ghastly burden. A soft breeze sprung from the sea, herald of the advancing eventide, following the drowsy languor of the perfect autumnal day. The faintly stirred air was full of its quickening exhilaration, but it found no human response in their heavy hearts. Solemn thoughts and silence came over all of them. Scarcely a word was spoken on the way to their destination.

By some chance, or at least it seemed like chance, Helen found herself a few steps behind the others, with Mr. Brown by her side. They, too, walked along in unbroken silence. His eyes were steadily fixed upon the ground, hers were wandering idly across the sparkling blue sea with its foam-crested furrows to the horizon. Whatever her thoughts were, they had changed her expression for the time; to a certain extent its late definiteness was gone, and a dreamy, refined abstraction had taken its place.

"If I had to die," she said, half to herself, "I would choose to die on such a day as this."

He raised his dark eyes and looked at her.

"Why?"

"I scarcely know," she said hesitatingly. "And yet, in my own mind, I do. It is so beautiful! It seems to give one a sense of peace and hope—I cannot explain it. It is the sort of thing one feels, and feels only."

He looked down again.

"I know what you mean. You would fear annihilation less?"

"Annihilation! Is that your creed?"

"Sometimes, if it were not for scenes like this, I might believe it possible," he answered slowly. "As it is, I do not! The exquisite beauty of the earth denies it! I pin my faith to a great analogy. The natural world is a reflex of the spiritual, and in the natural world there is no annihilation. Nothing can ever die. Nor can our souls ever die."

She looked at him keenly. The dreamy speculation had gone from her eyes. The fire of her former purpose had returned.

"It is well to feel like that. You would rather be Sir Geoffrey Kynaston, then, than his murderer, even now?"

He raised his hand quickly to his forehead, as though in pain. It was gone in an instant, but she had been watching.

"Yes, I would," he answered fervently. "Sir Geoffrey was a wicked man, but he may have repented. He had his opportunities."

"How do you know that he was wicked?" she asked quickly.

"I heard of him abroad—many years ago. Will you excuse me, Miss Thurwell. I must hurry on and open the door for them."

He walked swiftly on, leaving her alone. When they reached their destination, he was there waiting for them.

It was a strangely situated and strangely built abode. A long low building of deep yellow stone, half hidden by various creepers, and inaccessible on the side from which they approached it save to foot passengers. From the bottom of the winding path which they had to climb it seemed to hang almost sheer over the cliff side. A thickly growing patch of stunted pine trees rising abruptly in the background literally overtopped the tiled roof. From the summit of this plantation to the sea was one abrupt precipice, thickly overgrown for the first hundred feet or so by pine trees growing out from the side of the cliff in strange huddled fashion, the haunt of sea birds and a few daring rabbits.

They passed in at the hand-gate, and toiled up the steep path, threading their way among a wilderness of overgrown box shrubs, long dank grass and strange weeds. Helen, with her eyes fixed upon an open window on the right wing of the cottage, fell a little behind. The others came to a halt before the open door.

Mr. Brown met them and preceded them along the passage.

"I think he had better be carried in here," he said, motioning toward the room on the left-hand side, the side remote from the sea. "I have brought a sofa."

They stood on the threshold and looked in. The room was absolutely unfurnished, and the shutters had only just been thrown back, letting in long level gleams of sunlight, which fell upon the bare floor and damp walls, from which the discolored paper was commencing to peel off. Long cobwebs hung from the ceiling, waving slowly backward and forward in the unaccustomed draught. Helen Thurwell, who had just joined the little group, with a curious light in her eyes, and a deep spot of color in her pale cheeks, looked around and shivered. Mr. Thurwell, with a landlord's instinct, began to wonder who was at fault, his agent or his tenant.

The four men tramped in, their footsteps sounding dreary and mournful on the uncarpeted floor, and awakening strange rumbling echoes. Helen looked at them for a moment, all clustered round the single sofa which stood in the middle of the apartment, and then stepped softly back again into the hall. She looked around her eagerly, yet with no idle curiosity.

The whole interior of the place appeared bare and comfortless. There were no rugs in the hall, no carpet on the stairs, nor a single sign of habitation. Nor was there any servant about. She looked again into the room out of which she had just stepped. They were preparing to lift the body from the gate, which they had laid upon the floor, on to the sofa. She stepped back into the hall, and listened. There was no sound from any other part of the house. They were all too deeply engrossed to think of her. It was her chance!

She was very pale, and very resolute. The look which had come into her face for so short a time ago had had its meaning. The time for action had come. It was sooner than she had expected; but she was ready.

E. PHILLIPS OPPENHEIM

With swift noiseless step she crossed the hall and softly turned the handle of the door on the opposite side. It opened at once, and she stepped inside. She listened again. As yet she was undetected. She drew a little breath and glanced searchingly around her.

This room, too, was unfurnished, save that the floor was covered with cases full of books. Straight in front of her was another door, leading, as she knew, into a smaller apartment. Dare she go forward? She listened for a moment. There was no sound save the low muffled voices of the men who were lifting Sir Geoffrey on to the couch. Supposing she were discovered here? At the most, she would be suspected of a vulgar curiosity. It all flashed through her mind in a moment, and her decision was taken. Gathering her skirts in her hand lest they should catch against the edges of the cases, she threaded her way through them, and stood before the door of the inner room. She tried the handle. It yielded easily to her touch. She had gone too far to draw back now. In a moment she had passed the threshold, and the whole contents of the little room were disclosed to her.

Of all the senses, the eyes seem to carry the most lasting impression to the brain. One eager glance around, and the whole seemed photographed into her memory. A little strip of faded carpet only half covering the floor, piles upon piles of books, and a small table littered all over with foolscap, a few fine prints and etchings roughly hung upon the walls, a group of exquisite statuettes all huddled together, and an oak cabinet strongly bound with brass clasps—they were the things she chiefly remembered. The whole room was in the wildest disorder, as though the contents had been just shot inside and left to arrange themselves.

After that single cursory glance, Helen looked no more around her. Her whole attention was riveted upon the window exactly opposite. As she had seen from the outside, it was wide open, and several branches of a shrub growing up against it were broken off. From the leaves of the same shrub several drops of water were hanging, and on the ground below was a wet patch. She looked back into the room again. In one corner was an empty basin, and by its side, rolled up tightly, was a rough towel.

Before she could make any movement in that direction, another thing struck her. On a certain spot close by the side of the basin a pile of books was arranged in disorderly fashion enough, but with some little method. An idea flashed in upon her. They were arranged in that manner to hide something upon the floor.

She made a quick motion forward. Then she stopped short, and lifted her eyes to the door. Her cheeks burned, and her heart beat fast. Sir Allan Beaumerville was standing on the threshold, looking at her in mute amazement, and over his shoulder was the pale stern face of Mr. Brown.

VI

A Terrible Enemy

Afterwards Helen looked back upon those few moments as the most uncomfortable of her life. She was caught in the very act of a most unwarrantable and even immodest intrusion, which in the eyes of these two men could only appear like the attempted gratification of a reprehensible and vulgar curiosity. She made one spasmodic attempt to kindle her suspicions into a definite accusation, to stand upon her dignity, and demand an explanation of what she had seen. But she failed utterly. Directly she tried to clothe the shreds of this idea of hers with words, and to express them, she seemed to vividly realize the almost ludicrous improbability of the whole thing. One glance into the pale, dignified face which was bent upon her full of unconcerned surprise— and hateful to her with a gentle shade of pity at her confusion already creeping into it—and her attempt collapsed. She felt her cheeks burn with shame, and her eyes drooped before his steady gaze. She began to long feverishly for something to dissolve the situation. The silence was dreadful to her, but she could think of nothing to say. It was Mr. Brown, at last, who spoke.

"I was afraid you would not be able to find your way, Miss Thurwell," he said quietly. "I must apologize for asking you to come into such a den. The small engraving on the wall is the proof 'Bartolozzi' I spoke to you about. The head is perfect, is it not? Some day I should like to show you my 'Guido.' I am afraid, just now, I could not expect you to appreciate them."

She murmured something—what, she scarcely knew, and he did not appear to hear. The cold surprise disappeared from Sir Allan's face. Evidently he believed in Mr. Brown's mercifully offered explanation of her presence here.

"What! are you an enthusiast, Miss Thurwell?" he exclaimed. "Well, well, I was worse myself once in my younger days, before my profession made a slave of me. Surely, that is a genuine 'Velasquez,' Mr. Brown. Upon my word! Fancy coming across such a treasure here!"

He picked his way across the disorderly chamber, and, adjusting his eyeglass, stood looking at the picture. Helen made a hasty movement towards the door, and Mr. Brown followed her into the adjoining room.

"If I had known that I was to be honored by a visit from a lady," he said, "I would have endeavored—"

She turned suddenly round upon him with flaming cheeks.

"Don't," she interrupted, almost beseechingly. "Mr. Brown, you were very good to me just then. Thank you! I was most abominably rude to go into that room without your permission."

Her eyes were fixed upon the floor, and her distress was evident. It was clear that she felt her position acutely.

"Pray say no more about it," he begged earnestly. "It isn't worth a second thought."

She stopped with her back to one of the great cases filled with books, and hesitated. Should she confess to him frankly why she had gone there, and ask his pardon for such a wild thought? She raised her eyes slowly, and looked at him. Of course it was absurd. She has been out of her mind, she knew that now; and yet—

She looked at him more closely still. He had not seemed in any way disturbed when they had found her in that room—only a little surprised and bewildered. And yet, after all, supposing his composed demeanor had been only assumed. He was certainly very pale, very pale indeed, and there was a slight twitching of his hands which was out of character with his absolute impassiveness. Supposing it should be a forced composure. He looked like a man capable of exercising a strong control over his feelings. Supposing it should be so. Was there not, after all, just a chance that her former suspicions were correct?

The action of the mind is instantaneous. All these thoughts and doubts merely flashed through it, and they left her very confused and undecided. Her sense of gratitude towards him for shielding her before Sir Allan Beaumerville, and the intuitive sympathy of her nature with the delicacy and tact which he had shown in his manner of doing so, were on the whole stronger than her shadowy suspicions. And yet these latter had just sufficient strength to check the impulse of generosity which prompted her to confess everything to him. She did not tell him why she had started on the quest which had come to such an ignominious conclusion. She offered him no explanation whatever.

"It was very good of you," she repeated. "I did not deserve it at all. And now I must go and look for my father."

Mr. Thurwell was waiting in the hall, somewhat surprised at her absence. But he asked no questions. His thoughts were too full of the terrible thing which had happened to his friend and neighbor—and withal his daughter's betrothed.

They walked back across the moor together, saying very little, for there was only one possible subject for conversation, and both of them shrank a little from speaking about it. But when they were more than half-way to their destination, she asked a question.

"Nothing has been discovered, I suppose, of the murderer?"

Her father shook his head.

"Nothing. The dagger is our only clue as yet—except this."

He drew a folded piece of paper from his pocket, and touched it lightly with his finger.

"What is it? May I see?"

He handed it to her at once.

"It was in his pocket," he said. "I am keeping it to hand over to the proper authorities. Mr. Brown offered to take care of it, but I felt that, as a magistrate, I was in a measure responsible for everything in the shape of a clue, so I brought it away with me. Read it."

She opened the half sheet of notepaper and glanced down it. It was written in a queer cramped handwriting—evidently disguised.

"Sir Geoffrey Kynaston, you are doing a very rash and foolish thing in coming back to your own country, and thereby publishing your whereabouts to the world. Have you forgotten what hangs over you—or can you be so mad as to think that he has forgiven? Read this as a warning; and if life is in any way dear to you, go back to that hiding which alone has kept you safe for so many years. Do not hesitate or delay for one half-hour—one minute may be too long. If, after reading this, you linger in England, and disregard my warning, take care that you look into your life and hold yourself prepared to die."

She gave it back to him. There was some one, then, whom he had injured very deeply. It was like an echo from that stormy past of which many people had spoken.

"He had an enemy," she murmured, passing her arm through her father's.

"It seems so," he answered. "A terrible enemy."

VII

HELEN THURWELL'S SUSPICIONS

On a certain September day, about six weeks after the funeral of Sir Geoffrey Kynaston, Mr. Brown was spending what appeared to be a very pleasant afternoon. He was lying stretched out at full length on a dry mossy bank, with a volume of Shelley in his hand, and a case of thick Egyptian cigarettes by his side. In his ears was the whispering of the faint breeze amongst the pines, and the soft murmuring of the sea, hundreds of feet below, seen like a brilliant piece of patchwork through the fluttering leaves and dark tree-trunks which surrounded him. There was nothing to disturb the sweet silence of the drowsy afternoon. It was a charming spot which he had chosen, and he was quite alone. People, amongst whom for the last few weeks his name had become a fruitful source of conversation, were already beginning to fancy him flying across the country in an express train, or loitering on the docks at Liverpool, waiting for an Atlantic liner, or sitting at home trembling and fearful, struggling to hide his guilt beneath a calm exterior. But, as a matter of fact, he was doing none of these things. The harsh excitement of the busy gossips, and their stern judgment, troubled him nothing, for he was unconscious of them. He was away in thoughtland, dreaming of a fair, proud young face seen first on the rude pavement of an old Italian town, where its sweet composed freshness, amongst a pile of magnificent ruins, had captivated his artist's sense almost before it had touched his man's heart. He thought of the narrow street shutting in the sky till, looking upwards, it seemed like one deep band of glorious blue—of the ruined grey palace, with still some traces left of its former stately grace, and of the fountain playing in the moss-encrusted courtyard, gleaming like silver in the sunlight as it rose and fell into the worn stone basin. Here, where the very air seemed full of the records of a magnificent decay, everything seemed to form a fitting framework in his memory for that one face. It had been an artist's dream—or had it been the man's? Never the latter; he told himself sadly. Such were not for him. It had been better far that he had never seen her again. Before, the memory had been a very sweet one, stored away in his mind amongst all the great and beautiful things he had seen in his wanderings, always with a dainty freshness clinging to it, as though it had lain carefully preserved in perfume and spices. Was this new joy, of having seen and spoken to her, a better thing? this vague unsettlement of his being, which played havoc with his thoughts, and stirred up a whole host of strange new feelings in his heart? Surely not! It seemed to him like the breathing of warm new life into what had been a crystallized emotion—the humanizing of something spiritual. Surely, for him, it had better have remained in that first stage.

There was the sound of a light footstep on the springy turf. He started to his feet. A girl, tall and slim, was coming swiftly along the winding path through the plantation towards him. He knew at once that it was Helen Thurwell.

They were both equally surprised. As she looked up and saw him standing upright in the narrow path, tall, thin, and unnaturally pale, with the cigarette still burning between his fingers, and his book in his other hand, she felt strangely stirred. Neither was he unmoved by her sudden appearance, for though not a feature twitched, not a single gleam of color relieved the still pallor of his face, there was a new light in his dry brilliant eyes. But there was a vast difference between the thoughts which flashed into his mind and those which filled hers. To him there had stolen a sweetness into the summer's day surpassing the soft sunlight, and a presence which moved every pulse in his being, and crept like maddening fire through every sense. And to her, the sight of him was simply a signal to brace up all her powers of perception; to watch with suspicion every change of his features, and every tone of his voice. Had he shown any emotion at the sight of her, she would have attributed it to a guilty conscience, and would have made note of it in her mind against him. And as he showed none—none, at least, that she could detect—she put it down to the exercise of a strong will, and was a little disappointed. For she had gone with the tide, and, womanlike, having embraced an idea, it had already become as truth to her. Mr. Brown was the man who had murdered Sir Geoffrey Kynaston. It was a murderer with whom she was standing side by side among the glancing shadows of the rustling pine groves. It must be so!

Yet she did not shrink from him. After her first hesitation at the sight of a man's figure standing up amongst the dark tree-trunks, she had walked steadily on until she had reached him. And he, without any change of countenance, had simply stood and watched her. God! how beautiful she was! The sunlight, gleaming through the tops of the trees in long slanting rays, played like fire upon her red-gold hair; and the plain black gown, which yielded easily to her graceful movements, seemed to show every line of her supple yet delicate figure. She came nearer still, so near that he could trace the faint blue veins in her forehead, and once more recall the peculiar color of her eyes. Then he spoke to her, raising his hand with a suddenly returning instinct of conventionality for his cap; but he had risen without it, and was standing before her bare-headed.

"I am a trespasser, I fear," he said hesitatingly.

She came to a standstill by his side, and shook her head slowly.

"No, this is common land. There is a footpath, you see, although it is seldom used. It leads nowhere but to the Court."

"It is a favorite walk of mine," he said.

"Yes, it is pleasant. You bring a companion with you," she remarked, pointing to his book.

He glanced down at it, and then up at her again.

"Yes; a faithful friend, too. We spend a good deal of time out of doors together."

She read the title, and glanced up at him with a shade of interest in her face.

"Shelley was a great poet, I suppose," she said; "but I do not understand him."

For the first time his expression changed. A sudden light swept across his face, and in a moment it was glowing with sensibility and enthusiasm. She looked at him astonished. He stood before her revealed in a new light, and, although unwillingly, she saw him with different eyes.

"Not understand Shelley! Ah! but that is because you have not tried, then. If you had, you would not only understand, but you would love him."

She shook her head. In reality she felt that he was right, that her languid attempts to read him by a drawing-room fire, with the *Queen* beside her, and her mind very full of very little things, had not been the spirit in which to approach a great poet. But, partly out of womanly perversity, and partly out of curiosity to hear what he would say, she chose to dissent from him.

"I find him too mystical," she said; "too incomprehensible."

He looked down at her from his superior height with kindling eyes. It was odd how greatly she was surprised in him. She had imagined him to be a cynic.

E. PHILLIPS OPPENHEIM

"Mystical!" he repeated. "Yes, in a certain sense, he is so; and it is his greatest charm. But incomprehensible!—no. The essence of all artistic poetry is in the perfect blending of matter and form, so that the meaning creeps in upon us, but with a certain vagueness, a certain indefiniteness, which reaches us more in the shade of a dreamy consciousness than through the understanding. May I give you an illustration? We stand upon a low plain and gaze upon a far-off range of hills, from the sides of which thick clouds of white mist are hanging. Gradually, as the sun rises higher in the heavens, they float away, and we begin dimly to see through a clearer atmosphere the yellow corn waving on the brown hillside, the smoke rising from the lonely farmhouse, and, if we have patience and wait still, by-and-by we can even distinguish the brilliant patches of wild flowers, the poppies and the cornflowers in the golden fields, and the marsh marigolds in the meadows at the foot of the hill. It is a question of waiting long enough. So it is with what people call mysticism in poetry."

For the first time for many months a faint color had found its way into his wan cheeks. His face was alight with interest, and his dark eyes shone from their deep hollows with a new, soft fire. From that moment he assumed a new place in her thoughts. She was loath to grant it to him, but she had no alternative. Guilty or innocent, this man had something in him which placed him high above other men in her estimation. She felt stirred in a manner peculiarly grateful to her. It was as though every chord of her being had been tuned into fresh harmony; as though the hand of a magician had lifted the curtain which had enclosed her too narrow life, and had shown her a new world glowing with beauty and promise. She, too, wanted to feel like that; to taste the pleasures which this man tasted, and to feel the enthusiasm which had lit up his pale scholarly face.

At that moment her mind was too full to harbor those dark suspicions. With a sudden effort she threw them overboard, trampled on them, scouted them. Was this the face and the tongue of a murderer? Surely not!

"Thank you," she said softly. "I shall like to think over what you have said. Now I must go."

Her words seemed to bring him back to his old self. He stooped down and picked up his cap.

"You are going back to the Court?" he asked. "Let me walk to the end of the plantation with you."

She assented silently, and they turned along the narrow path side by side. Below them a bracken-covered cliff, studded with dwarfed trees, ran down to the sea; and on their left hand the black firs, larger and growing more thickly together, shut out completely the open moorland beyond. He had walked there before beneath a sky of darker blue, and when there had been only stray gleams of moonlight shining through the cone-laden boughs to show him the rough path; and he had been there when the tree-tops had bent beneath the shrieking wind, when the black clouds had been flying over his head, and the roar of the angry sea had filled the air with thunder. And these things had stirred him—one of nature's sons—in many ways. Yet none of them had sent the warm blood coursing through his veins like quicksilver, or had stolen through his senses with such sweet heart-stirring impetuosity as did the presence of this tall, fair girl, walking serenely by his side in thoughtful silence. Once, when too near the edge of the cliff, she put her foot on a fir-cone and stumbled, and the touch of her hand, as he caught hold of it to steady her, sent a thrill of keen, exquisite pleasure through his whole frame. He held it perhaps a little longer than necessary, and she let him. For the moment she had lost the sense of physical touch, and the firm grasp of his fingers upon hers seemed to her, in a certain sense, only an analogy to the sudden sympathy which had sprung up between them. Even when realization came, she drew her hand away gently, without anger, without undue haste even. One glance into his face at that moment would have told her everything; the whole horror of the situation would have flashed in upon her, and she would have been overwhelmed. But she did not look, and long before they had come to the end of the path the passionate light had died out from his eyes, and had left no trace behind. Once more he was only a plain, sad-looking man, hollow-eyed and hollow-cheeked, with bent head and stooping frame.

VIII

Did You Kill Sir Geoffrey Kynaston?

At the extremity of the plantation they came to a small wicket-gate opening out on to the cliff top. From here there was a path inland to the Court, whilst Falcon's Nest was straight in front of them. At the parting of the ways they hesitated, for it seemed necessary that they should part.

And whilst they looked around a little dazzled, having just emerged from the darkness of the plantation, they were conscious of a new glory in the heavens. Far away across the moorland the autumn sun had shot its last rays over the level plain and sea, and had sunk quietly to rest. It was not one of Turner's wild sunsets. There were no banks of angry clouds full of lurid coloring, flashing their glory all over the western sky. But in a different fashion it was equally beautiful. Long level streaks of transparent light, emerging from an ethereal green to a deep orange, lay stretched across the heavens, and a faint golden haze rising from the land seemed to mingle with them, and form one harmonious mass of coloring. And the air too was different—purer and rarer than the enervating atmosphere of the drowsy afternoon. Together they stood and became subject to the subtle charm of their environment. It seemed to Helen Thurwell then that a change was creeping into her life. Impersonal thought had attained a new strength and a new sweetness. But at that time she had no knowledge of what it meant.

"See!" he exclaimed softly, pointly westward, "there is what Coleridge made dear to us for ever, and Byron vainly scoffed at—the 'green light that lingers in the west.'"

He repeated the stanza absently, and half to himself, with a sudden oblivion of her presence—

> *"It were a vain endeavor,*
> *Though I should gaze for ever*
> *On that green light that lingers in the west.*
> *I may not hope from outward forms to win*
> *The passion and the life whose fountains are within."*

She watched him as his voice sank lower and lower, and though his eyes were dry and bright, she saw a look of intense sadness sweep across his face. Almost she felt inclined to let her natural sympathy escape her—to let loose the kind and tender words which had leapt up from her heart, and even trembled upon her lips. But a rush of consciousness came, and she choked them back. Thus much she could do, but no more. She could not at that moment look upon him as the man already suspected in many quarters of a most brutal murder. For the instant, all was blotted out. Had she tried she could not at that moment have revived her own suspicions. They seemed to her like some grotesque fungi of the mind—poisonous weeds to be crushed and destroyed. But the seed was there.

"Those are the saddest lines I ever read," she said quietly. "It is a true ode to dejection."

"And therefore they are very precious," he answered. "It is always sweet to find your own emotions so exquisitely expressed. It is like a spiritual narcotic."

"And yet—yet such poems encourage sadness, and that is morbid."

He shook his head.

"To be sad is not necessarily to be unhappy," he answered. "That sounds like a paradox, but it isn't! You remember the 'gentle melancholy' which Milton loved. There is something sweet in that, is there not?"

"But it is not like that with you," she said quickly.

He threw his arms up into the air with a sudden wild gesture of absolute despair. She had touched a chord in his nature too roughly, and it had not stood the strain. For a moment he had thrown off his mask. His white face was ghastly, and his eyes were burning with a hopeless passion.

"My God! No!" he cried. "I am in the depths of hell, with never a gleam of hope to lead me on. And the sin—the sin—"

He stopped suddenly, and his hands fell to his side. Slowly he turned round and looked at her, half doubtfully, half fearfully. What had he said? What had she heard? What did that look in her face mean—that look of anguish, of fear, of horror? Why did she not speak, even though it were to accuse him? Anything rather than that awful silence.

Twice she moved her white lips, but no sound came. The power of articulation seemed gone. Then she caught him by the arm, and turned him slowly round so that he faced his cottage. Only a few yards below them was the spot where she and her sister-in-law that was to have been had lolled in their low chairs by the luncheon-table, and had begun to feel impatient for the coming of one who had never come. Further away still, across the moor, was that dark circular patch of plantation behind which Sir Geoffrey Kynaston had been found, and away upon the cliffs overlooking the scene of the murder was Falcon's Nest.

The grasp on his arm tightened. Then she stretched out her other hand, and with shaking fingers pointed downwards—pointed to the very spot where the deed had been done. The memory of it all came back to her, and hardened her set white face. She looked him straight in the eyes without a quiver, and clenched her teeth.

"Did you—do that?" she asked in a firm, hard tone.

A curious mind slumber seemed to have crept over him. His eyes followed her outstretched hand, and his lips idly repeated her words.

"Did you kill Sir Geoffrey Kynaston?"

Her words fell sharp and clear upon the still air. A tremor passed through his whole frame, and the light of a sudden understanding flashed across his face. He was his old self again, and more than his old self.

"You are joking, of course, Miss Thurwell?" he said quietly. "You do not mean that seriously?"

She caught her breath, and looked at him. After all, it is only a step from tragedy to commonplace. He was deathly pale, but calm and composed. He had conquered himself just in time. Another moment, and she felt assured that she would have known all. Never mind! it should come, she told herself. The end was not yet.

"No; of course I did not mean it seriously," she repeated slowly. "Who are those men coming up the hill? Can you see?"

He moved a little nearer to her, and looked downward. On the slope of the hill were three men. She had recognized them already, and she watched him steadily.

"Your father is one," he said quietly. "The other two are strangers to me."

"Perhaps I can tell you something about them," she said, still watching him intently. "One is the constable from Mallory, and the other is a detective."

There was a slight hardening of his face, and she fancied that she saw his under lip quiver for a moment. Had he shown any guilty fear, had he shrunk back, or uttered a single moan, her sympathy would never have been aroused. But as it was, she was a woman, and her face softened, and the tears stood in her eyes. There was something almost grand in the composure with which he was waiting for what seemed inevitable—something of the magnificent resignation with which the noblemen of France one by one took their place at the block, and the simile was heightened by the slightly contemptuous, slightly defiant poise of his finely shaped head. She saw him cast one lingering glance around at the still sea, with its far-off motionless sails; at the clear sky, from which the brilliancy of coloring was fading away, and at the long sweep of moorland with its brilliant patches of heather and gorse, now slightly blurred by the mists rising from the earth. It was as though he were saying a last farewell to things which he had loved, and which he would see no more—and it had a strange effect upon her. The memory of that hideous crime left her. She could think only of the abstract pathos of the present situation, and she felt very miserable. It was wrong, unnatural of her; but at that moment, if she could have helped him to escape, she would have done her best in the face of them all.

They were almost at hand now, and she lifted her eyes, in which the tears were fast gathering. She thought nothing of her own situation—of their finding her alone with the murderer. With characteristic unselfishness she thought only of him.

She met her father's surprised gaze with indifference. She had a sort of feeling that nothing mattered much. What was going to happen eclipsed everything else.

And so it did. Her apathy changed in a moment to amazement, and her heart stood still. Her father had raised his hat to Mr. Brown with even more than the usual courtesy of his salute, and the two officials had saluted in the most correct fashion.

"Mr. Brown," he said, "we have all come in search of you to tender our most sincere apologies for an unfortunate mistake. Police Constable Chopping here is mostly to blame, and next to him, I am."

She glanced at the man by her side. His face was absolutely impenetrable. It showed no signs of the relief which was creeping into hers. His composure was simply wonderful.

"The fact is," her father continued, "Chopping came to see me with a long tale and a certain request which, under the circumstances—which I will explain to you afterwards—I could not as a magistrate refuse. I was compelled to sign a search warrant for him to go over Falcon's Nest. It was against my inclination, and a most unpleasant duty for me to perform. But I considered it my duty, and I attended there myself in order that it might not be abused. I hope to have your forgiveness for the liberty which we were compelled to take."

There was still no change in Mr. Brown's face, but, standing close to him, she heard him take a quick deep breath. Curiously enough, it was a relief to her to hear it. Such great self-restraint was almost unnatural.

"You only did your duty, Mr. Thurwell," he answered quietly. "You owe me no apology."

"I am very glad that you see it in that light," Mr. Thurwell said, "very glad indeed. But I have a further confession to make."

He drew Mr. Brown a little on one side, out of hearing of the others, but nearer to her than any of them, and commenced talking earnestly to him. This time she could tell that he was disturbed and uneasy, but she could not follow connectedly all her father said. Only a few stray words reached her.

"Very sorry indeed. . . Quite accidental. . . Will preserve. . . discovery."

"Then I may rely upon you to keep this absolutely to yourself?" she heard Mr. Brown say earnestly.

"I give you my word, sir!" her father answered. Then they turned round, and she saw that Mr. Brown looked distinctly annoyed.

"However did you come here, Helen?" her father asked, suddenly remembering her presence.

"I came for a walk, and met Mr. Brown in the plantation," she explained.

"Well, since you are here," he remarked good humoredly, "you must help me to induce Mr. Brown to come back to the Court. So far, we have been wretched neighbors. We shall insist upon his dining with us, just to show that there's no ill-feeling," he added, smiling. "Now, no excuses."

"Thank you, but I never go out," Mr. Brown answered. "I have not even any clothes here. So—"

"Please come, Mr. Brown," she said softly.

He flashed a sudden glance at her from his dark eyes, which brought the color streaming into her cheeks. Fortunately, twilight was commencing to fall, and she was standing a little back in the shadow of the plantation.

"If Miss Thurwell wishes it," he said, in a tone of a man who offers himself to lead a forlorn hope, "it is settled. I will come."

IX

Mr. Brown Dines at the Court

B oth to him and to her there was something strangely unreal in the little banquet to which they three—Mr. Thurwell, his daughter, and his tenant—sat down that evening. For many months afterwards, until, indeed, after the culmination of the tragedy in which she was the principal moving figure, Helen Thurwell looked back upon that night with strangely mingled feelings. It was the dawn of a new era in her existence, a fact which she never doubted, although she struggled vainly against it. And to him it was like a sudden transition into fairyland. The long years of lonely life and rigorous asceticism through which he had passed had been a period of no ordinary self-denial. Instinctively and with his whole nature the man was an artist. His homely fare, ill-cooked and ill-served among dreary surroundings, had for long been a horror to him. Whatever his reasons for such absolute isolation had been, they had sprung from no actual delight in rough living or non-appreciation of the refinements of civilized society. He realized to the full extent the sybaritic pleasures which now surrounded him. The white tablecloth flaming with daintily modeled plate and cut glass, the brilliant coloring of the scarlet and yellow flowers, the aromatic perfume of the chrysanthemums mingling with the faint scent of exotics, the luscious fruits, and the softly shaded table lights which threw a rich glow over the lovely face opposite to him—all these things had their own peculiar effect in the shape of a certain subtle exhilaration which was not slow to show itself. With scarcely an effort he threw off the old mask of reserve, with all the little awkwardnesses and gaucheries which it had entailed, and appeared as the shadow of the self of former days—a cultured, polished man of the world. Even Mr. Thurwell's good breeding was scarcely sufficient to conceal his surprise at the metamorphosis. Never before, at his table, had there been such a brilliant flow of conversation—conversation which had all the rare art of appearing general, whereas it was indeed nothing less than a monologue on the part of this strange guest. He had traveled far, he had seen great things in many countries, and he had known great men; and he talked lightly about them all, with the keen appreciation of the artist, and the graceful diction of the scholar. He was a man who had lived in the world—every little action and turn of speech denoted it. The French dishes—Mr. Thurwell was proud of his chef—were no secret to him, and he knew all about the vintages of the wines he was drinking. In the whole course of his experience, Mr. Thurwell had never entertained such a guest as this, and it was a sore trial to his good manners to abstain from any astonished comment on the lonely life his tenant had been lately leading.

And Helen sat listening to it all with a sort of dreamy content stealing over her, out of which she was stirred every now and then into enthusiasm by some brilliant criticism or fresh turn to the conversation. At such times her gray luminous eyes, with their strange dash of foreign color, would light up and flash their sympathetic approval across the few feet of tablecloth blazing with many-colored flowers and fruits and glittering silver. And he grew to look for this, and to receive it with an answering glance from his own dark eyes, full of a strange light and power. She, watching him more keenly than her father could, was conscious of something that altogether escaped him, a sort of undercurrent of suppressed excitement which never rose to the surface, and revealed itself in none of his mannerisms or his tone. But it was there, and she felt it—felt it more than ever when their eyes met, and hers were forced to droop before the steady fire in his, which more than once brought the faint color into her cheeks, and sent a new sensation quivering through her being.

Dinner came to an end at last, but when she rose to go her father protested. She generally sat with him while he smoked a cigarette and drank his coffee. Why should she go away now? They were making no stranger of Mr. Brown. And so she stayed.

Presently she found herself strolling round the room by his side, showing him the pictures which hung lightly upon the high oak panels, and the foreign bric-à-brac and Italian vases ranged along the wide black ledge a little below. Her father had been obliged to go out and speak to the head gamekeeper about some suspected poaching, and they were alone.

"This is where I like to sit after dinner, when we are alone," she said; and, lifting some heavy drooping curtains, she led him into a quaint recess, almost as large as an ordinary room. A shaded lamp was burning on a small Burmese table, and the faint fragrance of burning pine logs stole up from the open hearth and floated about on the air, already slightly perfumed with the odor of chrysanthemums clustered together in quaint blue china bowls, little patches of gold-and-white coloring, where everything else was somber and subdued. She sank into a low basket chair before the fire, and, obeying her gesture, he seated himself opposite to her.

"Now, talk to me, please," she said, half hiding her face with a feather screen to protect it from the fire. "No commonplacisms, mind! I have heard nothing else all my life, and I am weary of them. And, first, please to light a cigarette. You will find some in the silver box by your side. I like the perfume."

He did as he was bidden in silence. For a moment he watched the faint blue smoke curl upward, stole a glance around him, and drew a long breath as though he were drinking in to the full the artistic content of the exquisite harmony and coloring, of his surroundings. Then he threw a sudden, swift look upon the beautiful girl who was leaning back in her low chair, with her fair head resting upon a cushion of deep olive green, and her eyes fixed expectantly upon him. She was so near that, by stretching out his hand, he could have seized her small shapely fingers; so near, that he could even detect the delicate scent of lavender from the lace of her black dinner gown. He took in every detail of her dainty toilette from the single diamond which sparkled in the black velvet around her throat, to the exquisitely slippered feet resting lightly upon a tiny sage-green footstool, and just visible through the gossamerlike draperies which bordered her skirts. In the world of her sex she had become an era to him.

X

The Tragedy of Rachel Kynaston

I wonder whether you know that we have met before, Miss Thurwell?" he asked her suddenly.

She moved her screen and looked at him.

"Surely not! Where?"

In a few words he reminded her of that quaint street in the old Italian town, and of the half-ruined Palazzo di Vechi. He had seen her only for a few minutes, but her face had never been forgotten; the way in which he told her so, although he did not dwell upon it, told her also that it had been no ordinary memory—that it had held a separate place in his thoughts, as was indeed the case. Something in the manner of his allusion to it showed her too, as though he had laid his whole mind bare, with what interest, almost reverence, he had guarded it, and all that it had meant to him; and as she listened a faint color stole into her cheeks, with which the fire had nothing to do. She held her screen the closer, and bent her head lest he should see it.

But there was no fear of that; indeed, he had no thought of the kind. Leaving the dangerous ground behind him, he glided easily and naturally into impersonal subjects. From Italy he began to talk of Florence, of Pico della Mirandola, and the painters of the Renaissance. He strove his utmost to interest her, and with his vast stock of acquired knowledge, and his wonderfully artistic felicity of expression, he talked on and on, wandering from country to country, and age to age, till it all seemed to her like a strangely beautiful poem, full of yellow light and gleaming shadow, sometimes passionate and intense, at others fantastic and almost ethereal. Now and then she half closed her eyes, and his words, and their meaning, the form and the substance, seemed to come to her like richly blended music, stirring all her senses and quickening all her dormant faculties. Then she opened them again, and looked steadily upon the dark, wan face, with its sharp thin outline and strange poetic abstraction. By chance he spoke for a moment of De Quincey, and a shudder passed through all her being. Could such a face as that be a murderer's face? The utter morbidness of such a thought oppressed her only for a moment. If to-morrow it was to be her duty to loathe this man, then it should be so; but those few minutes were too precious to be disturbed by such thoughts. A new life was stirring within her, and its first breath was too sweet to be crushed on the threshold. After to-night—anything! But to-night she would have for her own.

And so the time passed on, and the evening slipped away. Mr. Thurwell had looked in, but seeing them so engrossed he had quietly retreated and indulged in his usual nap. A dainty tea equipage had been brought in, and she had roused herself to prepare it with her own hands, and it seemed to him that this little touch of domesticity had been the one thing wanted to make the picture perfect. There had been a momentary silence then, and she had found herself asking him questions.

"Do you never feel that you would like to be back in the world again?" she asked. "Yours is a very lonely life!"

"I do not often find it so," he answered, with his eyes fixed upon the fire. "One's books, and the thoughts one gets from them, are sufficient companions."

"But they are not human ones, and man is human. Do you think a lonely life quite healthy—mentally healthy, I mean?"

"It should be the healthiest of all lives. It is only in theory that solitude is morbid. If you knew more of the world, Miss Thurwell, you would understand something of its cramping influence upon all independent thought. I am not a pessimist—at least, I try not to be. I do not wish to say that there is more badness than goodness in the world, but there is certainly more littleness than greatness. To live in any manner of society without imbibing a certain form of selfishness is difficult; to do so and to taste the full sweetness of the life that never dies is impossible!"

"But there must be some exceptions!" she said hesitatingly. "If people care for one another, and care for the same things—"

He shook his head.

"People never do care for one another. Life is so full nowadays, there are so many things to care about, that any concentration of the affections is impossible. Love is the derision of the modern world. It has not even the respect one pays to the antique."

For several minutes there was deep silence. A piece of burning wood tumbled off from the log and fell upon the tiles, where it lay with its delicate blue smoke curling upward into the room, laden with the pungent odor of the pine. She moved her feet, and there was the slight rustling of her skirts. No other sound broke the stillness which they both remembered for long afterwards—the stillness before the storm.

Suddenly it came to an end. There was a sound of doors being quickly opened and shut, voices in the hall, and then a light, firm tread, crossing the main portion of the room. They both glanced toward the curtains, and there was a second's expectancy. Then they were thrown on one side with a hasty movement, and a tall dark woman in a long traveling cloak swept through them.

She paused for a moment on the threshold, and her flashing black eyes seemed to take in every detail of the little scene. She saw Helen, fair and comely, with an added beauty in her soft, animated expression, and she saw her companion, his face alight with intelligence and sensibility, and with the glow of a new life in his brilliant eyes. The perfume of the Egyptian tobacco which hung about the room, the tea tray, their two chairs drawn up before the fire—nothing escaped her. It all seemed to increase her wrath.

For she was very angry. Her form was dilated with passion, and her voice, when she spoke, shook with it. But it was not her anger, nor her threatening gestures, before which they both shrank back for a moment, appalled. It was her awful likeness to the murdered Sir Geoffrey Kynaston.

"Helen!" she cried, "they told me of this; but if I had not seen it with my own eyes, I would never have believed it."

Helen rose to her feet, pale, but with a kindling light in her eyes, and a haughty poise of her fair shapely head.

"You speak in riddles, Rachel," she said quietly. "I do not understand you."

A very storm of hysterical passion seemed to shake the woman, who had approached a little further into the room.

"Not understand me! Listen, and I will make it plain. You were engaged to marry my brother. I come here, almost from his funeral, and I find you thus—with his murderer! Girl, I wonder that you do not die of shame!"

His murderer! For a moment the color fled from cheeks and lips, and the room seemed whirling around her. But one glance at him brought back her drooping courage. He was standing close to her side, erect and firm as a statue, with his head thrown back, and his eyes fixed upon Rachel Kynaston. Blanched and colorless as his face was, there was no flinching in it.

"It is false!" she said proudly. "Ask him yourself."

"Ask him!" She turned upon him like a tigress, her eyes blazing with fury. "Let him hear what I have to say, and deny it. Is it not you who followed him from city to city all over the world, seeking always his life? Is it not you who kept him for many years from his native land for fear of blood-shed—yours or his? Is it not you who have fought with him and been worsted, and sworn to carry your enmity with you through life, and bury it only in his grave? Look at me, man, if you dare, look me in the face and tell me whether you did not seek his life in Vienna, and whether you did not fight with him on the sands at Boulogne. Oh, I know you! It is you! It is you! And then you come down here and live alone, waiting your chance. He is found foully murdered, and you are the only man who could have done it. Ask you whether you be guilty? There is no need, no need. Can anyone in their senses, knowing the story of your past hate, doubt it for one moment? And yet, answer me if you can. Look me in the face, and let me hear you lie, if you dare. Tell me that you know nothing of my brother's death!"

He had stood like marble, with never a change in his face, while she had poured out her passionate accusation. But when silence came, and she waited for him to speak, he could not. A seal seemed set upon his lips. He could not open them. He was silent.

A fearful glare of triumph blazed up in her eyes. She staggered back a little, and leaned upon the table, with her hand clasped to her side.

"See, Helen," she cried, "is that innocence? O God! give me strength to go on. I will see Mr. Thurwell. I will tell him everything. He shall sign a warrant. Ah!"

A terrible scream rang through the room, and echoed through the house. Mr. Thurwell and several of the servants came hurrying in. In the middle of the floor Rachel Kynaston lay prostrate, her fingers grasping convulsively at the empty air, and an awful look in her face. Helen was on her knees by her side, and Mr. Brown stood in the background, irresolute whether to stay or leave.

They crowded round her, but she waved them off, and grasping Helen's wrist, dragged her down till their heads nearly touched.

"Helen," she moaned, "I am dying. Swear to me that you will avenge Geoffrey's murder. That man did it. His name—his name—"

Suddenly her grasp relaxed, and Helen reeled back fainting into her father's arms.

"It is a fit," some one murmured.

But it was death.

E. PHILLIPS OPPENHEIM

XI

LEVY & SON, PRIVATE AGENTS

Anything in the letters, guv'nor?"

"Nothing so far, Ben, my boy," answered a little old gentleman, who was methodically opening a pile of envelopes, and carefully scrutinizing the contents of each before arranging them in separate heaps. "Nothing much yet. A letter from a despairing mother, entreating us to find her lost son. Description given, payment—tick! Won't do. Here's a note from Mr. Wallis about his wife's being at the theater the other night, and a line from Jack Simpson about that woman down St. John's Wood way. Seems he's found her, so that's off."

"Humph! business is slack," remarked a younger edition of the old gentleman, who was standing on the hearth rug, with his silk hat on the back of his head, in an attitude of unstudied grace.

"Say, guv'nor, you couldn't let me have a fiver, could you? Must keep up the credit of the firm, don't you know, and I'm awfully hard up. 'Pon my word, I am."

"I couldn't do anything of the sort!" exclaimed the old gentleman testily. "Certainly not. The way you spend money is grievous to me, Benjamin, positively grievous!"

He turned round in his chair, and with his spectacles on the top of his head surveyed his son and heir with a sorrowful interest.

"Oh, hang it all, some one must spend the money if we're to keep the business at all!" retorted Mr. Benjamin testily. "I can't live as I do without it, you know; and how are we to get the information we want? Look at the company I keep, too."

The old gentleman seemed mollified.

"There's something in that, Ben," he remarked, slowly wagging his head. "There's something in that, of course. Bless me, your mother was telling me you was with a lord the other day!"

Mr. Benjamin expanded a little with the recollection, and smiled gently.

"That was quite true, dad," he remarked with a grandiloquent air. "I was just going into the Cri—let me see, on Tuesday night it was— when whom should I run up against but little Tommy Soampton with a pal, and we all had drinks together. He was a quiet-looking chap, not dressed half so well as—er—"

"As you, Ben," interposed his father proudly.

"Well, I wasn't thinking of myself particularly," Mr. Benjamin continued, twirling an incipient mustache, and looking pleased. "But when Tommy introduced him as Lord Mossford, I was that surprised I nearly dropped my glass."

"What did you say to him, Ben?" asked the little old gentleman in an awed tone.

Ben drew himself up and smiled.

"I asked him how his lordship was, and whether his lordship'd take anything."

"And did he, Ben?" asked his father eagerly.

"Rather! He was just as affable as you like. I got on with him no end."

The little old gentleman turned away to his letters again to hide a gratified smile.

"Well, well, Ben, I suppose you must have it," he said leniently. "Young men will be young men. Only remember this, my boy—wherever you are, always keep an eye open for business. Never forget that."

Benjamin, junior, slapped his trousers pocket and grinned.

"No fear, dad. I don't forget the biz."

"Well, well; just wait till I've gone through the letters, and we'll see what we can do. We'll see. Ha! this reads well. I like this. Ben, we're in luck this morning. In luck, my boy!"

Mr. Benjamin abandoned his negligent attitude, and, drawing close to his father, peered over his shoulder. The letter which lay upon the desk was not a long one, but it was to the point.

> Thurwell Court,
> *Thursday*
>
> Dear Sirs,
>
> "I am recommended to consult your firm on a matter which requires the services of a skilled detective and the utmost secrecy. I am coming to London to-morrow, and will call at your office at about half-past ten. Please arrange to be in at that time.
>
> Yours truly,
> Helen Thurwell

To Messrs. Levy & Son,
Private Agents,
—— Street, Strand, London

Mr. Levy, senior, drew his hand meditatively down the lower part of his face once or twice, and looked up at his son.

"Something in it, I think, Benjamin, eh? Thurwell Court! Coat of Arms! Lady signs herself Miss Thurwell! Money there, eh?"

Mr. Benjamin was looking thoughtfully down at the signature.

"Thurwell, Thurwell! Where the mischief have I heard that name lately. Holy Moses! I know," he suddenly exclaimed, starting up with glistening eyes. "Dad, our fortune's made. Our chance has come at last!"

In the exuberance of his spirits he forgot the infirmities of age, and brought his hand down upon his father's back with such vehemence that the tears started into the little old gentleman's eyes, and his spectacles rattled upon his nose.

"Don't do that again, Benjamin," he exclaimed nervously. "I don't like it; I don't like it at all. You nearly dislocated my shoulder, and if you had, I'd have stopped the doctor's bill out of your allowance. I would, indeed! And now, what have you got to say?"

Mr. Benjamin had been walking up and down the office with his hands in his trousers' pockets whistling softly to himself. At the conclusion of his father's complaint he came to a standstill.

"All right, guv'nor. Sorry I hurt you. I was a bit excited. Don't you remember having heard that name Thurwell lately?"

Mr. Levy, senior, shook his head doubtfully.

"I'm afraid my memory isn't what it used to be, Benjamin. The name sounds a bit familiar, and yet—no, I can't remember," he wound up suddenly. "Tell me about it, my boy."

"Why, the Kynaston murder, of course. That was at Thurwell Court. Sir Geoffrey Kynaston was engaged to Miss Thurwell, you know, and she was one of the first to find him."

"Dear me! Dear me! I remember all about it now, to be sure," Mr. Levy exclaimed. "The murderer was never found, was he? Got clean off?"

"That's so," assented Mr. Benjamin. "Dad, it's a rum thing, but I was interested in that case. There was something queer about it. I read it every bit. I could stand a cross-examination in it now. Dad, it's a lucky thing. She's coming here to consult us about it, as sure as my name is Ben Levy. And, by jabers, here she is!"

There was the sound of a cab stopping at the door, and through a chink in the blinds Mr. Benjamin had seen a lady descend from it. In a moment his hat was off and on the peg, and he commenced writing a letter at the desk.

"Dad," he said quickly, without looking up, "leave this matter to me, will you? I'm up in the case. A lady, did you say, Morrison?"—turning toward the door. "Very good. Show her in at once."

XII

A Jewel of a Son

For the first time in her life Helen was taking a definite and important step without her father's knowledge. The matter was one which had caused her infinite thought and many heart searchings. The burden of Rachel Kynaston's dying words had fallen upon her alone. There seemed to be no escape from it. She must act, and must act for herself. Any sort of appeal to her father for help was out of the question. She knew beforehand exactly what his view of the matter would be. In all things concerning her sex he was of that ancient school which reckoned helplessness and inaction the chief and necessary qualities of women outside the domestic circle. He might himself have made some move in the matter, but it would have been half hearted and under protest. She knew exactly what his point of view would be. Rachel Kynaston had been excited by a fancied wrong—her last words were uttered in a veritable delirium! She could not part with the responsibility. The shadow of it lay upon her, and her alone. She must act herself or not at all. She must act herself, and without her father's knowledge, or be false to the charge laid upon her by a dying woman. So with a heavy heart she had accepted what seemed to her to be the inevitable.

She was shown at once into the inner sanctuary of Messrs. Levy & Son. Her first glance around, nervous though she was, was comprehensive. She saw a plainly but not ill-furnished office, the chief feature of which was its gloom. Seated in an easy chair was a little old gentleman with white hair, who rose to receive her, and a little farther away was a younger man who was writing busily, and who did not even glance up at her entrance. Although it was not a particularly dark morning, the narrowness of the street and the small dusty windows seemed effectually to keep out the light, and a jet of gas was burning.

Mr. Levy bowed to his visitor, and offered her a chair.

"Miss Thurwell, I presume," he said in his best manner.

The lady bowed without lifting her veil, which, though short, was a thick one.

"We received a letter from you this morning," he continued.

"Yes; I have called about it."

She hesitated. The commencement was very difficult. After all, had she done wisely in coming here? Was it not all a mistake? Had she not better leave the thing to the proper authorities, and content herself with offering a reward? She had half a mind to declare that her visit was an error, and make her escape.

It was at this point that the tact of the junior member of the firm asserted itself. Quietly laying down his pen, he turned toward her, and spoke for the first time.

"We gathered from your letter, Miss Thurwell, that you desired to consult us concerning the murder of Sir Geoffrey Kynaston."

Helen was surprised into assenting, and before she could qualify her words, Mr. Benjamin had taken the case in hand.

"Exactly. Now, Miss Thurwell, we have had some very delicate and very difficult business confided to us at different times, and I may say, without boasting, that we have been remarkably successful. I may so, father, may I not?"

"Most decidedly, Benjamin. There was Mr. Morris's jewels, you know."

"And Mr. Hadson's son."

"And that little affair with Captain Trescott and Bella B——"

Mr. Benjamin dropped the ruler, which he had been idly balancing on his forefinger, with a crash, and shot a warning glance across at his father.

"Miss Thurwell will not be interested in the details of our business," he remarked. "Our reputation is doubtless known to her."

Considering what the reputation of Messrs. Levy & Son really was, this last remark was a magnificent piece of cool impudence. Even Mr. Levy could not refrain from casting a quick glance of admiration at his junior, who remained perfectly unmoved.

"What I was about to remark, Miss Thurwell, was simply this. The chief cause of our success has been that we have induced our clients at the outset to give us their whole confidence. We lay great stress on this. Everything that we are told in the way of business we consider absolutely secret. But we like to know everything."

"I shall keep nothing back from you," she said quietly. "I have nothing to conceal."

Mr. Benjamin nodded approval.

"Then, in order that the confidence between us may be complete, let me ask you this question, Why have you brought this matter to us, instead of leaving it to the ordinary authorities?"

Helen Thurwell lifted her veil for the first time, and looked at the young man who was questioning her. Mr. Benjamin Levy, as a young man of fashion, was an ape and a fool. Mr. Benjamin Levy, taking the lead in a piece of business after his own heart, was as shrewd a young man as you could meet with. Looking him steadily in the face, and noticing his keen dark eyes and closely drawn lips, she began for the first time to think that, after all, she might have done a wise thing in coming here.

"The ordinary authorities have had the matter in hand two months, and they have done nothing," she answered. "I am very anxious that it should be cleared up, and I am naturally beginning to lose faith in them. They have so many other things to attend to. Now, if I paid you well, I suppose you would give your whole time to the matter."

"Undoubtedly," assented Mr. Levy, senior, gravely.

"Undoubtedly," echoed his son. "I am quite satisfied, Miss Thurwell, and I thank you for your candor."

"I suppose you will want me to tell you all about it," she said, with a faint shudder.

"Not unless you know something fresh. I have every particular in my head that has been published."

Helen looked surprised.

"You read all about it, I suppose?" she asked.

"Yes; such things interest us, naturally. This one did me particularly, because, from the first, I saw that the police were on the wrong tack."

"What is your idea about it, then?" she asked.

"Simply this," he answered, turning round and facing her for the first time. "All the time and trouble spent in scouring the country and watching the ports and railway stations was completely wasted. The murder was not committed by an outsider at all. The first thing I shall want, when we begin to work this, is the name and address of all the people living within a mile or two of the scene of the murder, and then every possible particular concerning Mr. Bernard Brown, of Falcon's Nest."

She could not help a slight start. And from his looking at her now for the first time so fixedly, and from the abrupt manner in which he had brought out the latter part of his sentence, she knew that he was trying her.

"There is one more question, too, Miss Thurwell, which I must ask you, and it is a very important one," he continued, still looking at her. "Do you suspect any one?"

She answered him without hesitation.

"I do."

Mr. Levy, senior, stirred in his chair, and leaned forward eagerly. Mr. Benjamin remained perfectly unmoved.

"And who is it?" he asked.

"Mr. Brown."

Mr. Benjamin looked away and made a note. If she could have seen it, Helen would certainly have been surprised. For, though her voice was low, she had schooled herself to go through her task without agitation. Yet, here was the note.

"Query: Connection between Mr. Brown and Miss T. Showed great agitation in announcing suspicion."

"Do you mind telling us your reasons?" he went on.

She repeated them after the manner of one who has learned a lesson.

"Mr. Brown came to our part of the country just at the time that Sir Geoffrey came from abroad. They had met before, and there was some cause of enmity between them—"

"Stop! How do you know that?" Mr. Benjamin interrupted quickly.

She told him of Mr. Brown's admission to her, and of the tragedy of Rachel Kynaston's last words. He seemed to know something of this too.

"Any other reason?"

"He seemed agitated when he came out from the cottage, after the crime was discovered. From its situation he could easily have committed the murder and regained it unseen. It would have been infinitely easier for him to have done it than anyone else."

Mr. Benjamin looked at his father, and his father looked at him.

"Can you tell me anything at all of his antecedents?" he continued.

She shook her head.

"We knew nothing about him when he came. He never talked about himself."

"But he was your father's tenant, was he not?"

"Yes."

"Then he gave you some references, I suppose?"

"Only his bankers and his lawyers."

"Do you remember those?"

"Yes. The bankers were Gregsons, and the lawyer's name was Cuthbert."

Mr. Benjamin made a note of both.

"There is nothing more which it occurs to you to tell us, Miss Thurwell?" he asked.

"There is one circumstance which seemed to me at the time suspicious," she said slowly. "It was after the body had been carried to Mr. Brown's house, and I was waiting for my father there. I think I must have suspected Mr. Brown then, in a lesser degree, for I took the opportunity of being alone to look into his sitting room. It was rather a mean thing to do," she added hurriedly, "but I was a little excited at the notion of his guilt, and I felt that I would do anything to help to bring the truth to light."

"It was very natural," interposed Mr. Levy, senior, who had been watching for some time for the opportunity of getting a word in. "Very natural, indeed."

His son took no notice of the interruption, and Helen continued.

"What I saw may be of no consequence, but I will just tell you what it was, and what it suggested to me. The window was open, and the leaves of a laurel shrub just outside were dripping with wet. A little way in the room was an empty basin, and on the floor by the side was a pile of books. They might have been there by accident, but it seemed to me as if they had been purposely placed there to hide something—possibly a stain on the floor. Before I could move any of them to see, I was disturbed."

"By Mr. Brown?"

"By Mr. Brown and Sir Allan Beaumerville."

"Did you gather from his appearance that he was alarmed at finding you there?"

Helen shook her head.

"No. He was surprised, certainly, but that was natural. I cannot say that he looked alarmed."

Mr. Benjamin put away his notes and turned round on his stool.

"A word or two with regard to the business part of this matter, Miss Thurwell. Are you prepared to spend a good deal of money?"

"If it is necessary, yes."

"Very good. Then I will give you a sketch of my plans. We have agents in Paris, Vienna, Venice, and other towns, whom I shall at once employ in tracing out Sir Geoffrey Kynaston's life abroad, concerning which I already have some useful information. During the rest of the day I shall make inquiries about Mr. Brown in London. To-morrow I shall be prepared to come down to Thurwell in any capacity you suggest."

"If you know anything of auditing," she said, "you can come down and go through the books of the estate at the Court. I can arrange that."

"It will do admirably. These are my plans, then. We shall require from you, Miss Thurwell, two hundred guineas to send abroad, and forty guineas a week for the services of my father and myself and our staff. If in twelve months we have not succeeded, we will engage to return you twenty-five per cent of this amount. If, on the other hand, we have brought home the crime to the murderer, we shall ask you for a further five hundred. Will you agree to these terms?"

"Yes."

Mr. Benjamin stretched out his hand for a piece of writing paper, and made a memorandum.

"Perhaps you would be so good as to sign this, then?" he said, passing it to her.

She took the pen, and wrote her name at the bottom. Then she rose to go.

"There is nothing more?" she said.

"Nothing except your London address," he reminded her.

"I am staying with my aunt, Lady Thurwell, at No. 8, Cadogan Square."

"Can I call and see you to-morrow morning there?"

She hesitated. After all, why not. She had put her hand to the plow, and she must go on with it.

"Yes," she answered; "as the auditor who is going to Thurwell Court."

He bowed, and held the door open for her.

"That is understood, of course. Good morning, Miss Thurwell."

She was standing quite still on the threshold, as if lost in thought for a moment. Suddenly she looked up at him with a bright spot of color glowing in her cheeks.

"Let me ask you a question, Mr. Levy."

"Certainly."

"You have read the account of this—terrible thing, and you have heard all I can tell you. Doubtless you have formed some idea concerning it. Would you mind telling it to me?"

Mr. Benjamin kept his keen black eyes fixed steadily upon her while he answered the question, as though he were curious to see what effect it would have on her.

"Certainly, Miss Thurwell. I think that the gentleman calling himself Mr. Brown will find himself in the murderer's dock before a month is out."

She shuddered slightly, and turned away.

"Thank you. Good morning."

"Good morning, Miss Thurwell."

She was gone, and as the sound of her departing cab became lost in the din of the traffic outside, a remarkable change took place in the demeanor of Mr. Benjamin Levy. His constrained, almost polished manner disappeared. His small, deep-set eyes sparkled with exultation, and all his natural vulgarity reasserted itself.

"What do you think of that, guv'nor, eh?" he cried, patting him gently on the shoulder. "Good biz, eh?"

"Benjamin, my son," returned the old man, with emotion, "our fortune is made. You are a jewel of a son."

XIII

A Strange Meeting

Grayness reigned everywhere—in the sky, on the hillside, and on the bare moor, no longer made resplendent by the gleaming beauty of the purple heather and fainter flashes of yellow gorse. The dry, springy turf had become a swamp, and phantom-like wreaths of mist blurred and saddened the landscape. The sweet stirring of the summer wind amongst the pine trees had given place to the melancholy drip of raindrops falling from their heavy, drooping branches on to the soddened ground. Every vestige of coloring had died out of the landscape—from the sea, the clouds, and the heath. It was the earth's mourning season, when the air has neither the keen freshness of winter, the buoyancy of spring, the sweet drowsy languor of summer, or the bracing exhilaration of autumn. It was November.

Daylight was fast fading away; but the reign of twilight had not yet commenced. After a blustering morning, a sudden stillness had fallen upon the earth. The wild north wind had ceased its moaning in the pine trees, and no longer came booming across the level moorland. The dull gray clouds which all day long had been driven across the leaden sky in flying haste, hung low down upon the sad earth, and from over the water a sea fog rose to meet them. Nature had nothing more cheerful to offer than silence, a dim light, and indescribable desolation.

A solitary man, with his figure carved out in sharp relief against the vaporous sky, stood on the highest point of the cliff. Everything in his attitude betokened the deepest dejection—in which at least he was in sympathy with his surroundings. His head drooped upon his bent shoulders, and his dark, weary eyes were fixed upon the rising sea fog in a vacant gaze. Warmly clad as he was, he seemed chilled through his whole being by the raw lifelessness of the air. Yet he did not move.

The utter silence was suddenly broken by the rising of a little flock of gulls from among the stunted firs hanging down over the cliff. Almost immediately afterwards there came another sound, denoting the advance of a human being. The little hand gate leading out of the plantation was opened and shut, and light footsteps began to ascend the ridge of the cliffs on which he was standing, hesitating now and then, but always advancing. As soon as he became sure of this, he turned his head in the direction from which they came, and found himself face to face with Helen Thurwell.

It was the first time they had come together since the terrible night at Thurwell Court, when their eyes had met for an awful moment over the dead body of Rachel Kynaston. The memory of that scene flashed into the minds of both of them; from hers, indeed, it had seldom been absent. She stood face to face with the man whom she had been charged, by the passionate prayers of a dying woman, to hunt down and denounce as a murderer. They looked at one another with the same thoughts in the minds of both. The first step she had already taken. Henceforth he would be watched and dogged, his past life raked up, and his every action recorded. And she it was who had set the underhand machinery at work, she it was whom he, guilty or innocent, would think of as the woman who had hunted him down. If he should be innocent, and the time should come when he discovered all, what would he think of her? If he could have seen her a few days back in the office of Messrs. Levy & Son, would he look at her as he was doing now? The thought sent a shiver through her. At that moment she hated herself.

It was no ordinary meeting this, for him or for her. Had she been able to look him steadily in the face, she might have seen something of her own nervousness reflected there. But that was just what at first she was unable to do. One rapid glance into his pale features, which suffering and intellectual labor seemed in some measure to have etherealized, was sufficient. She had all the poignant sense of a culprit before an injured but merciful judge, and at that moment the memory of those dying words was faint within her. And so, though it is not usually the case, it was he who appeared the least disturbed, and he it was who broke that strange silence which had lasted several moments after she had come to a standstill before him.

"You do not mind speaking to me, Miss Thurwell?"

"No; I do not mind," she answered in a low, hesitating tone.

"Then may I take it that Miss Kynaston's words have not—damaged me in your esteem?" he went on, his voice quivering a little with suppressed anxiety. "You do not—believe—that—"

"I neither believe nor disbelieve!" she interrupted. "Remember that you had an opportunity of denying it which you did not accept!"

"That is true!" he answered slowly. "Let it remain like that, then. It is best."

She had turned a little away as though to watch a screaming curlew fly low down and vanish in the fog. From where he stood on slightly higher ground he looked down at her curiously, for in more than one sense she was a puzzle to him. There was a certain indefiniteness in her manner toward him which he felt a passionate desire to construe. She seemed at once merciful and merciless, sympathetic and hard. Then, as he looked at her, he almost forgot all this wilderness of suffering and doubt. All his intense love for physical beauty, ministered to by the whole manner of his life, seemed rekindled in her presence. The tragedy of the present seemed to pass away into the background. From the moment when he had first caught a glimpse of her in the courtyard of the Palazzo Vechi, he had chosen her face and presence with which to endow his artist's ideal—and, since that time, what change there had been in her had been for the better. The animal spirits of light-hearted girlhood had become toned down into the more refined and delicate softness of thoughtful womanhood. In her thin supple figure there was still just the suspicion of incomplete development, which is in itself a fascination; and her country attire, the well-cut brown tweed ulster, the cloth cap from beneath which many little waves of fair silky hair had escaped, the trim gloves and short skirts—the most insignificant article of her attire—all seemed to bespeak that peculiar and subtle daintiness which is at the same time the sweetest and the hardest to define of nature's gifts to women.

Even in the most acute crisis, woman's care for the physical welfare of man seems almost an instinct with her. Suddenly turning round, she saw how ill-protected he was against the weather, and a look of concern stole into her face.

"How ridiculous of you to come out without an overcoat or anything on such a day as this!" she exclaimed. "Why, you must be wet through!—and how cold you look!"

He smiled grimly. That she should think of such a thing just at that moment, seemed to him to be a peculiar satire upon what had been passing through his mind concerning her. Then a sudden thrill shook every limb in his body—his very pulses quickened. She had laid her gloved hand upon his arm, and, having withdrawn it, was regarding it ruefully. It was stained with wet.

"You must go home at once!" she said, with a decision in her tone which was almost suggestive of authority. "You must change all your things, and get before a warm fire. Come, I will walk with you as far as Falcon's Nest. I am going round that way, and home by the footpath."

They started off side by side. The first emotion of their meeting having passed away, he found it easier to talk to her, and he did so in an odd monosyllabic way which she yet found interesting. All her life she had been somewhat peculiarly situated with regard to companionship. Her father, having once taken her abroad and once to London for the season, considered that he had done his duty to her, and having himself long ago settled down to the life of a country squire, had expected her to be content with her position as his daughter and the mistress of his establishment. There was nothing particularly revolting to her in the prospect. She was not by any means emancipated. The "new woman" would have been a horror to her. But, unfortunately, although she was content to accept a comparatively narrow view of life, she was slightly epicurean in her tastes. She would have been quite willing to give up her life to a round of such pleasures as society and wealth can procure, but the society must be good and entertaining, and its pleasures must be refined and free from monotony. In some parts of England she might have found what would have satisfied her, and under the influence of a pleasure-seeking life, she would in due course have become the woman of a type. As she grew older the horizon of her life would have become more limited and her ideas narrower. She would have lived without tasting either the full sweetness or the full bitterness of life. She would have filled her place in society admirably, and there would have been nothing to distinguish her either for better or worse from other women in a similar position. But it happened that round Thurwell Court the people were singularly uninteresting. The girls were dull, and the men bucolic. Before she had spent two years in the country, Helen was intensely bored. A sort of chronic languor seemed to creep over her, and in a fit of desperation she had permitted herself to become engaged to Sir Geoffrey Kynaston, for the simple reason that he was different from the other men. Then, just as she was beginning to tremble at the idea of marriage with a man for whom she had never felt a single spark of love, there had come this tragedy, and, following close upon it, the vague consciousness of an utter change hovering over her life. What that change meant she was slow to discover. She was still unconscious of it as she walked over the cliffs with the grey mists hanging around them, side by side with her father's tenant. She knew that life had somehow become a fairer thing to her, and that for many years she had been living in darkness. And it was her companion, this mysterious stranger with his wan young face and sad thoughtful eyes, who had brought the light. She could see it flashing across the whole landscape of her future, revealing the promise of a larger life than any she had ever dreamed of, full of brilliant possibilities and more perfect happiness than any she had ever imagined. She told herself that he was the Columbus who had shown her the new land of culture, with all its fair places, intellectual and artistic. This was the whole meaning of the change in her. There could be nothing else.

XIV

Helen Thurwell asks a Direct Question

A t the summit of the little spur of cliff they paused. Close on one side were the windows of Falcon's Nest, and on the other the batch of black firs which formed the background to it ran down the steep cliff side to the sea. The path which they were following curved round the cottage, and crossed the moor within a few yards of the spot where Sir Geoffrey had been found. As they stood together for a moment before parting, she noticed, with a sudden cold dismay, that thick shutters had recently been fitted to the windows of the little room into which she had stolen on the day of Sir Geoffrey's murder.

"Are you afraid of being robbed?" she asked. "One would imagine that your room there held a secret."

She was watching him, and she told herself the shot had gone to its mark.

He followed her finger with his eyes, and kept his face turned away from her.

"Yes, that is so," he answered quietly. "That little room holds its secret and its ghost for me. Would to God," he cried, with a sudden passion trembling in his tones, "that I had never seen it—that I had never come here!"

Her heart beat fast. Could it be that he was going to confess to her? Then he turned suddenly round, and in the twilight his white face and dark luminous eyes seemed to her like mute emblems of an anguish which moved her woman's heart to pity. There was none of the cowardice of guilt there, nothing of the criminal in the deep melancholy which seemed to have set its mark upon his whole being. And yet he must be very guilty—very much a criminal.

Her eyes strayed from his face back to the window again. There was no light anywhere in the house. It had a cold desolate look which chilled her.

"Is that the room where you sit?" she asked, pointing to it.

"Yes. There is no other furnished, except my housekeeper's, and she is away now."

"Away! Then who is with you in the house?"

"At present, no one," he answered. "She was taken ill, and went home this morning. She is generally ill."

She looked at him perplexed.

"But who does your cooking for you, and light the fires, and that sort of thing?"

"I haven't thought about it yet," he answered. "I did try to light the fire this afternoon, but I couldn't quite manage it. I—I think the sticks must have been damp," he added hesitatingly.

She looked at him, wet through and almost blue with cold, and at the dull cheerless-looking cottage. Again the woman in her triumphed, and her eyes filled with tears.

"I never heard anything so preposterous," she exclaimed almost angrily. "You must be out of your senses, Mr. Brown. Now, be so good as to obey me at once. Go into the house and get a thick overcoat, the thickest you have, and then come home with me, and I will give you some tea."

He hesitated, and stood quite still for a moment, with his face turned steadily away from her. All the subtle sweetness of that last visit of his to her home had come back to him, and his heart was sick with a great longing. Was he not a fool to refuse to enter into paradise, when the gates stood open for him? No words could describe the craving which he felt to escape, just for a brief while, from the lashings of his thoughts and the icy misery of his great loneliness. What though he were courting another sorrow! Could his state be worse than it was? Could any agony be keener than that which he had already tasted? Were there lower depths still in the hell of remorse? If so, he would sound them. Though he died for it, he would not deny himself this one taste of heaven. He turned suddenly round, with a glow in his eyes which had a strange effect upon her.

"You are very good to me, Miss Thurwell," he said. "I will come."

"That is sensible of you," she answered. "Get your coat, and you can catch me up. I think we had better go back the same way, as it is getting late."

She walked slowly down the path, and he hurried into the cottage. In a few minutes he overtook her, wrapped in a long Inverness cape from head to foot, and they walked on side by side.

The grey afternoon had suddenly faded into twilight. Overhead several stars were already visible, dimly shining through a gauze-like veil of mist stretched all over the sky, and from behind a black line of firs on the top of a distant hill the moon had slowly risen, and was casting a soft weird light upon the saddened landscape. Grey wreaths of phantom-like mist were floating away across the moor, and a faint breeze had sprung up, and was moaning in the pine plantation when they reached the hand-gate. They paused for a moment to listen, and the dull roar of the sea from below mingled with it in their ears. She turned away with a shudder.

"Come!" she said; "that sound makes me melancholy."

"I like it," he answered. "Nature is an exquisite musician. I never yet heard the sea speak in a tone which I did not love to hear. Listen to that slow mournful rise of sound, reaching almost to intensity, and then dying away so sadly—with the sadness that thrills. Ah! did you hear that? The shrieking of those pebbles dragged down to the sea, and crying out in almost human agony. I love the sea."

"Is that why you came to this desolate part of the world?" she asked.

"Partly."

"Tell me the whole reason," she said abruptly. "Was there anything special which made you fix on this neighborhood? You may think me curious, if you like—but I want to know."

"I had a vow to keep," he answered hoarsely. "You must ask me no more. I cannot tell you."

Her heart sank like lead. A vow to keep. There was something ominous in the sound of those words. She stole a glance at him as they walked on in silence, and again her judgments seemed put to confusion and her hopes revived. His face, dimly seen in the shadows of the plantation, was suddenly illuminated by a pale quivering moonbeam, as they passed through a slight opening. Could these be the features of a murderer? Her whole heart rebelled against her understanding, and cried out "No!" For the first time she realized the æsthetic beauty of his face, scarred and wasted though it was by the deep lines of intellectual toil and consuming sorrow. There was not a line out of place, save where his cheek-bones projected slightly, owing to his extreme thinness, and left deep hollows under his eyes. Nor was his expression the expression of a guilty man, for, notwithstanding the intense melancholy which dwelt always in his dark eyes, and seemed written into every feature, there was blended with it a strange pride, the slight yet wholesome contempt of a man conscious of a certain superiority in himself, neither physical nor in any way connected with material circumstances, over the majority of his fellows. And as the realization of this swept in upon her, and her faith in him suddenly leaped up with a new-born strength, there came with it a passionate desire to hear him proclaim his innocence with his own lips, and, having heard it, to banish for ever doubts and suspicions, and give herself up to this new sweetness which was hovering around her life. She caught hold of his hand, but dropped it almost at once, for the fire which flashed into his face at the touch of her fingers half frightened her. He had come to a sudden standstill, and before his eyes she felt hers droop and the hot color burn her cheeks. What had come to her? She could not tell. She was nervous, almost faint, with the dawning promise of a bewildering happiness. Yet her desire still clung to her, and she found words to express it.

"I cannot bear this any longer," she cried. "I must ask you a question, and you must answer it. The thought of it all is driving me mad."

"For God's sake, ask me nothing!" he said in a deep hollow tone. "Let me go back. I should not be here with you."

"You shall not go," she answered. "Stand there where the light falls upon your face, and answer me. Was it you who killed Sir Geoffrey Kynaston? Tell me, for I will know."

There was a dead silence, which seemed to her fevered nerves intolerable. From all around them came the quiet drip, drip, of the rain, from the bending boughs on to the damp soaked ground, and at that moment a slight breeze from over the moorland stirred amongst the branches, and the moisture which hung upon them descended in little showers. From below, the dull roar of the sea came up to them in a muffled undertone, like a melancholy background to the slighter sound. There was an indescribable dreariness about it all which quickened the acute agony of those few moments.

More awful than anything to her was the struggle which she saw in that white strained face half hidden in his clasped hands. What could hesitation mean but guilt? What need was there for it? Her feet seemed turned to stone upon the cold ground, and her heart almost stopped beating. There was a film before her eyes, and yet she saw his face still, though dimly, and as if it were far off. She saw his hands withdrawn, and she saw his ashen lips part slowly.

"I did not kill Sir Geoffrey Kynaston," he said in a low constrained voice. "If my life could have saved his, I would have given it."

A warm golden light seemed suddenly to banish the misty gloom of the damp plantation. The color rushed into her cheeks, and her heart leaped for joy. She heard, and she believed.

"Thank God!" she cried, holding out both her hands to him with a sudden impulsive gesture. "Come! let us go now."

She was smiling softly up at him, and her eyes were wet with tears. He took one quick passionate step towards her, seizing her hands, and drawing her unresistingly towards him. In a moment she would have been in his arms—already a great trembling had seized her, and her will had fled. But that moment was not yet.

Something seemed to have turned him to stone. He dropped her fingers as though they were burning him. A vacant light eclipsed the passion which had shone a moment before in his eyes. Suddenly he raised his hands to the sky in a despairing gesture.

"God forgive me!" he cried. "God forgive me!"

For very shame at his touch, and her ready yielding to it, her eyes had fallen to the ground. When she raised them he was gone. There was the sound of his retreating footsteps, the quick opening and closing of the hand-gate, and through the trees she saw him walking swiftly over the cliffs. Then she turned away, with her face half hidden in her hands, and the hot tears streaming down her cheeks.

Again there was silence, only broken by the louder roar of the incoming tide, and the faint rustling of the leaves. Suddenly it was broken by a human voice, and a human figure slowly arose from a cramped posture behind a clump of shrubs.

"Holy Moses! if this ain't a queer start," remarked Mr. Benjamin Levy, shaking the wet from his clothes, and slowly filling a pipe. "Wants him copped for murder, and yet tries to get him to make up to her. She's a deep un, she is. I wonder if she was in earnest! If only she was, I think I see my way to a real good thing—a real good thing," he repeated, meditatively.

XV

A Literary Celebrity

It was Tuesday afternoon, and the Countess of Meltoun was at home to the world—that is to say, her world. The usual throng of men of fashion, guardsmen, literary men, and budding politicians were bending over the chairs of their feminine acquaintances, or standing about in little groups talking amongst themselves. The clatter of teacups was mingled with the soft hum of voices; the pleasantly shaded room was heavy with the perfume of many flowers. People said that Lady Meltoun was the only woman in London who knew how to keep her rooms cool. It was hard to believe that outside the streets and pavements were hot with the afternoon sun.

Helen Thurwell, who had come late with her aunt, was sitting on a low couch near one of the windows. By her side was Sir Allan Beaumerville, and directly in front of her the Earl of Meltoun, with a teacup in his hand, was telling her stories of his college days with her father. There had been a great change in her during the last six months. Looking closely into her face, it seemed as though she had felt the touch of a deep sorrow—a sorrow which had left all its refining influences upon her without any of the ravages of acute grief. Those few minutes in the pine grove by the sea had left their indelible mark upon her life, and it was only the stimulating memory of his own words to her concerning the weakness of idle yielding to regret, and the abstract beauty of sorrow which had been her salvation. They had come back to her in the time of her suffering fresh and glowing with truth; she had found a peculiar comfort in them, and they had become her religion. Thus she had set herself to conquer grief in the highest possible manner—not by steeping herself in false excitement, or rushing away for a change of scene, but by a deliberate series of intellectual and artistic abstractions, out of which she had come, still in a manner sorrowful, but with all her higher perceptions quickened and strengthened until the consciousness of their evolution, gradually growing within her, gave a new power and a new sweetness to her life.

And of this victory she showed some traces in her face, which had indeed lost none of its physical beauty, but which had now gained a new strength and a new sweetness. She was more admired than ever, but there were men who called her difficult—even a little fastidious, and others who found her very hard to get on with. The great artist who had just taken Sir Allan Beaumerville's place by her side was not one of these.

"I am so glad that you are here to-day, Miss Thurwell," he said, holding her grey-gloved hand in his for a moment. "I have been looking for you everywhere."

"That is very nice of you," she answered, smiling up at him.

"Ah! but I didn't mean only for my own sake. I know that you like meeting interesting people, and to-day there is an opportunity for you."

"Really! and who is it, Mr. Carlyon? How good of you to think of me!"

"You remember telling me how much you admire Maddison's work."

"Why, yes! But he is not here, surely?" she exclaimed. "It cannot be he!"

Mr. Carlyon smiled at her sudden enthusiasm. After all, this woman had fire. She was too much of the artist to be without it.

"He is not here now, but he will be. I could not believe it myself at first, for I know that he is a perfect recluse. But I have just asked Lady Meltoun, and there is no doubt about it. It seems that they came across him in a lonely part of Spain, and he saved the life of Lady Meltoun's only child—a little boy. It is quite a romantic story. He promised to come and seem them directly he returned to England, and he is expected here to-day."

"I shall like to see him very much," she said thoughtfully. "Lately I have been reading him a great deal. It is strange, but the tone of his writings seems always to remind me of some one I once knew."

"There is no one of to-day who writes such prose," the artist answered. "To me, his work seems to have reached that exquisite blending of matter and form which is the essence of all true art."

"All his ideas of culture and the inner life are so simple and yet so beautiful."

"And the language with which he clothes them is divine. His work appeals everywhere to the purest and most artistic side of our emotional natures; and it is always on the same level. It has only one fault—there is so little of it."

"Do you know him?" she asked, deeply interested.

"I do. I met him in Pisa some years ago, and, although he is a strangely reserved man, we became almost intimate. I am looking forward to introducing him to you."

"I shall like it very much," she answered simply.

"Who is the fortunate individual to be so highly favored?" asked a pleasant voice close to her side.

"You have returned, then, Sir Allan?" she said, looking up at him with a smile. "Have you heard the news? Do you know who is expected?"

He shook his head.

"I have heard nothing," he said. "If I am to have a sensation, it will be you who will impart it to me. Don't tell me all at once. I like expectancy."

She laughed.

"What an epicure you are, Sir Allan! Come, prepare for something very delightful, and I will tell you."

"Is it the prince?" he asked.

She shook her head.

"The Mikado in disguise? The Khedive incognito? Mr. Gladstone?"

She shook her head again.

"The sensation will be more delightful than you imagine, evidently. There have been many Khedives, and many Mikados, but there can never be another Bernard Maddison."

A disturbed shade seemed to fall upon the baronet's face. She followed his eyes, riveted upon the door. The hum of conversation had suddenly ceased, and every one was looking in the same direction. On the threshold stood a tall, gaunt man, gazing in upon the scene before him with an expression of distinct aversion, mingled with indifference. He was dressed just like the other men, in a long frock coat, and he had a white gardenia in his buttonhole. But there was something about him distinct and noticeable—something in the quiet easy manner with which he at last moved forward to greet his hostess, which seemed to thrill her through and through with a sense of sweet familiarity. And then she caught a turn of his head as he stooped down over Lady Meltoun's hand, and a great wave of bewilderment, mingled with an acute throbbing joy, swept in upon her. This man, whom every one was gazing at with such eager interest, was her father's tenant, Mr. Bernard Brown.

XVI

A Snub for a Baronet

Those few moments were full of a strange, intense interest to the three persons who side by side had watched the entrance of Mr. Bernard Maddison. To Helen Thurwell, whose whole being was throbbing with a great quickening joy, they were passed in a strenuous effort to struggle against the faintness which the shock of this great tumult of feeling had brought with it. To the artist, who loved her, they brought their own peculiar despair as he watched the light playing upon her features, and the new glow of happiness which shone in those sweet, sad eyes. And to Sir Allan Beaumerville, who had reasons of his own for surprise at this meeting, they brought a distinct sensation of annoyance.

The artist was the first to recover himself. He knew that the battle was over for him, that this woman already loved, and that his cause was hopeless. And with little of man's ordinary selfishness on such occasions, his first thought was for her.

"You would like to change your seat," he whispered. "Come with me into the recess yonder. I will show you some engravings."

She flashed a grateful look up at him, and saw that he knew her secret.

"I should like it," she said. "Walk that side of me, please."

They rose and made their way to one of the little screened recesses which people—especially young people—said made Lady Meltoun's rooms so delightful. He placed a chair for her, and taking up a book of engravings buried himself in it.

"Don't speak to me for five minutes, please," he said. "I am looking for a design."

At the end of that time he closed the book, and looked up at her. There was no fear of her fainting now. She was very pale, but she seemed quite calm.

"I am going to speak to Maddison," he said quietly. "Do you—may I bring him and introduce him to you?"

She looked up at him with luminous eyes.

"If you please. Don't tell him my name, though."

"It shall be as you wish," he answered.

By moving her chair a few inches she could see into the room. He was still standing by Lady Meltoun's side, listening with an absent smile to her chatter, and every now and then bowing gravely to the people whom she introduced to him. The hum of conversation had been renewed, but many curious glances were cast in his direction, of which he seemed altogether unconscious. Even had there not been his great fame as a critic and a writer, and the romance of his strange manner of life to interest people, his personal appearance alone was sufficient to attract attention. He was taller by several inches than any man in the room, and his thin oval face, refined yet strong and full of a subtle artistic sensibility, was in itself a deeply interesting study. How different he appeared here in his well-fitting, fashionable clothes, and calm distinctive manner, and with just that essence of wearied languor in his dark eyes which men of the world can only imitate! He had changed, and yet he had not changed, she thought. He was the same, and yet there was a difference. Presently she saw Mr. Carlyon reach his side, and the greeting which passed between the two men was marked with a certain quiet cordiality which bore out Mr. Carlyon's words, that they had once been fellow-workers. Watching his opportunity, the artist drew him a little on one side, and made his request. Helen drew back trembling with expectancy. But a few minutes later Mr. Carlyon came back to her alone.

"I am sorry," he said simply, "but, even to oblige me, Maddison won't come. I had no idea he was such a misogynist. He is here, he says, to keep a promise, but he wishes for no acquaintances, and he absolutely declines to be introduced to any woman, unless it is forced upon him. What shall I do? Shall I tell him your name?"

She hesitated.

"No, don't tell him that," she said. "Do you remember a few lines of poetry of his at the end of his last volume of criticisms? There is a little clump of firs on the top of a bare wind-swept hill, with the moon shining faintly through a veil of mist, and a man and woman standing together like carved figures against the sky, listening to the far-off murmur of the sea."

"Yes, I remember it," he said slowly.

"Then will you tell him that some one—some one who has seen such a place as he describes, is—?"

"I will tell him," Mr. Carlyon answered. "I think that he will come now."

He left her again, and went back towards Mr. Maddison. Just as he got within speaking distance he saw a slight quiver pass across the white face, as though he had recognized some one in the crowd. Mr. Carlyon hesitated, and decided to wait for a moment.

They were standing face to face, Sir Allan Beaumerville, the distinguished baronet, who had added to the dignity of an ancient family and vast wealth, a great reputation as a savant and a *dilettante* physician, and Mr. Bernard Maddison, whose name alone was sufficient to bespeak his greatness. In Sir Allan's quiet, courteous look, there was a slightly puzzled air as though there were something in the other's face which he only half remembered. In Mr. Maddison's fixed gaze there was a far greater intensity—something even of anxiety.

"Surely we have met before, Mr. Maddison," the baronet said easily. "Your face seems quite familiar to me. Ah! I remember now, it was near that place of Lord Lathon's, Mallory Grange, upon the coast. A terrible affair, that."

"Yes, a terrible affair," Mr. Maddison repeated.

"And have you just come from ——shire?" Sir Allan asked.

"No; I have been abroad for several months," Mr. Maddison answered.

"Abroad!" Sir Allan appeared a little more interested. "In what part?" he asked civilly.

"I have been in Spain, and the south of France, across the Hartz mountains, and through the Black Forest."

"Not in Italy?" Sir Allan inquired.

There was a short silence, and Sir Allan seemed really anxious for the reply. It came at last.

"No; not in Italy."

Sir Allan seemed positively pleased to think that Mr. Maddison had not extended his travels to Italy. There was a quiet gleam in his eyes which seemed almost like relief. Doubtless he had his reasons, but they were a little obscure.

"Ah! Shall you call upon me while you are in town, Mr. Maddison?" he asked, in a tone from which all invitation was curiously lacking.

"I think not," Mr. Maddison answered. "My stay here will be brief. I dislike London."

Sir Allan laughed gently.

"It is the only place in the world fit to live in," he answered.

"My work and my tastes demand a quieter life," Mr. Maddison remarked.

"You will go into the country then, I suppose."

"That is my intention," was the quiet reply.

"Back to the same neighborhood."

"It is possible."

Sir Allan looked searchingly into the other's calm, expressionless face.

"I should have thought that the associations—"

Mr. Maddison was evidently not used to society. Several people said so who saw him suddenly turn his back on that charming old gentleman, Sir Allan Beaumerville, and leave him in the middle of a sentence. Lady Meltoun, who happened to notice it, was quite distressed at seeing an old friend treated in such a manner. But Sir Allan took it very nicely, everybody said. There had been a flush in his face just for a moment, but it soon died away. It was his own fault, he declared. He had certainly made an unfortunate remark, and these artists and literary men were all so sensitive. He hoped that Lady Meltoun would think no more of it, and accordingly Lady Meltoun promised not to. But though, of course, she and every one else who had seen it sympathized with Sir Allan, there were one or two, with whom Sir Allan was not quite such a favorite, who could not help remarking upon the grand air with which Mr. Maddison had turned his back upon the baronet, and the dignity with which he had left him.

Mr. Carlyon, who had been watching for his opportunity, buttonholed Maddison, and led him into a corner.

"I've got you now," he said triumphantly. "My dear fellow, whatever made you snub poor Sir Allan like that?"

"Never mind. Come and make your adieux to Lady Meltoun, and let us go. I should not have come here."

"One moment first, Maddison," the artist said seriously. "Do you remember those lines of yours in which a man and woman stand on a bare hill by a clump of pines, and watch the misty moonlight cast weird shadows upon the hillside and over the quivering sea? 'A Farewell,' you called it, I think?"

"Yes; I remember them."

"Maddison, the woman to whom I wished to introduce you bids you to go to her by the memory of those lines."

There was very little change in his face. It only grew a little more rigid, and a strange light gleamed in his eyes. But the hand which he had laid on Carlyon's arm to draw him towards Lady Meltoun suddenly tightened like a band of iron, till the artist nearly cried out with pain.

"Let go my arm, for God's sake, man!" he said in a low tone, "and I will take you to her."

"I am ready," Mr. Maddison answered quietly. "Ah! I see where she is. You need not come."

He crossed the room, absolutely heedless of more than one attempt to stop him. Mr. Carlyon watched him, and then with a sore heart bade his hostess farewell, and hurried away. He was generous enough to help another man to his happiness, but he could not stay and watch it.

XVII

Bernard Maddison and Helen Thurwell

And so it was in Lady Meltoun's drawing-room that they met again, after those few minutes in the pine plantation which had given color and passion to her life, and which had formed an epoch in his. Neither were unmindful of the fact that if they were not exactly the centre of observation, they were still liable to it in some degree, and their greeting was as conventional as it well could have been. After all, she thought, why should it be otherwise? There had never a word of love passed between them—only those few fateful moments of tragic intensity, when all words and thoughts had been merged in a deep reciprocal consciousness which nothing could have expressed.

He stood before her, holding her hand in his for a moment longer than was absolutely necessary, and looking at her intently. It was a gaze from which she did not shrink, more critical than passionate, and when he withdrew his eyes he looked away from her with a sigh.

"You have been living!" he said. "Tell me all about it!"

She moved her skirts to make room for him by her side.

"Sit down!" she said, "and I will try."

He obeyed, but when she tried to commence and tell him all that she had felt and thought, she could not. Until that moment she scarcely realized how completely her life had been moulded by his influence. It was he who had first given her a glimpse of that new world of thought and art, and almost epicurean culture into which she had made some slight advance during his absence, and it was certain vague but sweet recollections of him which had lived with her and flowed through her life—a deep undercurrent of passion and poetry, throwing a golden halo over all those new sensations—which had raised her existence, and her ideals of existence on to a higher level. How could she tell him this? The time might come when she could do so, and if ever it did come, she knew that it would be the happiest moment of her life. But it was not yet.

"Tell me a little of yourself," she said evasively. "You have been traveling, have you not?"

"Yes, I have been traveling a little!" he answered. "In Spain I was taken ill, and Lady Meltoun was kind to me. That is why I am here."

"But you do not say how it was that you were taken ill," she said, her cheeks suddenly glowing. "You saved her son's life. We saw all about it in the papers, but of course we did not know that it was you. It was splendid!"

"If you saw it in the papers at all, depend upon it, it was very much exaggerated!" he answered quietly. "Your father received my letter, I suppose?"

"Yes; the cottage has been shut up, just as you desired. Are you ever coming to take possession again?"

"I hope so—some day—and yet I do not know. There are strange things in my life, Miss Thurwell, which every now and then rise up and drive me away into aimless wanderings. Life has no goal for me—it cannot have. I stand for ever on the brink of a precipice."

There was a sadness in his voice which almost brought the tears into her eyes—mostly for his sake, partly for her own. For, though he might never know it, were not his sorrows her sorrows?

"Are they sorrows which you can tell to no one?" she asked softly. "Can no one help you?"

He shook his head.

"No one."

"And yet no sorrow can last for ever that has not guilt at its root," she said.

"Mine will last while life lasts," he answered; "and there is—no guilt at the root."

"You have taken up another's burden," she said. "Is it well? Do you owe nothing to yourself, and your own genius? Sorrow may shorten your life, and the world can ill spare your work."

"There are others who can do my work," he said. "No other can—But forgive me. I wish to talk of this no more. Tell me of your life since I left you. Something in your face tells me that it has been well spent. Let me hear of it."

And, gathering up all her courage, she told him. Piece by piece she took up the disconnected thoughts and ideas which had come to her, and wove them together after the pattern of her life—to which he listened with a calm approval, in which was sometimes mingled a deeper enthusiasm, as she touched a chord which in his own being had often been struck to deep tremulous music. And as she went on he grew sad. With such a companion as this woman, whose sensibilities were his sensibilities, and whose instincts so naturally cultured, so capable of the deeper coloring and emotional passion which his influence could speedily develop—with such a woman as this—whom already he loved, what might not life mean for him? Well, it must pass. Another of those bright butterfly visions of his fancy, gorgeous with hope and brilliancy—another one to be crushed by the iron hand of necessity. He had gone away wounded, and he had come back to find the wound still bleeding.

Gradually the rooms were thinning, and at last Lady Thurwell, impatient of her niece's long absence, came to fetch her. When she found her *tête-à-tête* with the lion of the day, however, her manner was most gracious.

"I hope you have been able to persuade Mr. Maddison to come and see us," she said to her niece. "We are at home on Thursdays at Cadogan Square, and we lunch every day at two," she added, turning towards him. "Come whenever you like."

"You are very good, Lady Thurwell," he said, accepting her offered hand. "I am only passing through London, but if I have the opportunity I shall avail myself of your kindness."

She left them together for a moment while she made her adieux to her hostess. In that moment Helen found courage to yield to a sudden impulse.

"Please come," she said softly.

He had no time to answer, for Lady Meltoun had come up to them.

"Miss Thurwell," she said good-naturedly, "I don't know when I shall forgive you for monopolizing Mr. Maddison in this shameful manner. Why, there were quite a crowd of people came this afternoon only to catch a glimpse of him, and there was nothing to be seen but his boots behind that screen. I am in terrible disgrace, I can assure you!"

"The fault was mine," he interposed, "altogether mine. In an ungovernable fit of shyness, I took refuge with the only person except yourself, Lady Meltoun, whom I was fortunate enough to know. I simply refused to come away."

"Well, I suppose I must forgive you, or you won't come again," Lady Meltoun said. "But now you are here, you must really stop and see Edgar. When every one has gone we will go up to the nursery, and in the meantime you may make yourself useful by taking Lady Thurwell out to her carriage. I'm afraid there's rather a crush."

So they all three went out together, and while they stood waiting for Lady Thurwell's victoria, he managed to say a word to her alone.

"I will come and see you," he whispered.

She looked up at him a little shyly, for in handing her into the carriage he had assumed a certain air of proprietorship which had brought a faint color into her cheeks.

"Come soon," she whispered. "Good-bye!"

She nodded brightly, and Lady Thurwell smiled as the horses started forward, and the carriage drove away.

"I wonder who Mr. Maddison really is?" she said, half to herself, just as they reached home.

Lady Thurwell shrugged her shoulders.

"Do you mean who his family are?" she asked. "My dear, it isn't of the slightest consequence. Bernard Maddison is Bernard Maddison, and his position would be just what it is, even though his father were a coal heaver."

Which remark showed that Lady Thurwell, as well as being a woman of society, was also a woman of sense. But Helen was not thinking of his family.

XVIII

A Cheque for £1,000

I t was ten o'clock in the morning, and the usual routine of business had commenced in the office of Messrs. Levy & Son. Mr. Levy, senior, was sitting at his desk opening his letters, and Mr. Benjamin, who had only just returned from a long journey on business of the firm, and did not feel inclined for office work, was leaning back in the client's chair, with his feet up against the mantelpiece, and a partly smoked cigar in his mouth. He had just finished a long account of his adventures, and was by no means inclined to quit the subject.

"Altogether, dad," he was saying, "it's about the prettiest piece of business we ever struck. But one thing is very certain. We must get some more tin from Miss Thurwell. Why, I've been at it five months now, and the expenses at some of those foreign hotels were positively awful. Not knowing the confounded lingo, you see, I was forced to stump up, without trying the knocking-off game."

"Yes, Benjamin. Yes, my son. We must certainly have some more of the rhino. Your expenses have been positively e-normous, e-normous," declared the old man, with uplifted hands and eyes. "Some of your drafts have brought tears into my eyes. Positively tears," he echoed mournfully.

"Couldn't be helped, guv'nor. The thing had to be done."

"And you have got it nearly all in order now, Benjamin, eh? You've got him under your thumb, eh? He can't escape?"

"Not he! Mark my words, dad. The rope's already woven that'll go round his neck."

The old man looked doubtful.

"If he's such a learned, clever man as you say—writes books and such like—they'll never hang him, my son. They'll reprieve him. That's what they'll do."

"I don't care a blooming fig which it is, so long as it comes off. Do you remember what I told you when Miss Thurwell first came here, dad?"

"Perfectly, my son, perfectly. You said that our fortune was made. Those were your very words," he added, with glistening eyes. "Our fortune is made."

"And what I said I'll stick to," Mr. Benjamin declared. "When this case comes off, it'll be the biggest thundering sensation of the day. And who'll get the credit of it all? Who tracked him down for all his false name and sly ways; hunted him all over Europe, found out who he really was, and why he hated Sir Geoffrey Kynaston so much that he murdered him? Why, I did, dad—Benjamin Levy, of Levy & Son, Carle Street, Strand. Ain't it glorious, guv'nor? Ain't it proud?"

Mr. Benjamin's enthusiasm was catching. It was reflected in his father's face, and something glistened in his eyes. He removed his spectacles, and carefully wiped them. After all, he was a father, and he had a father's feelings.

"When will the time come, Benjamin?" he inquired.

"A month to-day, I hope," was the prompt reply. "I have one more journey to take, and it will be all square."

"Where to? How far?" inquired the old gentleman uneasily.

Mr. Benjamin looked at him, and shook his head. "Come, dad, I know what you are thinking of," he said. "It's the expense, ain't it?"

"It is, Benjamin," his father groaned. "I hate parting with hard-earned money for exorbitant bills and these long journeys. Couldn't it be done without it, Ben?" he inquired, in a wheedling tone. "There's piles of money gone already in expenses. Piles and piles."

"And if there is, ain't it Miss Thurwell's, you old stupid?" remarked Mr. Benjamin. "'Tain't likely that we should find the money ourselves."

"Of course, of course. But, Benjamin, my son, the money is thrown away for all that. We could charge it, you know—charge it always. We must have a margin—we must positively have a margin to work with."

"Dad, dad, what an old sinner you are!" exclaimed his hopeful son, leaning back in his chair and laughing. "A margin to work with. Ha! ha! ha!"

Mr. Levy looked uncertain whether to regard his son's merriment as a compliment, or to resent it. Eventually, the former appeared to him the wisest course, and he smiled feebly.

"Dad, just you leave this matter with me," Mr. Benjamin said at last. "I know what I'm doing, and unless I'm very much mistaken, I see my way to make this a bigger thing, even as regards the cash, than you and I ever dreamed of. Leave it to me. Hullo! who's that?"

He peered up over the office blind, and sat down again at once. In a moment his cigar was behind the grate, and his expression completely changed.

"Ah! Miss Thurwell, dad," he said coolly, "and I'll bet ten to one I know what she wants. Mind you leave it all to me. I've no time to explain, but you'll spoil it if you interfere. Come in. Why, Miss Thurwell, we were this moment talking of you," he continued, springing to his feet and offering her a chair. "Please come in."

Helen advanced into the room, and lifted her veil. One swift glance into her flushed face confirmed Mr. Benjamin's idea as to the reason of her visit, and he commenced talking rapidly.

"I'm glad you've come this morning, Miss Thurwell. I only got back from Spain yesterday, and I'm thankful to tell you our case is nearly complete. Thankful for your sake, because you will have the satisfaction of seeing the murderer of Sir Geoffrey Kynaston brought to book, and thankful for ours, because we shall at one stroke establish our reputation. I need not tell you that that is far more to us than the reward will be, for our expenses have been enormous."

"Enormous!" groaned Mr. Levy, senior.

"However, we have decided not to take another penny of money from you, Miss Thurwell," he continued, casting a warning glance at his father. "After all, the money is not so much to us as our reputation, and this will be made for ever, now."

Mr. Benjamin paused, a little out of breath, but quite satisfied with himself. Opposite, his father was purple with anger, and almost choking at his son's folly. Take no more money from Miss Thurwell! Was the boy mad?

"I'm afraid, from what you say, Mr. Levy," Helen said hesitatingly, "that you will be rather disappointed when I tell you the reason of my visit."

Mr. Benjamin, who knew perfectly well what she was going to say, assumed an expression of deep concern.

"I find," she continued, "that we must have been making a mistake all along, and you have evidently been misled. This Mr. Brown, who appeared such a mysterious personage to us, and whom we therefore suspected, is no other than Bernard Maddison."

"Yes. I knew that," Mr. Benjamin remarked quietly. "I found that out very soon, of course. Author, and all that sort of thing, isn't he? Well, go on, Miss Thurwell, please. I am anxious."

She looked surprised.

"Don't you see that this does away with our theory at once? It is quite impossible that a man like Bernard Maddison could have committed a horrible crime like this."

Mr. Benjamin looked ingenuously perplexed.

"I can't say that I follow you, Miss Thurwell," he said, shaking his head. "All I know is that I can prove this Mr. Bernard Brown, or Bernard Maddison, or whatever else he chooses to call himself, guilty of that murder. That's what we want, isn't it?"

A cold chill passed over her, and she was compelled to sink into the chair which stood by her side. Like a flash she suddenly realized the impossibility of convincing such men as these of his innocence. Yet, even then, the worst side of the situation did not occur to her.

"Perhaps we had better put it in this way, Mr. Levy," she said. "I gave you certain instructions to follow out, which I now rescind. I wish nothing further done in the matter."

Mr. Benjamin's face was a study. He had contrived to conjure up an expression which combined the blankest surprise with the keenest disappointment. Helen began to feel still more uncomfortable.

"Under the circumstances," she said, "and as you seem rather disappointed, I will pay you the reward just as though the thing had gone on."

Mr. Benjamin shook his head slowly.

"Do you know, Miss Thurwell, that you are proposing a conspiracy to me?"

"A conspiracy!" she repeated. "I don't understand."

"It's very simple," he went on gravely. "I have in my possession, or shortly shall have, every particular of this Mr. Maddison's life. I can show the connection between him and Sir Geoffrey Kynaston, and, in short, I can prove him guilty of murder. What you ask me to do is to suppress this. That is the moral side of the question. Then, with regard to the practical side, if this thing is gone on with, we shall get the reward you promised and, what is far more important to us, a reputation which we have looked forward to as a certain foundation for a great extension of our business. If, on the other hand, we drop it, we get simply the reward, which, pardon my saying so, would be a miserable return for all our labor. That is how the matter stands from our point of view. I think I've expressed it fairly, father?"

Mr. Levy, who had assumed a far more contented expression, solemnly assented. What a son this was of his, he thought. Bless him!

Helen was very pale, and her heart was beating fast. Why had she come to this place, and put herself in the power of these men? It was too dreadful.

"I do not desire to hear a word of Mr. Maddison's history," she said. "This thing must be stopped. I have my cheque book with me. Cannot you take money to withdraw from it?"

Mr. Benjamin looked at his father gravely, and Mr. Levy shook his head.

"My dear young lady," he said, "this is a very serious thing, a very serious thing."

"The fact is," said Mr. Benjamin, "I was going to Scotland Yard for a warrant this morning."

Helen looked from one to the other appealingly, with tears in her eyes. Mr. Benjamin appeared to be somewhat moved thereby.

"Look here, dad," he said, "suppose we go into the other room and talk this thing over for a few minutes. Miss Thurwell will not mind excusing us."

"Oh, no. Only don't be long!" she pleaded.

They left her for barely five minutes, although to her, waiting in an agony of impatience, it seemed much longer. When they returned, they both looked very solemn.

"We have talked this matter over thoroughly, Miss Thurwell," said Mr. Benjamin, taking up his old position at the desk, "and we cannot help seeing that it is a great risk for us to run to suppress our information, and a great disappointment."

"Quite so, quite so," interrupted Mr. Levy. "A great risk, and a great disappointment!"

"Still, we are willing and anxious to help you," Mr. Benjamin continued, "and, if you like, we will do so on these terms. If you like to give us a cheque for a thousand pounds, we will agree to let the matter stand over for the present. We cannot give you any undertaking to absolutely destroy or suppress any evidence we may have against Mr. Maddison, as that would be a distinct conspiracy, but we will agree to suspend our present action, and to do nothing without communicating with you."

She moved to the desk, and drew out her cheque book.

"I will do it," she said. "Give me a pen, please."

There was not the slightest sign of emotion on either of their faces. They received the cheque, bowed her out, and watched her disappear into the street without making any sign. Then Mr. Benjamin's exultation broke out.

"Dad, I told you that our fortune was made, didn't I. Was I right or wrong?"

Mr. Levy was so overcome with parental affection, that he could scarcely command his voice. But he did so with an effort.

"You were right, my son," he exclaimed. "You were right, Benjamin. We will go together and cash the cheque."

XIX

AN UNPLEASANT DISCOVERY
FOR BERNARD BROWN

A March wind was roaring over the open moorland, driving huge masses of black clouds across the angry sky, and whistling amongst the dark patches of pine trees, until it seemed as though their slender stems must snap before the strain. All around Falcon's Nest the country, not yet released from the iron grip of a late winter, lay wasted and desolate; and the heath, which had lost all the glowing touch of autumn, faded into the horizon bare and colorless. Nowhere was there any relief of outline, save where the white front of Thurwell Court stretched plainly visible through a park of leafless trees.

And of all the hours of the day it was at such a season the most depressing. Faint gleams of the lingering day still hung over the country, struggling with the stormy twilight, and a pale, wan glare, varied with long black shadows, moved swiftly across the sea and the moor—the reflection of the flying clouds overhead.

A single human being, the figure of a tall man clad in an ulster buttoned up to the throat, was making his way across the open country. He walked rapidly—and, indeed, there was nothing to tempt any one to linger—and his destination was obvious. He was on his way to Falcon's Nest.

A drearier abode than it appeared that afternoon never raised its four walls to the sky. The grounds which surrounded it had been swept bare by the storms of winter, and nothing had been done to repair the destruction which they had accomplished. Uprooted shrubs lay dead and dying upon the long dank grass, and the creepers torn from the walls hung down in pitiful confusion. Every window reflected back the same blank uninviting gloom. There was no light, no single sign of habitation. Mr. Thurwell had evidently respected his tenant's wish to the letter. The place had not been touched or entered during his absence.

The pedestrian, Mr. Bernard Brown himself, leaned over the gate for a moment, silently contemplating the uninviting scene with a grim smile. He had reasons of his own for being satisfied that the place had not been interfered with, and it certainly seemed as though such were the case.

After a few minutes' hesitation he drew a key from his pocket and fitted it in the lock. There was a resistance when he tried to turn it that he did not understand. Stooping down, he suddenly tried the handle. It opened smoothly. The gate was unlocked. He withdrew the key with trembling fingers. All his relief at the dismantled appearance of the cottage had disappeared. A strange unquiet look shone in his eyes, and his manner suddenly became nervous and hurried. He had locked the gate on his departure, he was sure, and Mr. Thurwell's steward had told him that there was no duplicate set of keys. How could it have been opened save with a skeleton key.

He walked quickly up the path to the front door. Here a greater shock still awaited him. The latch-key which he held ready in his hand was not needed. He tried the handle, and the door opened.

Mr. Brown grew white to the lips, and he shrank back as though afraid or reluctant to enter the house. The door stood ajar. He pushed it open with his stick, and peered in upon the darkness. Everything was silent as the grave. He listened for a moment, and then, his natural courage returning, he stepped inside, and closed the door after him. The shutting out of the few gleams of daylight which lingered in the sky left him in utter darkness. Fumbling in his pocket, he produced a wax candle wrapped in a piece of newspaper, and a box of matches, one of which he carefully struck.

At first the gloom seemed too profound to be dispersed by the feeble flickering light, but gradually, as his eyes became accustomed to it, he began to distinguish the more familiar objects. Half fearfully he glanced towards the door on the right-hand side. It stood half open. There was no longer room for any doubt. The house had been opened during his absence.

The full realization of any disaster often brings with it a calm which, to all outward appearance, contrasts favorably with the prior state of anxiety. This appeared to be the case with Mr. Bernard Brown. His entrance to the house had been hesitating and anxious, but as soon as he was convinced that what he dreamed had really come to pass, his nervousness seemed to fall away from him, and he was his old self again, calm and resolute. Holding the flickering candle high above his head, he moved steadily forward into the room on the right-hand side of the entrance.

Everything here was exactly as he had left it. The cases filled with books, some half emptied, some untouched, still lay about the floor, with the dust thick upon them. He cast one swift glance around, and then walked across and opened the door of the small inner room. The sudden draught extinguished his candle, and he found himself suddenly in total darkness. The closely barred shutters, which protected the low window, were securely fastened, and effectually shut out the lingering remnants of daylight. Stooping down, he re-lit the candle which he was still carrying, and holding it high over his head, looked anxiously around. One glance was sufficient. In the corner of the room opposite to him was a small table, where he always kept a basin of cold water and some clean towels. Round here the carpet had been torn up, and rearranged, with little pretence at concealment. Nearer the window stood a large oak cabinet, the most important piece of furniture in the room, and this he saw again in a moment had been tampered with. It had been moved a little out of its position, and one of the lower drawers stood partly open.

Like a man in a dream he slowly walked across to it and drew out a bunch of keys from his pocket. The final test had yet to be applied, and the final blow to fall.

He unlocked the topmost partition, and revealed a number of small drawers. Eagerly he drew out the topmost one, and looked inside. Then he knew the worst. It was empty. There was no longer any doubt whatever. His cottage had been entered by no ordinary housebreaker, for the purpose of plunder, but with a set of false keys, and with a far more serious object. The secret on which more than his life depended was gone!

E. PHILLIPS OPPENHEIM

XX

God! that I May Die!

For a certain space of time, which seemed to him indefinite, but which was indeed of no great length, he stood there stunned, gazing at the rifled cabinet. Then, as consciousness returned to him, the roar of the storm without fell upon his ears, and struck some strange note of accord with the tumult in his brain. Turning round, he unbarred the shutters, and, opening the window, stepped outside. With slow, uncertain steps he made his way through the dense black plantation of shrieking fir trees, and out on to the cliffs. Here he paused, and stood quite still, looking across the sea. There was no light in the sky, but the veil of absolute darkness had not yet fallen upon the earth. Far away on the horizon was a lurid patch of deep yellow storm-clouds, casting a faint glimmer upon the foaming sea, which seemed to leap up in a weird monotonous joy to catch the unearthly light. From inland, rolling across the moorland, came phantom-like masses of vaporous cloud, driven on by the fierce wind which boomed across the open country, and shrieked and yelled amongst the pine plantations as though mad with a sudden hellish joy. On the verge of the cliff he stretched out his arms, as though to welcome the wild din of the night. The thunder of the ocean, seething and leaping against the rocks below, shook the air around him. The salt spray leaped up into his white face, and the winds blew against him, and the passionate cry of saddened nature rang in his deafened ears. At that moment those things were a joy to him.

And there came to him then something of that strange sweet calm which lays its soothing hand for a moment upon those who stand face to face with death, or any other mighty crisis. Looking steadfastly far away, beyond the foaming waste of waters to where one faint streak of stormlight shone on the horizon, pictures of the past began to rise up before his eyes. He saw himself again a happy, light-hearted child, riding gaily upon his father's shoulder, and laughing up into the beautiful face of his youthful mother. The memories of that time, and of his first home, came back to him with a peculiar freshness and fragrance, like a painting by one of the old masters, perfect in design, and with its deep rich coloring softened and mellowed by age. He remembered the bright beauty of those sunny southern gardens, where he had passed long hours listening to the gentle splashing of the water in the worn grey fountain bowl, and breathing in the soft spring-like air, faint with the sweetness of Roman violets. And, half unconsciously, his thoughts travelled on to the time when all the pure beauty of his surroundings— for his had been an artist's home—had begun to have a distinct meaning for him, and in the fervor of an esthetic and unusually thoughtful youth, he had dreamed, and felt, and tasted deep of pleasures which the world yields only to those who stoop to listen to her secrets, with the quickened sensibilities and glowing imagination of the artist—one of her own children. He had read her in such a way that he found himself struggling, even in early boyhood, for some means of expression—but at that time none had come to him. The fruits of his later life had been the result of his early experience, but how embittered, how saddened by the unchanging gloom, which, at one period, had seemed as though it must dry up for ever all enthusiasm from his boyish heart. What a fire of passions had blazed up and died away within him; and as he thought of that sudden dying away, he thought of the moment when they had been quenched for ever, and of the voice which had quenched them. Again he crouched on his knees by the side of the sofa drawn up close to the high open windows of the Italian villa, and felt that thin white hand laid gently upon his trembling lips, checking in a moment the flood of angry words which in his heart had been but the prelude to a curse. The calm of that death-white face, with its marble passionless pallor and saint-like beauty, lingered still, faithfully treasured up in the rich store-house of his memory. Death alone would wipe it out. It was one of the experiences of his life, written alike into his undying recollection, and into his heart.

And then had come that period of severe struggle with himself, out of which he had emerged not only a conqueror, but with all the spoils of conquest. For he had found himself, after the battle was fought out and won, possessed of a more triumphant self-control, and a complete mastery over those fierce earthly passions which, had they held sway for long, would in time most surely have weakened that higher and purer part of his nature from which all the good of his life had come. It was, indeed, in some measure owing to the wholesome discipline of this struggle that he had found at last the long-sought-for gift of expression, and, taking up the pen, had sent forth golden words and thoughts into an age where such metal was rare indeed. Always there had been this dark cloud of anxiety looming over him, and leading him into many countries and constantly denying him the peace for which he longed. Then had come the climax of it all, the tragedy which had thrown over him the lowering cloud of a hideous danger. Failure was his. The moment of trial had come, and he had been unequal to it; and day and night there rang ever in his ears the faint far-off whisper of those tremulous lips, and the pleading light in those burning eyes seemed ever before him. Again he felt the touch of that icy cold hand, and again he remembered the words of the oath which, alas! he had not kept. Oh, it was horrible!

Once more his thoughts moved on a stage, and this time they reached their climax. Before his fixed eyes there floated the image of a sweet, wistful face glowing with healthy physical life, and yet with all that delicate refinement of coloring and feature which had made her face linger in his artist's memory for years before she had dwelt in his man's heart. It was a torture of hell, this, that the fairest and sweetest part of a man's life—his love—should come to him at such a time. And then for one brief moment all memory of his misery passed away from him, and his whole being became absorbed in a luxury of recollection. He thought of the change which his love had wrought in him. What had life been before? A long series of artistic and philosophical abstractions, bringing their own peculiar content, but a content never free from disquieting thought and restless doubts. How could it be otherwise? Was he not human like other men? Asceticism and intellect, and a certain purity of life which an almost epicurean refinement had rendered beautiful to him, these, easily keeping in sway his passionate temperament through all the long years of his life, now only served to fan the flame of that great pure love which had suddenly leaped up within him, a blazing, unquenchable fire. Human emotion once aroused, had thrilled through all his being with a sweet, heart-stirring music, and his whole nature was shaking from its very foundation. To him such a love seemed like the rounding of his life, the panacea for all that vague disquiet which, even in the moments of most perfect intellectual serenity, had sometimes disturbed him. The love of such a man was no light thing. It had mingled with his heart's blood, with the very essence of all his being. No death, no annihilation was possible for it. It was a part of himself, woven unchangeably into his life in a glowing skein, the brilliant colors of which could never fade. He looked into the future, golden with the light of such a love, and he saw a vision of perfect happiness, of joy beyond all expression, of deep, calm content, surpassing anything which he had known. Hand in hand he saw two figures, himself and her, gliding through the years with a sort of effortless energy, tasting together of everything in life that was sweet, and pure, and beautiful; scattering all trouble and worldly vexation to the winds, by the touchstone of their undying love. There was intoxication—ethereal intoxication in such a vision. The winds blew against him, and the torrents of driven rain, cold and stinging, dashed themselves against his pale, steadfast face. Down on the beach below the mad sea was thundering upon the cliffs, flinging its white spray so high that it glittered like specks of luminous white light against the black waters. Yet he noticed none of it. Until the brilliancy of that vision which glowed before him faded, nothing external could withdraw his thoughts.

And fade away it did at last, and neither the cold rain nor the howling wind had given him such a chill as crept through all his body, when memory and realization drove forth this sweet flower of his imagination. All the cruel hopelessness, the horror of his position, rushed in upon him like a foul nightmare. He saw himself shunned and despised, the faces of all men averted from him; all that had gone to make his life worthy, and even famous, forgotten in the stigma of an awful crime. He saw her eager, beautiful face, white and convulsed with horror, shrinking away from him as from some loathsome object. God! it was madness to think of it! Let this thought go from him, fade away from his reeling brain, or he would surely go mad.

Heedless of the fury of the winds that roared over the moorland, and sobbed and shrieked in the pine grove, he threw himself upon his knees close to the very verge of the cliff, and stretched out his hands to the darkened heavens in a passionate gesture of despair. It was the first time during all the fierce troubles of a stormy life that he had shrunk down, beaten for the moment by the utter hopelessness of the struggle which seemed to him now fast drawing toward its end.

"God! that I may die!" he moaned. "That I may die!"

And, as though in answer to his prayer, life for him suddenly became a doubtful thing. A wild gust of wind had uprooted a young fir tree from the plantation, and bearing it with a savage glee toward the cliff side, dashed it against the kneeling man. There was no chance for him against it. Over they went, man and tree together, to all appearance bound for inevitable destruction.

Even in that second, when he felt himself being hurled over the cliff, by what force he knew not, the consciousness of the sudden granting of his prayer flashed across his mind, and, strange though it may seem, brought with it a deep content. It was as he would have it be, death sudden and unfelt. But following close upon it came another thought, so swiftly works the brain in the time of a great crisis. He would be found dead, and everyone, in the light of what would soon be made known, would surely call it suicide. She would think so, too. Death on such terms he would not willingly have.

Effort followed swiftly upon thought. He clutched wildly at the cliff side during the first second of that flying descent, and the wind bending it almost double, brought a stunted fir tree sapling within his reach. He grasped it, and he was saved. Only a yard or two away, the cliff side was black with them growing so closely together that he pulled himself with ease from one to another till he climbed over the cliff top, and stood again upright on the ground.

His hands were bleeding, and his clothes were hanging round him in rags. Yet, in a certain sense, his narrow escape had done him good, for it had brought very vividly before him the impiety of his prayer. He had given way too long to maddening thoughts, and they had unnerved him. With the consciousness of his escape, all the manliness of his nature reasserted itself. He had faced this thing so long that he would face it now to the end. Let it come when it would, he would summon up all his strength, and meet it like a man. After death was peace for everlasting. God keep him in that faith!

He turned away from the cliff, and walked quickly back to the cottage, making his plans as he went. First he changed all his clothes, and then opening again his rifled cabinet, he transferred the remaining papers to a small handbag. These were all his preparations, but when he stepped out again and walked down the path of his garden, a change had fallen upon the earth. Faint gleams of dawn were breaking through the eastern sky, and though the sea was still troubled and crested with white-foamed breakers, the wind had gone down. Compared with the violence of the storm a few hours back, the stillness of the gray twilight was full of a peculiar impressiveness. Peace after the storm. Rest after trouble.

And something of this saddened peace crept into the heart of the solitary figure crossing the moorland—on his way back to face a doom which seemed closing in fast around him.

XXI

Sir Allan Beaumerville has a Caller

Sir Allan Beaumerville, Bart., *dilettante* physician and man of fashion, was, on the whole, one of the most popular men in London society. He was rich, of distinguished appearance, had charming manners, and was a bachelor, which combination might possibly account in some measure for the high esteem in which he was held amongst the opposite sex. He had made his *début* in society quite late in life, for he had succeeded to the baronetcy, which was one of the oldest and richest in the country, unexpectedly; and, as a young man, London—fashionable London, at any rate—had seen or known nothing of him. Nor, indeed, had he at any time had much to say to anyone about the earlier period of his life. It was generally understood that he had lived abroad, and that he had been in some sort of practice, or how else could he have acquired his knowledge of the technical part of his profession? Beyond this, nothing was known; and although he was evidently a traveled man, having much to say at times about all the interesting parts of Southern Europe, no one ever remembered meeting him anywhere. For the rest, he had passed through none of the curriculum of English youth. No public school had had his name upon its books, nor had he even graduated in his own country. But he had taken a very high degree indeed at Heidelberg, which had won him considerable respect among those who knew anything about such matters, and his diplomas included half the letters of the alphabet, and were undeniable. And so when he had suddenly appeared in London on the death of his uncle and cousin, a middle-aged, distinguished gentleman, with manners a little foreign, but in their way perfect, society had voted him a great improvement on the former baronet, and had taken him by the hand at once. That was a good many years ago, and very soon after his first introduction to the London world he had become a notable figure in it. He had never missed a town season, and at all its chief functions was a well-known and popular figure, always among the best and most exclusive set, and always welcome there. He had a yacht at Cowes, a share in a Scotch moor, a dozen or so hunters at his little place near Melton, a shooting box in Derbyshire, and a fine old mansion and estate in Kent, where everyone liked to be asked; and where he had more than once had the honor of entertaining royalty. There was only one thing in the world wanted to make Sir Allan Beaumerville perfect, women declared, and that one thing was a wife. But although no one appeared to appreciate more highly the charms of feminine society—as he showed in more ways than one, both in St. John's Wood and in Belgravia—he had never shown the least inclination to perform his duty to society in this respect. How he managed to steer clear of the many snares and pitfalls laid for him in the course of his career puzzled a good many men. But he did it, and what was more remarkable still, he made no enemies. He had friendships among the other sex such as no man save he dared have indulged in to a like extent; but with infinite skill he always seemed to be able to drop some delicate insinuation as to the utter absence of any matrimonial intention on his part, which left no room for doubt or hope. He was, in short, possessed of admirable powers of diplomacy which never failed him.

Of course his impregnability gave rise to all manner of stories. He had been jilted in his youth, he had a wife alive, or he had had one, and she was dead, none of which rumors met any large amount of credence. As to the first, the idea of anyone jilting Sir Allan Beaumerville, even before his coming into the baronetcy, found no favor in the feminine world. No woman could have shown such ill judgment as that; and, besides, he had very little of the melancholy which is generally supposed to attend upon such a disappointment. As to the second, it was never seriously entertained, for if any woman had once claimed Sir Allan Beaumerville as a husband, she was scarcely likely to keep away from him, especially now that he was occupying such a distinguished position. The third was quite out of the question, for even had he ever been married—which nobody believed—he was scarcely the sort of man to wear the willow all his life, and, indeed, it was very evident that he was not doing anything of the sort. Everyone knew of a certain little establishment beyond Kensington way, where Sir Allan's brougham was often seen, but of course no one thought the worse of him for that. And without a doubt, if Sir Allan had yielded to that gentle wish so often expressed, and commenced domestic life in a more conventional manner in the great house at Grosvenor Square, he would have forfeited at once a great deal of his popularity, at any rate among the feminine part of his acquaintance. As it was, there was always a faint hope of winning him to add a zest to his delightful companionship, and Sir

Allan, who was a very shrewd man, was perfectly aware of this. He was a sybarite of refined taste, with an exquisite appreciation of the finer and more artistic pleasures of life; and the society of educated and well-bred women was one of the chief of them. Rather than run any risk of deterioration in its quality he preferred to let things remain as they were, and that he might enjoy it the more thoroughly without the restraint placed upon other men, was the sole reason that he had not altogether abandoned his profession. He never took any fee, nor did he ever accept any casual patient. But on certain days of the week, at certain hours, he was at home as a physician to certain of his lady acquaintances to whom he had already offered his services. The number was always few, for the invitations were rarely given, and the patients generally remained upon the sick list for an indefinite period. But there were few invitations more sought after. Something—perhaps the very slight spice of impropriety which certain prudes, who had not been asked, affected to see in such an arrangement—had made them the fashion; and, then, Sir Allan was undeniably clever. Altogether, the idea was a great success for him.

It had been one of Sir Allan's afternoon receptions, and, as usual, every patient on his list had paid him a visit. Having seen the last and most favored to her carriage, Sir Allan returned to his study with a slight smile on his handsome face, and the recollection of some delightfully confidential little speeches still tingling in his ears. For a moment he stood on the hearth rug recalling them, then he looked round the room and rang the bell. A servant appeared almost immediately.

"Clear these things away, Morton," Sir Allan said, pointing to some dainty marvels of china and a Japanese teapot, which stood on a little round table between two chairs, "and bring me a loose jacket from my room. I am dining in Downing Street to-night, and shall not want to dress before eight."

The man obeyed, and Sir Allan, lighting a thick Egyptian cigarette, took up a French novel, and stretched himself out in his easy chair.

"You are not at home to anyone else this afternoon, sir?" the servant inquired before quitting the room.

"Certainly not," Sir Allan answered, yawning. "Has anyone been inquiring for me?"

"Yes, sir."

"Lady or gentleman?"

"Gentleman, sir—at least, I think so. He looks like one."

"Any name?"

"I didn't inquire, sir. I said that you were not at home; but, as he seemed very pressing, I promised to try and ascertain when you would be at liberty."

"Ask him his name," Sir Allan directed.

The man withdrew, and returned in a moment or two looking a little puzzled.

"His name is Brown, sir—Mr. Bernard Brown."

Sir Allan was seldom clumsy in little things, but at that moment he dropped the book which he had been reading upon the floor. The servant hastened toward it, but Sir Allan waved him away. He preferred to pick it up himself.

"I'm afraid I've lost my place," he remarked, turning over the leaves. "You can show Mr. Brown in here, Morton," he added. "I may as well see what he wants."

The man withdrew, and Sir Allan recommenced the chapter. Then the door was opened again, and the visitor was admitted. Sir Allan laid the paper knife carefully in his place, and shutting the book, rose from his chair.

"Mr. Brown," he said, "I am very pleased to see you. Come and take a seat here."

He stood up in an easy attitude upon the hearthrug, and pointed with a smile to the chair which his last visitor had occupied. But he did not offer his hand to Mr. Brown, nor did Mr. Brown appear to expect it.

The apartment was in the semi-gloom of twilight, for the silver lamp burning on the bracket by Sir Allan's side was covered with a rose-colored shade, and threw all its light downward. The art treasures with which the room was crowded, and the almost voluptuous grace of its adornment and coloring, were more suggested than seen. Mr. Brown, who had advanced only a few steps from the closed door, covered his eyes with his hand, and looked a little dazed.

"Do you live in darkness?" he said in a low tone. "I want to see your face."

Sir Allan shrugged his shoulders, and turned up the lamp a little higher than it was. The faces of the two men were now distinctly visible to each other, and the contrast between them was rather startling. Sir Allan's was placid, courteous, and inquiring. Mr. Brown's was white almost to ghastliness, and his eyes were burning with a strange light.

"I wish you'd sit down, my dear fellow!" Sir Allan remarked in a tone of good-natured remonstrance. "It worries me to see you standing there, and I'm sure you look tired enough."

Mr. Brown took no notice whatever of the invitation.

"I have come to see you, Sir Allan Beaumerville," he said slowly, "to lay certain facts before you, and to ask your advice concerning them—as a disinterested party."

"Very happy, I'm sure, to do the best I can," Sir Allan murmured, lighting a fresh cigarette. "I wish you'd sit down to it, though. I suppose it's about that murder we were mixed up in? Horrid affair it was."

"Yes, it was a very horrid affair," Mr. Brown repeated slowly.

"They haven't caught the man yet, I suppose?"

"They have not—yet."

Sir Allan shrugged his fine shoulders.

"I fancy their chance is a poor one now, then," he remarked, emitting a little cloud of smoke from his lips, and watching it curl upward in a faint blue wreath to the ceiling. "How differently they manage affairs on the Continent! Such a crime would not go undetected a day there."

"It will not be undetected here many more days," Mr. Brown said. "My own belief is that a warrant is already issued for the apprehension of the supposed murderer, and I should not be surprised to hear that at this very moment the police were watching this house."

Sir Allan looked hard at his guest, and elevated his eyebrows.

"This is a very serious matter, Mr. Brown," he said, looking at him steadily in the face. "Do I understand—?"

"I will explain," Mr. Brown interrupted quietly. "On my return to Falcon's Nest yesterday, I find that during my absence the cottage has been entered, apparently by some one in authority, for keys have been used. My cabinet has been forced open, and a number of my private letters and papers have been taken away. Certain other investigations have also been made, obviously with the same object."

Sir Allan maintained his attitude of polite attention, but he had stopped smoking, and his cigarette was burning unnoticed between his fingers.

"I scarcely see the connection yet," he said suavely. "No doubt I am a little dense. You speak about a number of private papers having been abstracted from your cabinet. Do I understand—is it possible that anything in those papers could lead people to fix upon you as the murderer of Sir Geoffrey Kynaston?"

The two men looked steadily into each other's faces. There was nothing in Sir Allan's expression beyond a slightly shocked surprise; in Mr. Brown's there was a very curious mixture indeed.

E. PHILLIPS OPPENHEIM

"Most certainly!" was the quiet reply. "Those letters plainly point out a motive for my having committed the crime."

"They are from—"

"Stop!"

Sir Allan started. The word had burst from Mr. Brown's lips with a passion which his former quietude rendered the more remarkable. There was a dead silence between them for fully a minute. Then Mr. Brown, having resumed his former manner, spoke again.

"Those letters," he said, "tell the story of a certain episode in the life of Sir Geoffrey Kynaston. No other person is mentioned or alluded to in them. Yet the fact of their having been found in my possession makes them strong evidence against me."

Sir Allan nodded.

"I don't know why on earth you've come to me for advice," he remarked. "I'm not a lawyer."

"Neither do I quite know. Still, I have come; and, as I am here, give it me."

"In a word, then—bolt," said Sir Allan laconically.

"That is your advice, is it?"

"I don't see anything else to do. I don't ask you whether you are guilty or not, and I do ask myself whether I am doing my duty in giving you any advice calculated to defeat the ends of justice. I simply consider the facts, and tell you what I should do if I were in your unfortunate position. I should bolt."

"Thank you, Sir Allan, for your advice so far," Mr. Brown said quietly. "There is just one little complication, however, which I wish to tell you of."

"Yes. Might I trouble you to put the matter in as short a form as possible, then?" Sir Allan remarked, looking at his watch. "I am dining with the Prime Minister to-night, and it is time I commenced to dress."

"I will not detain you much longer," Mr. Brown said. "The complication, I fear, will scarcely interest you, for it is a sentimental one. If I fled from England to-night, I should leave behind me the woman I love."

"Then why the devil don't you take her with you?" asked Sir Allan, with a shrug of the shoulders. "She'll go right enough if you ask her. Women like a little mystery."

"The woman whom I love appears to be of a different class to those from whom you have drawn your experience," Mr. Brown answered quietly. "I am not married to her."

Sir Allan shrugged his shoulders lightly.

"Well, if she's a prude, and won't go, and you haven't pluck enough to run away with her, I don't know how to advise you," he remarked.

Mr. Brown looked steadily into the other's face. Sir Allan met his gaze blandly.

"Your speech, Sir Allan, betrays a cynicism which I believe is greatly in fashion just now," Mr. Brown said slowly. "Sometimes it is altogether assumed, sometimes it is only a thin veneer adopted in obedience to the decree of fashion. Believing that, so far as you are concerned, the latter is the case, I beg you to look back into your past life, and recall, if possible, some of its emotions. Again I tell you that if I fly from England, I shall leave behind me the woman I dearly love. I have come to you, Sir Allan Beaumerville, with an effort. I lay all these facts before you, and I ask you to decide for me. What shall I do?"

"And I repeat, my dear fellow," answered Sir Allan suavely, "that the only advice I can give you is, to leave England to-night!"

Mr. Brown hesitated for a moment. Then he turned away toward the door without a word or gesture of farewell.

"By the by," Sir Allan remarked, "one moment, Mr. Brown! Have you any objection to telling me the name of the lady who has been honored with your affection. Do I know her?"

"You do. Her name is no concern of yours, though."

Suddenly an unpleasant idea seemed to flash across Sir Allan's mind. He was more disturbed than he had been during the whole of the interview.

"Of course you don't mean that charming Miss Thurwell?" he said quickly.

The limits of Mr. Brown's endurance seemed to have been passed. He turned suddenly round, his eyes blazing with passion, and walked across the room to within a few feet of Sir Allan. He stood there with one hand grasping the back of a chair, and looked at him.

"And if I did mean her, sir, what is that to you? By what right do you dare to—"

Suddenly his upraised hand fell. Both men stood as though turned to stone, listening, yet scarcely daring to glance toward the door. It was the sound of Morton's quiet voice and the trailing of skirts which had checked Mr. Brown's passionate speech.

"Lady and Miss Thurwell!"

There was no time to move, scarcely time for thought. Morton stood respectfully at the door, and the two ladies were already on the threshold.

"My dear Sir Allan"—in Lady Thurwell's silvery voice—"what will you think of such a late visit? I felt ashamed to ask for you, only we have been at the Countess of Applecorn's in the next square, and I could positively not pass your door when I remembered that it was your afternoon. But you are all in darkness; and you have a visitor, haven't you?"

The figures of the two men were barely visible in the deep gloom of the apartment, for the lamp had burned low, and gave little light. Lady Thurwell had stopped just inside the room, surprised.

If only Sir Allan's companion had been a patient! What a delightful piece of scandal it would have been!

"Lady Thurwell! Ah, how good of you!" exclaimed Sir Allan, coming forward out of the shadow; "and you, too, Miss Helen. I am honored indeed. Morton, lights at once!"

"We must not stay a moment," declared Lady Thurwell, shaking hands. "No, we won't sit down, thanks! You know why we've called? It's about the opera to-night. You got my note?"

"I did, Lady Thurwell, and I can trustfully say that I never read one from you with more regret."

"Then you have an engagement?"

"Unfortunately, yes! I am dining at Downing Street."

"Well, we must send for that schoolboy cousin of yours, Helen!" said Lady Thurwell, laughing. "You see how dependent we are upon your sex, after all. Why, is that really you, Mr. Maddison!" she broke off suddenly, as a tall figure emerged a little out of the gloom. "Fancy meeting you here! I had no idea that you and Sir Allan Beaumerville were friends. Helen, do you see Mr. Maddison?"

"I can't say that I do," she answered, with a low happy laugh; "but I'm very glad he's here!"

The lights were brought in as she finished her little speech, and they all looked at one another. Lady Thurwell broke into a little laugh.

"Really, this is a singular meeting," she said, "but we mustn't stop a moment. Mr. Maddison, we were hoping to see you yesterday afternoon. Do come soon!"

He bowed with a faint smile upon his lips.

"Come out to the carriage with us, please, Mr. Maddison," Helen said to him in a low tone as Lady Thurwell turned to go; and he walked down the hall between them and out on to the pavement, leaving Sir Allan on the steps.

"You will come and dine with me soon, won't you, Mr. Maddison?" Lady Thurwell asked him, as she touched his hand stepping into the brougham.

"I will come whenever you ask me!" he answered rashly.

"Then come now!" said Helen quickly. "We are all alone for the evening, fancy that, and we can't go out anywhere because we haven't an escort. Do come!"

He looked at Lady Thurwell.

"It will be a real charity if you will," she said, smiling graciously. "We shall be bored to death alone."

"I shall be delighted," he answered at once. "About eight o'clock, I suppose?"

"Half-past seven, please, and we'll have a long evening," said Helen. "That will give you time to get to your club and dress. Good-by!"

They drove off, and Mr. Bernard Brown walked swiftly away toward Pall Mall. Once he stopped in the middle of the pavement and broke into an odd little laugh. It was a curious position to be in. He was expecting every moment to be arrested for murder, and he was going out to dine.

XXII

"GOD FORBID IT!"

M r. Maddison—to drop at this point the name under which he had chosen to become the tenant of Falcon's Nest—was a member of a well-known London club, chiefly affected by literary men, and after his acceptance of Lady Thurwell's invitation, he hastened there at once and went to his room to dress. As a rule a man does not indulge in any very profound meditation during the somewhat tedious process of changing his morning clothes for the monotonous garb of Western civilization. His attention is generally fully claimed by the satisfactory adjusting of his tie and the precaution he has to use to avoid anything so lamentable as a crease in his shirt, and if his thoughts stray at all, it is seldom beyond the immediate matter of his toilet, or at most a little anticipation with regard to the forthcoming evening. If on the right side of thirty, a pair of bright eyes may sometimes make him pause for a moment, even with the hair brushes in his hands, to wonder if she will be there to-night, and if by any fortunate chance he will be able to take her in to dinner. And if the reign of the forties has commenced, it is just possible that a little mild speculation as to the *entrées* may be admitted. But, as a rule, a man's thoughts do not on such an occasion strike deep beneath the surface, and there is no record of an author having laid the plan of his next work, or a soldier having marked out a campaign, while struggling with a refractory tie, or obstinate parting. Even if such had ever happened to be the case, we should not have cared to hear about it. We prefer to think of a Napoleon planning great conquests in the serene stillness of night among a sleeping camp and beneath a starlit sky, or of a Wordsworth writing his poetry in his cottage home among the mountains.

But Mr. Bernard Maddison, before he left his room that evening, had come to a great decision—a decision which made his step the firmer, and which asserted itself in the carriage of his head and the increased brightness of his eyes, as he slowly descended the wide, luxurious staircase. And he felt calmer, even happier, from having at least passed from amid the shoals of doubt and uncertainty. The slight nervousness had quite left him. He was still more than ordinarily pale, and there was a look of calm resignation in his thoughtful æsthetic face which gave to its intellectuality a touch of spirituality. One of the members of the club said, later on in the smoking room, that Maddison seemed to him to realize one's idea of St. Augustine in evening clothes. So far as appearance went the comparison was not inapt.

As he reached the hall the porter came up to him with his cloak.

"There is a gentleman waiting for you in the strangers' room, sir," he said.

Mr. Maddison turned away that the man might not see the sudden dread in his face. It was not a long respite he craved for—only one evening. Was even this to be denied him?

"Any name?" he asked quietly.

"He gave none," the man answered; "but I think it is Sir Allan Beaumerville."

"Ah!" Mr. Maddison felt a sudden relief which escaped him in that brief interjection. He was scarcely surprised at this visit. "I will go to him," he said. "Call me a hansom, Grey, will you?"

The porter went outside, and Mr. Maddison crossed the hall and in a small, dimly-lit room, found himself face to face with his visitor.

Sir Allan wore the brilliant uniform of a colonel in the yeomanry, for the dinner to which he was going was to be followed by an official reception. But he was very pale, and his manner had lost much of its studied nonchalance.

"I followed you here," he began at once, "because, after your departure, I began to realize more fully the seriousness of what you told me."

"Yes. I thought at the time that your indifference was a little remarkable," Mr. Maddison said quietly. The positions between them were entirely reversed. It was Sir Allan Beaumerville now who was placing a great restraint upon himself, and Mr. Maddison who was collected and at his ease.

"I was taken by surprise," Sir Allan continued. "Since you left me I have been picturing all manner of horrible things. Have you fully realized that you may be arrested at any moment on this frightful charge?"

"I have fully realized it," Mr. Maddison answered calmly. "In fact, when the porter told me that a gentleman wished to see me, I imagined at once that it had come."

"And have you considered, too," Sir Allan continued, "how overwhelming the evidence is against you?"

"I have considered it."

"Then why do you linger here for one moment? Why don't you escape while you have the chance?"

"Why should I?" Mr. Maddison answered. "I shall make no attempt to escape."

Sir Allan's face grew a shade more pallid, and betrayed an agitation which he strove in vain to conceal.

"But supposing you are arrested," he said quickly, "everything will go against you. What shall you do?"

"I shall accept my fate, whatever it may be," was the quiet reply. "I prefer this to flight. Life would not be very valuable to me as a skulking criminal in a foreign country. If it be declared forfeit to the law, the law shall have it."

There was a sudden choking in Sir Allan's voice, and an almost piteous look in his face.

"God forbid it!" he cried; "God forbid it!"

And suddenly this hardened man of the world, this professed cynic in an age of cynicism, sank down in a chair and buried his head in his arms on the green baize writing table, crushing the gold lace of his glittering uniform, and the immaculate shirt front, with its single diamond stud. It was only for a moment that a sudden rush of feeling overcame him. But when he looked up his face was haggard and he looked years older.

"Does anyone—know of this?" he asked in a hoarse tone.

Mr. Maddison shook his head.

"No one whatever as yet," he said shortly. "If I am free to-morrow, I shall go to Italy."

A sudden change swept into Sir Allan's face. He rose from his chair, drawing himself up to his full height. Again he was the stately, distinguished man of the world, with little feeling in his voice or looks. Between him and this other man in his sober black, with wasted face and thin stooping frame, there was a startling difference.

"I have no doubt that you will do your duty, Mr. Maddison," he said coldly; "although, if I may be forgiven for saying so, your method appears to me a little quixotic, and, in a certain sense, singularly devoid of consideration for others. I will not detain you any longer."

He wrapped his long cloak around him and left the room in dignified silence. Mr. Maddison followed him to the steps, and saw him get into his carriage. They parted without another word.

XXIII

Lovers

Bernard Maddison kept his engagement that evening, and dined alone with Lady Thurwell and Helen. There had been some talk of going to the opera afterwards, but no one seemed to care about it, and so it dropped through.

"For my part," Lady Thurwell said, as they sat lingering over their dessert, "I shall quite enjoy an evening's rest. You literary men, Mr. Maddison, talk a good deal about being overworked, but you know nothing of the life of a chaperon in the season. I tell Helen that she is sadly wanting in gratitude. We do everything worth doing—picture galleries, matinées, shopping, afternoon calls, dinners, dances, receptions—why, there's no slavery like it."

Helen laughed softly.

"We do a great deal too much, aunt," she said. "I am almost coming round to my father's opinion. You know, Mr. Maddison, he very seldom comes to London, and then only when he wants to pay a visit to his gunmaker, or to renew his hunting kit, or something of that sort. London life does not suit him at all."

"I think your father a very wise man," he answered. "He seeks his pleasures in a more wholesome manner."

She looked thoughtful.

"Yes, I suppose, ethically, the life of a man about town is on a very low level. That is why one meets so few who interest one, as a rule. Don't you think all this society life very frivolous, Mr. Maddison?"

"I am not willing to be its judge," he answered. "Yet it is a moral axiom that the higher we seek for our pleasures the greater happiness we attain to. I am an uncompromising enemy to what is known as fashionable society, so I will draw no conclusions."

"It is intellect and artistic sensibility *versus* sensuousness," yawned Lady Thurwell. "I'm a weak woman, and I'm afraid I'm too old to change my ways. But I'm on the wrong side of the argument all the same; at least, I should be if I took up the cudgels."

"Which are the greater sinners, Mr. Maddison?" asked Helen, smiling, "men of the world or women of the world?"

"Without doubt, men," he answered quickly. "However we may talk about the equality of the sexes, the fact remains that women are born into the world with lighter natures than men. They have at once a greater capacity, and more desire for amusement pure and simple. They wear themselves out in search of it, more especially the women of other nations. And after all, when their life has passed, they have never known the meaning of real happiness, of the pleasures that have no reaction, and that sweet elevation of mind that is only won by thought and study."

"Poor women!" murmured Lady Thurwell. "Mr. Maddison, you are making me quite uncomfortable. Paint my sex in more glowing colors, please, or leave them alone. Remember that I am the only middle-aged woman here. I don't count Helen at all. I see that she is something of your way of thinking already. Traitress! Do light a cigarette, Mr. Maddison. I adore the perfume of them, and so does Helen."

He took one from the box she passed him, and gravely lit it. They were doing everything in a very informal manner. Dinner had been served in the library, a cozy little apartment with a large open grate in which a cheerful fire had been lit. The ordinary table had been dispensed with in favor of a small round one just large enough for them, and now, with dessert on the table, they had turned their chairs round to the fire in very homelike fashion.

"Do you know, I like this," Helen said softly. "I think it is so much better than a dinner party, or going out anywhere."

"See what a difference the presence of a distinguished man of letters makes," laughed Lady Thurwell. "Now, only a few hours ago, we were dreading a very dull evening—Helen as well as myself. How nice it was of you to take pity on us, Mr. Maddison!"

"Especially considering your aversion to our society," put in Helen. "Are not you really thinking it a shocking waste of time to be here talking to two very unlearned women instead of seeking inspiration in your study?"

He looked at her reproachfully.

"I know nothing of Lady Thurwell's tastes," he said; "but you can scarcely call yourself unlearned. You have read much, and you have thought."

"A pure accident—I mean the thinking," she answered lightly. "If I had not been a country girl, with a mind above my station, intellectually, there's no telling what might have happened. Town life is very distracting, if you once get into the groove. Isn't it, aunt?"

Lady Thurwell, who was a thorough little *dame de société*, rose with a pout and shrugged her shoulders.

"I'm not going to be hauled over the coals by you superior people any longer," she answered. "I shall leave you to form a mutual improvement society, and go and write some letters. When you want me, come into the drawing room, but don't come yet. Thank you, Mr. Maddison," she added, as he held the door open for her; "be merciful to the absent, won't you?"

And so they were alone! As he closed the door and walked across the room to his seat, there came back to him, with a faint bewildering sweetness, something of the passionate emotion of their farewell in the pine grove on the cliff. He felt his pulses quicken, and his heart beat fast. It was in vain that the dying tenets of his old life, a life of renunciation and solitude, feebly reasserted themselves. At that moment, if never before, he knew the truth. The warm fresh sunlight lay across his barren life, brightening with a marvelous glow its gloomiest corners. The old passionless serenity, in which the human had been crushed out by the intellectual, was gone forever. He loved this woman.

And she was very fair. He stole a long glance at her as she leaned back in her low wicker chair—the fond glance of a lover—and he felt his keenly artistic sense stirred from its very depths by her purely physical beauty. The firelight was casting strange gleams upon the deep golden hair which waved about her oval face and shapely forehead in picturesque unrestraint, and there was an ethereal glow in her exquisite complexion, a light in her eyes, which seemed called up by some unusual excitement.

The setting of the picture, too, was perfect. Her ivory satin gown hung in long straight lines about her slim perfect outline with all the grace of Greek drapery, unrelieved save by one large bunch of Neapolitan violets nestling amongst the folds of old lace which filled up the open space of her bodice. He stood and looked at her with a strange confusion of feelings. A new life was burning in his veins, and for the first time since his boyhood he doubted his absolute self-mastery. Dared he stay there? Could he sit by her side, and bandy idle words with her?

The silence had lasted for several minutes, and was beginning to possess something of that peculiar eloquence which such silences usually have. At last she raised her eyes, and looked at him standing motionless and thoughtful amongst the shadows of the room, and at the first glance he felt his strength grow weak, and his passionate love rising up like a living force. For there was in her eyes, and in her face, and in her voice when she spoke, something of that softening change which transfuses a woman's being when she loves, and lets the secret go from her—a sort of mute yielding, an abandonment, having in it a subtle essence of unconscious invitation.

"Come and talk to me," she said softly. "Why do you stand out there?"

He made one last despairing effort. With a strangely unnatural laugh, he drew a chair to her side and began to talk rapidly, never once letting his eyes rest upon her loveliness, striving to keep his thoughts fixed upon his subject, but all the time acutely conscious of her presence. He talked of many things with a restless energy which more than once caused her to look up at him in wonderment. He strove even to keep her from answering him, lest the magic of her voice should turn the trembling scale. For her sake he unlocked the inmost recesses of his mind, and all the rich store of artistic sensations, of jealously preserved memories, came flooding out, clothed with all that eloquence of jeweled phrase and daintily turned sentence which had made his writings so famous. For her sake, too, he sent his imagination traveling through almost untrodden fields, bringing back exquisite word pictures, and lifting the curtain before many a landscape of sun-smitten thought. All the music of sweet imagery and pure bracing idealism thrilled through her whole being. This was indeed a man to love! And as his speech grew slower, and she heard again that peculiar trembling in his tone, the meaning of which her woman's heart so easily interpreted, she began to long for those few words from him which she felt would be the awakening of a new life in her. He could not fail to notice even that slight change, and wondering whether her attention was commencing to flag, he paused and their eyes met in a gaze full of that deep tragical intensity which marks the birth between man and woman of any new sensation. The fire which glowed in his eyes told her of his love as plainly as the dreamy yet expressive light which gleamed in hers spoke also to him, and when her head drooped before the gathering passion in his face, and the faint color streamed into her cheeks, no will of his could keep the words back any longer. He felt his breath come quickly, and his heart almost stop beating. His pulses were quickening, and a strange new delight stole through him. Surely this was the end. He could bear no more.

And it seemed as though it were indeed so, for with a sudden impulse he caught hold of her white, ringless hand, and drew it gently toward him. There was a slight instinctive resistance which came and went in a space of time only a thought could measure. Then she yielded it to him, and the sense of her touch stole through his veins with a sort of dreamy fascination, to give place in a moment to the overmastering fire of his great passion.

Her face was turned away from him, but he saw the faint color deepen in her cheeks and the light quivering of the lip. And then a torrent of feeling, before which his last shaking barriers of resistance crumbled away like dust, swept from his heart, striking every chord of his nature with a crash of wild music.

"Helen, my love, my love!" he cried.

And she turned round, her eyes dim with trembling tears, yet glowing with a great happiness—turned around to feel his arms steal around her and hold her clasped to his heart in a mad sweet embrace. And it seemed to her that it was for this that she had lived.

XXIV

A Woman's Love

It seemed to him in those few golden moments of his life that memory died away and time stood still. The past with its hideous sorrows, and the future over which it stretched its chilling hand, were merged in the present. Life had neither background nor prospect. The overpowering realization of the elysium into which he had stepped had absorbed all sense and all knowledge. They were together, and words were passing between them which would live to eternity in his heart.

But the fairest summer sky will not be fair forever. Clouds will gather, and drive before them the sweetness and joy from the smiling heavens, and memory is a mistress who may slumber but who never sleeps. Those moments of entrancing happiness, although in one sense they lasted a lifetime, were in the ordinary measure of time but of brief duration. For with something of the overmastering suddenness with which his passion had found expression, there swept back into his heart all the still cold flow of icy reminiscence. She felt his arms loosen around her, and she raised her head, wondering, from his shoulder, wonder that turned soon to fear, for he rose up and stood before her white, and with a great agony in his dark eyes.

"I have been mad!" he muttered hoarsely. "Forgive me! I must go!"

She stood up by his side, pale, but with no fear or weakness in her look. She, too, had begun to realize.

"Tell me one thing," she said softly. "You do—love me!"

"God knows I do!" he answered. The words came from his heart with a nervous intensity which showed itself in his quivering lips, and the vibration of his tone. She knew their truth as surely as though she had seen them written in letters of fire, and that knowledge, or rather her absolute confidence in it, made her in a measure bold. The dainty exclusiveness which had half repelled, half attracted other men had fallen away from her. She stood before him a loving tearful woman, with something of that gentle shame which is twin sister to modesty burning in her cheeks.

"Then I will not let you go," she said softly, taking both his hands in hers, and holding him tightly. "Nothing shall come between us."

He looked into the love light which gleamed in her wet eyes, and stooping down he took her again into his arms and kissed her.

"My darling!" he whispered passionately, "my darling! But you do not know."

"Yes, I do," she answered, drawing him gently back to their old place. "You mean about what Rachel Kynaston said that awful night, don't you?"

"More than that, alas!" he answered in a low tone. "Other people besides Rachel Kynaston have had suspicions about me. I have been watched, and while I was away, Falcon's Nest has been entered, and papers have been taken away."

She was white with fear. This was Benjamin Levy's doing, and it was through her. Ought she to tell him? She could not! She could not!

"But they do not—the papers, I mean—make it appear that—"

"Helen," he interrupted, with his face turned away from her, "it is best that you should know the truth. Those papers reveal the story of a bitter enmity between myself and Sir Geoffrey Kynaston. When you consider that and the other things, you will see that I may at any moment be arrested."

A spasm of pain passed across her face. At that moment her thoughts were only concerned with his safety. The terrible suggestiveness of what he had told her had very little real meaning for her then. Her one thought was, could she buy those papers? If all her fortune could do it, it should be given. Only let him never know, and let him be safe!

"Bernard," she whispered softly, "I am not afraid. It is very terrible, but it cannot alter anything. Love cannot come and go at our bidding. It is forever. Nothing can change that."

He stopped her lips with passionate kisses, and then he tried to tear himself away. But she would not let him go. A touch of that complete self-surrender which comes even to the proudest woman when she loves had made her bold.

"Have I not told you, Bernard," she whispered, "that I will not let you go?"

"Helen, you must," he said hoarsely. "Who knows but that to-morrow I may stand in the dock, charged with that hideous crime?"

"If they will let me, I shall gladly stand by your side," she answered.

He turned away, and his shaking fingers hid his face from her.

"Oh, this is too much for a man to bear!" he moaned. "Helen, Helen, there must be nothing of this between you and me."

"Nothing between you and me!" she repeated with a ring of gentle scorn in her voice. "Bernard, do you know so little of women, after all? Do you think that they can play at love in this give-and-take fashion?"

He did not answer. She stood up and passed one of her arms around his neck, and with the other hand gently disengaged his fingers from before his face.

"Bernard, dearest, look at me. All things can be changed by fashion or expediency save a woman's love, and that is eternal. Don't think, please, of any of these terrible things that may be in store for us, or what other people would think or say. I want you to remember that love, even though it be personal love, is far above all circumstance. No power in this world can alter or change it. It belongs to that better part of ourselves which lifts us above all misfortune and trouble. You have given me a great happiness, Bernard, and you shall not take it away from me. Whatever happens to you, it is my right to share it. Remember, for the future, it is 'we,' not 'I.' You must not think of yourself alone in anything, for I belong now to everything that concerns you."

And so it was that for the first time in his life Bernard Maddison, who had written much concerning them, much that was both faithful and beautiful, saw into the inner life of a true woman. Only for the man whom she loves will she thus lift the curtain from before that sweet depth of unselfishness which makes even the homeliest of her sex one of the most beautiful of God's creations; and he, if he be in any way a man of human sensibility and capacity, must feel something of that wondering awe, that reverence with which Bernard Maddison drank in the meaning of her words. The mute anxiety of her tearful gaze, the color which came and fled from her face—he understood all these signs. They were to him the physical, the material covering for her appeal. A life of grand thoughts, of ever-climbing ideas, of pure and lofty aims, had revealed to him nothing so noble and yet so sweetly human as this; had filled his being with no such heart-shattering emotion as swept through him at that moment. A woman's hand had lifted him out from his despair into a higher state, and there was a great humility in the silent gesture with which he yielded his will to hers.

And then again there were spoken words between them which no chronicles should report, and a certain calm happiness took up its settled place in his heart, defiant of that despair which could not be driven out. Then came that reawakening to mundane things which seems like a very great step indeed in such cases. She looked at the clock, and gave a little start.

"Bernard, it is nearly eleven o'clock," she cried. "We must go into the drawing-room at once. What will aunt think of us? You must come with me, of course; but you'd better say good night now. There, that will do, sir!"

She drew away and smoothed her ruffled hair back from her forehead, looking ruefully in the glass at her tear-stained cheeks, and down at the crushed violets in her corsage.

"May I have them?" he asked.

She drew them out and placed them in his hand.

"To-morrow—" she said.

"To-morrow I must go into the land of violets," he interrupted.

She turned round quickly.

"What do you mean? You are not going away without my permission, sir?"

"Then I must seek it," he answered, smiling. "You have given life such an exquisite sweetness for me, that I am making plans already to preserve it. My one hope lies in Italy."

"How long should you be away?" she asked anxiously.

"Not a week," he answered. "If I am permitted to leave England, which I fear is doubtful, to-morrow, I can be back perhaps in five days."

"Then you may go, Bernard," she whispered. "Take this with you, and think of me sometimes."

She had drawn out a photograph of herself from a folding case on the mantelpiece, and he took it from her eagerly.

"Nothing in the world could be so precious to me," he said.

"For a novice you say some very nice things," she answered, laughing softly. "And now you must go, sir. No, you needn't come into the drawing-room; I really couldn't show myself with you. I'll make your excuses to my aunt. Farewell—love!"

"Farewell—sweetheart!" he answered, hesitating for a moment over the words which seemed so strange to him. Then, as though loth to leave him, she walked down the hall by his side, and they looked out for a moment into the square. A footman was standing prepared to open the door, but Helen sent him away with a message to her maid.

"Do you know why I did that?" she asked, her clasp tightening upon his arm.

He shook his head, and looked down at her fondly.

E. PHILLIPS OPPENHEIM

"I can't imagine, unless—"

She glanced half fearfully behind and then up into his face again, with a faint blush stealing into her cheeks.

"I want one more kiss, please."

He looked into her soft trustful face, and he felt, with a sense almost of awe, the preciousness of such a love as this, a love which, comprehending the terrible period of anxiety through which he had to pass, was not ashamed to seek to sweeten it for him by the simple charm of such an offering. Then, at the sound of returning footsteps in the hall, he let go her hands, and with her fond farewell still lingering in his ears, he hurried out into the street.

XXV

Mr. Levy, Junior, Goes on the Continent

Mr. Benjamin Levy was standing in his favorite position before the office fireplace, with his legs a little apart, and his small keen eyes fixed upon vacancy. It was thus, in that very pose, and on that very hearthrug, that he had thought out more than one of those deep-laid schemes which had brought a certain measure of notoriety to the firm of which he was a shining light, and at that very moment he was engaged in deep consideration concerning the case in which his energies were at present absorbed.

A few feet away, his father was carefully calculating, with the aid of a ready reckoner, the compound interest on a little pile of bills of exchange which lay before him. Every now and then he paused, and, looking up from his task, glanced cautiously into his son's perplexed face. Curiosity at length culminated in speech.

"What was you thinking, Benjamin, my son?" he said softly. "The Miss Thurwell case is plain before us, is it not? There is nothing fresh, is there? No fresh business, eh, my son?"

Mr. Benjamin started, and abandoned his reflections.

"No; nothing fresh, dad. It was the Thurwell affair I was thinking of. Give me the keys, will you?"

Mr. Levy leaned back in his chair and produced from his trousers pocket a jingling bunch of keys.

Mr. Benjamin took them in thoughtful silence, and, opening the safe, drew out a packet of faded letters tied up with ribbon. From these he selected one, and carefully replaced the rest.

"Those letters again," remarked his fond parent, chuckling. "Take care of them, Benjamin, take care of them. They was worth their weight in gold to us."

"They're worth a great deal more than that," remarked Mr. Benjamin carelessly. "There's only one thing, dad, that puzzles me a bit."

"It must be a rum thing, my boy, that does that," his fond parent remarked admiringly. "I never praise undeservedly, but I must say this, Benjamin, you've managed this Thurwell affair marvelously— marvelously! Come, let me see what it is that is too deep for you."

He rose and looked over his son's shoulder at the letter which he was reading—one thin sheet of foreign note paper, covered with closely written lines of faint, angular writing, and emitting even now a delicate musky scent.

"What is it, Benjamin—what is it?"

His son laid his finger on a sentence toward the close of the letter, and read it aloud:—

"What that fear has been to me, and what it has grown into during my sad lonely life, I cannot hope to make you understand. Always those terrible words of vengeance ring in my ears as I heard them last. They seem to roll over sea and land, and in the middle of the night, and out in the sunlit street, I seem to hear them still. It is not you I fear, Bernard, so much as him!"

Mr. Levy listened, and nodded approvingly.

"All is plain there, Benjamin, I think. The meaning is quite clear."

Mr. Benjamin laid his finger upon the last sentence.

"What do you make of that, dad?" he asked.

Mr. Levy adjusted his spectacles and read it slowly.

"'It is not for you I fear, Bernard, so much as him.' Tut, tut, that's simple enough," he declared. "This woman, whoever she may be, is afraid of a meeting between Sir Geoffrey Kynaston and Mr. Bernard Maddison, to give him his right name, and she remarks that it is for him she fears, and not for Sir Geoffrey. Quite right, too, considering the affectionate tone of these letters."

"Yes, I suppose that's it," Mr. Benjamin remarked in an absent tone, folding up the letter, and putting it back amongst the rest.

Mr. Levy watched him narrowly, and returned to his desk with a sense of injury. His son—his Benjamin—had discovered something which he was not going to confide to the parental ear. It was a blow.

He was wondering whether it might have the desired effect if he were to produce a scrap of old yellow pocket handkerchief, and affect to be overcome, when they heard a hurried footstep outside. Both looked up anxiously. There was a quick knocking at the door, and a shabby-looking man dressed in black entered.

"Well, Leekson, what news?" Mr. Benjamin asked quickly.

"He's off," was the prompt reply. "Continent. Afternoon train. Waterloo, three o'clock."

Mr. Benjamin's eyes sparkled.

"I knew it!" he exclaimed triumphantly. "Job's over, Leekson. Get me a cab, and go to the office for your money."

"You're going to let him go!" cried Mr. Levy piteously.

"Not I. I'm going with him, dad. A fifty-pound note from the safe, quick."

Mr. Levy gave it to him with trembling fingers.

"Now, dad, listen to me," Benjamin said earnestly, reaching down his overcoat from the peg. "Miss Thurwell will be here some time to-day, I'm certain, to try and buy those letters. I've changed my mind about them. Sell."

"Sell," repeated Mr. Levy, surprised. "I thought that that was what we were not to do."

"Never mind, never mind. I'm playing a better game than that now," continued Mr. Benjamin. "I'll leave it to you to make the bargain. There's no one can beat you at that, you know, dad."

Mr. Levy acknowledged his son's compliment with a gratified smile.

"Well, well, Benjamin, we'll say nothing about that. I'll do my best, you may be sure," he declared fervently.

"I may as well just mention that I have ascertained how much money she has got," Mr. Benjamin went on. "She's worth, until her father dies, about fifteen thousand pounds. We won't be hard on her. Suppose we say five thousand the lowest, eh?"

"All right, Benjamin, all right," the old man murmured, rubbing his hands softly together. "Five thousand pounds! My eye! And how long shall you be away?"

"I can't quite tell, dad. Just keep your pecker up, and stick to the biz."

"Yes, Ben, yes. And of course you can't stop to tell me about it now, but won't this five thousand pounds from the young lady about put an end to this little game, eh? And, if so, need you go following this Mr. Maddison all over the country, eh? An expensive journey, Ben. You've got that fifty-pound note, you know."

Mr. Benjamin laughed contemptuously.

"You'll never make a pile, you won't, dad," he exclaimed. "You're so plaguedly narrow minded. Listen here," he added, drawing a little closer to him, and looking round over his shoulder to be sure that no one was listening to him. "When I come back, I'll make you open your eyes. You think this thing played out, do you? Bah! The letters aren't worth twopence to us. When I come back from abroad, I'm going to commence to play this game in a manner that'll rather astonish you, and a certain other person. Ta-ta, guv'nor."

Mr. Benjamin Levy was a smart young man, but he had a narrow escape that afternoon, for as he was sauntering up and down the platform at Waterloo, whom should he see within a dozen yards of him but Mr. Maddison and Miss Thurwell. He had just time to jump into a third-class carriage, and spread a paper out before his face, before they were upon him.

"Jove, that was a shave!" he muttered to himself. "Blest if I thought they were as thick as that. I wonder if she's going with him. No, there's no female luggage, and that's her maid hanging about behind there. Moses, ain't she a slap-up girl, and ain't they just spooney! D—d if he ain't kissed her!" he wound up as the train glided out of the station, leaving Helen Thurwell on the platform waving her handkerchief. "Well, we're off. So far, so good. I feel like winning."

But, unfortunately for Mr. Benjamin, there was a third person in that train whom neither he nor Mr. Maddison knew of, who was very much interested in the latter. Had he only mentioned his name, or referred in the slightest possible way to his business abroad before Mr. Benjamin, that young gentleman would have promptly abandoned his expedition and returned to town. But, as he did not, all three traveled on together in a happy state of ignorance concerning each other; and Mr. Benjamin Levy was very near experiencing the greatest disappointment of his life.

XXVI

Helen Decides to Go Home

Mr. Benjamin Levy's surmise had been an accurate one. Late in the afternoon of that day, Helen Thurwell called at the little office off the Strand, and when she left it an hour later, she had in her pocket a packet of letters, and Mr. Levy had in his safe a check and promissory note for five thousand pounds. Both were very well satisfied—Mr. Levy with his money, and Helen with the consciousness that she had saved her lover from the consequences of what she now regarded as her great folly.

She was to have dined out that evening with her aunt, but when the time to dress came, she pleaded a violent headache, and persuaded Lady Thurwell, who was a good-natured little woman, to take an excuse.

"But, my dear Helen, you don't look one bit ill," she had ventured to protest, "and the Cullhamptons are such nice people. Are you sure that you won't come?"

"If you please, aunt," she had begged, "I really do want to stay at home this evening;" and Lady Thurwell had not been able to withstand her niece's imploring tone, so she had gone alone.

Helen spent the evening as she had planned to. She took her work down into the room where they had been the night before, and where this wonderful thing had happened to her. Then she leaned back in her low chair—the same chair—and gave herself up to the luxury of thought; and when a young woman does that she is very far gone indeed. It was all so strange to her, so bewildering, that she needed time to realize it.

And as she sat there, her eyes, full of a soft dreamy light, fixed upon vacancy, and her lips parted in a happy smile, she felt a sudden longing to be back again upon the moorland cliffs round Thurwell Court, out in the open country with her thoughts. This town season with its monotonous round of gayety was nothing to her now. More than ever, in the enlarged and sweeter life which seemed opening up before her, she saw the littleness and enervating insipidity of it all. She would go down home, and take some books—the books he was fond of—and sit out on the cliffs by the sea and read and dream, and think over all he had said to her, and look forward to his coming; it should be there he would find her. They two alone would stand together under the blue sky, and wander about in the sunshine over the blossoming moors. Would not this be better than meeting him again in a crowded London drawing-room? She knew that he would like it best.

So when Lady Thurwell returned from her party, and was sitting in her room in a very becoming dressing gown, yawning and thinking over the events of the evening, there was a little tap at the door, and Helen entered, similarly attired.

"Please tell me all about it," she begged, drawing up a chair to the fire. "My headache is quite gone."

"So I should imagine," remarked Lady Thurwell. "I never saw you look better. What have you been doing to yourself, child? You look like Aphrodite 'new bathed in Paphian wells.'"

"If you mean to insinuate that I've had a bath," laughed Helen, "I admit it. Now, tell me all about this evening."

Which of course Lady Thurwell did, and found a good deal to say about the dresses and the menu.

"By the bye," she wound up, with a curious look at her niece, "Sir Allan Beaumerville was there, and seemed a good deal disappointed at the absence of a certain young lady."

"Indeed!" answered Helen. "That was very nice of him. And now, aunt, do you know what I came in to say to you?"

Lady Thurwell shook her head.

"Haven't any idea, Helen. Has anyone been making love to you?"

Helen shook her head, but the color gathered in her cheeks, and she took up a screen, as though to protect her face from the fire.

"I want to go home, aunt. Don't look so startled, please. I heard from papa this morning, and he's not very well, and Lord Thurwell comes back to-morrow, so you won't be lonely, and I've really quite made my mind up. Town is very nice, but I like the country best."

"Like the country best in May!" Lady Thurwell gasped. "My dear child, have you taken leave of your senses?"

"Not quite, aunt," Helen answered, smiling. "Only it is as I say. I like the country best, and I would really rather go home."

Lady Thurwell considered for a full minute. Being a very juvenile matron, she had by no means enjoyed her *rôle* as chaperon to an acknowledged beauty. She had offered it purely out of good nature, and because, although only related by marriage—Lord Thurwell was the elder brother of Mr. Thurwell, of Thurwell Court, and the head of the family—still there was no one else to perform such a service for Helen. But if Helen did really not care for it, and wished to return to her country life, why there was no necessity for her to make a martyr of herself any longer.

"You really mean this, Helen?"

"I do indeed, aunt."

"Then it is settled. Make your own arrangements. I have liked having you, child, and whenever you choose to come to me again you will be welcome. But of course, it is not everyone who cares for town life, and if you do not, you are quite right to detach yourself from it. I'm afraid I know several young men who'll take your sudden flight very much to heart; and one who isn't particularly young."

"Nonsense!" laughed her niece. "There'll be no mourning on my account."

"We shall see," remarked Lady Thurwell, sententiously. "If one person does not find his way down to Thurwell Court after you before long, I shall be surprised."

"Please don't let anyone do anything so stupid, aunt," pleaded Helen with sudden warmth. "It would be—no good."

Lady Thurwell lifted her eyebrows, and looked at her niece with a curious little smile.

"Who is it?" she asked quietly.

But Helen only laughed. Her secret was too precious to part with—yet.

XXVII

Mr. Thurwell Makes Some Inquiries

And so Helen had her own way, and went back to her home on the moors, where Mr. Thurwell, who had just finished his hunting season, was very glad to see her, although not a little surprised. But she told him no more than she had told her aunt, that she had no taste for London life. The time would soon come when he would know the whole truth, but until her lover's return the secret was her own.

She had one hasty note from him, posted in Paris on his way to Italy, and though there were only a few lines in it, she treasured up the little scrap of paper very tenderly, for, such as it was, it was her first love letter. He had given her an address in the small town to which he was bound, and she noticed, with a slight wonder at the coincidence, that it was the same place where he had first seen her. She had written to him, and now there had come a pause. She had nothing to do but to wait.

But though such waiting is at best but a tedious matter, those few days brought their own peculiar happiness to her. She would have found it impossible to have confided her secret to any human being; she had no bosom friend to whom she could go for sympathy. But her healthy, open-air life, her long solitary walks, and a certain vein of poetry which she undoubtedly possessed, had given her some of that passionate, almost personal, love of nature which is sweeter by far than any human friendship. For her those long stretches of wild moorland, with the dark silent tarns and far-distant line of blue hills, the high cliffs where the sea wind roared with all the bluster and fury of a late March, the sea itself with its ever-changing face, the faint streaks of brilliant color in the evening sky, or the wan glare of a stormy morning—all these things had their own peculiar meaning to her, and awoke always some echo of response in her heart. And it chanced that at that time all the sweet breezy freshness of a late spring was making glad the country which she loved, and the perfect sympathy of the season with her own happiness seemed to her very sweet, for it was springtime too in her heart. A new life glowed in her veins, and sometimes it seemed to her that she could see the vista of her whole future bathed in the warm sunlight of a new-born happiness. The murmuring pine groves, the gay reveling of the birds, the budding flowers and heath—all these things appealed to her with a strange sympathetic force. So she took long walks, and came home with sparkling eyes, and her cheeks full of a rich color, till her father wondered what had come to his proud silent daughter to give this new buoyancy to her frame, and added physical beauty to her face, which had once seemed to him a little too *spirituelle* and ethereal.

Once more Helen and her father sat at breakfast out on the sheltered balcony of Thurwell Court. Below them the gardens, still slightly coated with the early morning dew, were bathed in the glittering sunshine, and in the distance, and over the tops of the trees in the park, a slight feathery mist was curling upward. The sweet, fresh air, still a little keen, was buoyant with all the joyous exhilaration of spring, and nature, free at last from the saddened grip of winter, was reasserting itself in one glad triumphant chorus. Down in the park the slumberous cawing of the rooks triumphed over the lighter-voiced caroling of innumerable thrushes and blackbirds, and mingled with the faint humming of a few early bees, seemed to fill the air with a sweetly blended strain of glad music. It was one of those mornings typical of its own season, in which the whole atmosphere seems charged with quickening life. Summer with its warm luscious glow, and autumn with its clear calm repose, have their own special charms. But a spring morning, coming after the deep sadness of a hard winter, gains much by the contrast. There is overflowing energy and passionate joy in its newly beating pulses, the warm delight of reawakening life, happy to find the earth so fair a place, which the staider charms of a more developed season altogether lack.

It was in some measure owing to this influence, and also to the fact that she held in her hand a letter from her lover, which her father had handed her without remark, but with a somewhat curious glance, that Helen was feeling very happy that morning. The last year had dealt strangely with her. Tragedy had thrown its startling, gloomy shadow across her life, and had left traces which could never be altogether wiped out. Anxieties of another sort had come, perplexities and strange unhappy doubts, although these last had burned with a fitful, uncertain flame and now seemed stilled for ever. But triumphing over all these was this new-born love, the great deep joy of a woman's life, so vast, so sweet and beautiful, that it transfuses her whole being, and seems to lift her into another world.

And so Helen, leaning back in her chair, with her eyes wandering idly over the pleasant gardens and park below, to where, through a deep gap in the trees, was just visible a faint blue line of sea, was wrapped up very much in her own thoughts, and scarcely doing her duty toward entertaining her father. Indeed, she seemed almost unconscious of his presence until he looked up suddenly from a letter he was reading and asked her a question.

"By the bye, Helen," he said, "I've meant to ask you something every day since you've been home, but I have always forgotten it. Who was that young man who came down here to help Johnson with the auditing, and who went away so suddenly? A *protégé* of yours, I suppose, as he came here on your recommendation?"

"Yes, I was interested in him," she answered, looking steadily away, and with a faint color in her cheeks. "Why do you ask? Did he not do his work properly?"

"Oh, yes, he did his work very well, I believe," Mr. Thurwell said impatiently. "It was what he did after working hours, and which has just come to my notice, which makes me ask you. It seems he spent the whole of his spare time making covert, but I must say ingenious, inquiries respecting Sir Geoffrey's murder, and I am also given to understand that he paid Falcon's Nest an uninvited visit in the middle of the night. What does it all mean? Was it merely curiosity, or had he any object in it?"

"I think—he had an object," she answered slowly.

"Indeed!" Mr. Thurwell raised his eyebrows and waited for an explanation.

"You remember, papa, that awful scene here when Rachel Kynaston died, and what her last words to me were?"

"Yes, I remember perfectly," Mr. Thurwell answered gravely.

"Well, at that time I could not help having just a suspicion that Mr. Brown must be mixed up in it in some way, and it seemed to me that I should not be quite at ease if I let matters go on without doing anything, so I—well, this young man came down here to see whether he could find out anything."

Mr. Thurwell seldom frowned at his daughter, of whom he was secretly a little afraid, but he did so now. He was seriously angry.

"It was not a matter for you to have concerned yourself in at all," he said, rising from his seat. "At least, I should have been consulted."

"It was all very foolish, I know," she admitted humbly.

"It was worse than foolish; it was wrong and undutiful," he declared. "I am astonished that my daughter should have mixed herself up with such underhand work. And may I ask why I was kept in ignorance?"

"Because you would not have allowed me to do what I did," she said quietly, with downcast eyes. "I thought it was my duty. I have been punished—punished severely."

He softened a little, and resumed his seat. She was certainly very contrite. He was silent for a moment or two, and then asked her a question.

"Did this young man—detective, I suppose he was—find out anything about Mr. Brown?"

She looked up, a little surprised at the curiosity in his tone.

"Why, papa, it was I who found out how stupid I had been," she said. "When I discovered that our mysterious tenant was Bernard Maddison, of course I saw the absurdity of suspecting him at once."

Mr. Thurwell moved a little uneasily in his chair.

"He did not find out anything, then?" he asked.

She was silent. She had not expected this, and she scarcely knew how to answer.

"He found out what Mr. Brown—I mean Mr. Maddison—himself told me, that he had known Sir Geoffrey abroad."

"Nothing more?"

"I did not ask. To tell the truth, I was not interested. The idea of Mr. Maddison being connected with such a crime is simply ridiculous. I was heartily sorry that I had ever taken any steps at all."

Mr. Thurwell lit a cigarette, and drew his remaining letters toward him.

"I must confess," he said slowly, "that when his house was searched in my presence, and all that we discovered was that Mr. Brown was really Bernard Maddison, I felt very much as you feel; and, as you no doubt remember, I went out of my way to be civil to the man, and brought him up here to dine. But since then things have cropped up, and I'm bound to say that it looks a little queer. I hear that young man of yours told several people that he had in his pocket what would bring Mr. Brown to the scaffold any day."

"It is not true," she answered in a low firm tone. "I know that it is not true."

Mr. Thurwell shrugged his shoulders.

"I hope not, I'm sure. Still, I'd rather he did not come back here again. Some one must have done it, you see, and if it was a stranger, he must have been a marvelous sort of fellow to come into this lonely part of the country, and go away again without leaving a single trace."

"Criminals are all clever at disguises," she interposed.

"Doubtless; but they have yet to learn the art of becoming invisible," he went on drily. "I'm afraid it's no use concealing the fact that things look black against Maddison, and there is more than a whisper in the county about it. If he's a wise fellow, he'll keep away from here."

"He will not," she answered. "He will come back. He is innocent!"

Mr. Thurwell saw the rising flush in his daughter's face, but he had no suspicion as to its real cause. He knew that Bernard Maddison was one of her favorite authors, and he put her defence of him down to that fact. He was not a particularly warm advocate on either side, and suddenly remembering his unopened letters, he abandoned the discussion.

Helen, whose calm happiness had been altogether disturbed, rose in a few minutes with the intention of making her escape. But her father, with an open letter in his hand, checked her.

"Have you been seeing much of Sir Allen Beaumerville in town, Helen?" he asked.

"Yes, a great deal. Why?" she asked.

"He's coming down here," Mr. Thurwell said. "He asks whether we can put him up for a night or two, as he wants to do some botanizing. Of course we shall be very pleased. I did give him a general invitation, I remember, but I never thought he'd come. You'll see about having some rooms got ready, Helen!"

"Yes, papa, I'll see to it," she answered, moving slowly away.

What could this visit in the middle of the season mean? she wondered uneasily. It was so unlike Sir Allan to leave town in May. Could it be that what her aunt had once laughingly hinted at was really going to happen? Her cheeks burned at the very thought. She liked Sir Allan, and she had found him a delightful companion, but even to think of any other man now in such a connection seemed unreal and grotesque. After all, it was most improbable. Sir Allan had only shown her the attention he showed every woman who pleased his fastidious taste.

XXVIII

Sir Allan Beaumerville Visits the Court

On the following day Sir Allan duly arrived, and in a very short space of time Helen's fears had altogether vanished. His appearance was certainly not that of an anxious wooer. He was pale and haggard and thin, altogether a different person to the brilliant man about town who was such a popular figure in society. Something seemed to have aged him. There were lines and wrinkles in his face which had never appeared there before, and an air of restless depression in his manner and bearing quite foreign to his former self.

On the first evening Mr. Thurwell broached some plans for his entertainment, but Sir Allan stopped him at once.

"If I may be allowed to choose," he said, "I should like to be absolutely quiet for a few days. London life is not the easiest in the world, and I'm afraid I must be getting an old man. At any rate I am knocked up, and I want a rest."

"You have come to the right place for that," Mr. Thurwell laughed. "You could live here for months and never see a soul if you chose. But I'm afraid you'll soon be bored."

"I'm not afraid of that," Sir Allan answered quietly. "Besides, my excuse was not altogether a fiction. I really am an enthusiastic botanist, and I want to take up my researches here just where I was obliged to leave them off so suddenly last year."

Mr. Thurwell nodded.

"I remember," he said; "you were staying at Mallory, weren't you, when that sad affair to poor Kynaston happened?"

"Yes."

Sir Allan moved his chair a little, as though to escape from the warmth of the fire, and sat where the heavily shaded lamp left his face in the shadow.

"Yes, that was a terrible affair," he said in a low tone; "and a very mysterious one. Nothing has ever been heard of the murderer, I suppose?"

"Nothing."

"And there are no rumors, no suspicions?"

Mr. Thurwell looked uneasily around, as though to satisfy himself that there were no servants lingering in the room.

"It is scarcely a thing to be talked about," he said slowly; "but there have been things said."

"About whom?"

"About my tenant at Falcon's Nest—Bernard Maddison, as he turned out to be."

"Ah!"

Mr. Thurwell looked at his guest wonderingly. He could not quite make up his mind whether he was profoundly indifferent or equally interested. His tone sounded a little cold.

"There was a fellow down here in my employ," continued Mr. Thurwell, lighting a fresh cigar, "who turns out to have been a spy or detective of some sort. Of course I knew nothing of it at the time—in fact, I've only just found it out; but it seems he ransacked Falcon's Nest and discovered some papers which he avowed quite openly would hang Mr. Maddison. But what's become of him I don't know."

"I suppose he didn't disclose the nature of the papers?" Sir Allan asked quietly.

"No, he didn't go as far as that. By the bye, you know every one, Beaumerville. Who is this Bernard Maddison? Of course I know all about his writing and that; but what family is he of? He is certainly a gentleman."

Sir Allan threw away his cigarette, and rose.

"I think I have heard once, but I don't remember for the moment. Miss Helen promised us a little music, didn't she?" he added. "If you are ready, shall we go and remind her?"

Sir Allan brought the conversation to an end with a shrug of his shoulders, and during the remainder of his stay Mr. Thurwell noticed that he carefully avoided any reopening of it. Evidently his guest has no taste for horrors.

Sir Allan rose late on the following morning, and until lunch-time begged for the use of the library, where he remained writing letters and reading up the flora of the neighborhood. Early in the afternoon he appeared equipped for his botanizing expedition.

"Helen shall go with you and show you the most likely places," Mr. Thurwell had said at luncheon. But though Sir Allan had bowed courteously, and had expressed himself as charmed, he had not said another word about it, so when the time came he started alone. On the whole Helen, although she was by no means ill-pleased, was not a little puzzled. In London, when it was sometimes difficult to obtain a place by her side at all, Sir Allan had been the most assiduous and attentive of cavaliers; but now that they were quite alone in the country, and her company was even offered to him, he showed himself by no means eager to avail himself of it. On the contrary, he had deliberately preferred doing his botanizing alone. Well, she was quite satisfied, she thought, with a little laugh. It was far better this way than the other. Still she was puzzled.

Later in the afternoon she started for her favorite walk alone. She nearly always chose the same way along the cliffs, through the fir plantation, and sometimes as far as the hill by the side of which was Falcon's Nest. It was a walk full of associations for her, associations which had become so dear a part of her life that she always strove to heighten them even by choosing the same hour of the day for her walk as that well-remembered one when they had stood hand-in-hand for a single moment in the shadows of the darkening plantation. And again, as it had done many times before, her heart beat fast, and sweet memories began to steal back to her as she passed under those black waving branches moaning slightly in the evening breeze, and pressed under foot the brown leaves which in a sodden mass carpeted the winding path. Yes, it was here by that tall slender fir that they had stood for that one moment of intense happiness, when the thunder of the sea filling the air around them had almost forbidden speech, and the strange light had flashed in his dark eyes. She passed the spot with slow, lingering steps and quickening pulses, and opening the little hand-gate, climbed slowly up the cliff.

At the summit she paused and looked around. A low grey mist hung over the moor, and twilight had cast its mantle of half-veiled obscurity over sea and land. A wind too had sprung up, blowing her ulster and skirts around her, and driving the mist across the moor in clouds of small, fine rain. Before her she could just see the dim outline of the opposite hill, with its dark patch of firs, and Falcon's Nest, bare and distinct, close up against its side. The wind and the rain blew against her, but she took no heed. All personal discomforts seemed so little beside these memories tinged with such a peculiar sweetness. It is a fact that a woman is able to extract far more pleasure from memories than a man, for there is in his nature a certain impatience which makes it impossible for him to keep his thought fixed steadfastly

E. PHILLIPS OPPENHEIM

upon the past. The vivid flashes of memory which do come to him only incite a great restlessness for its renewal, which, if it be for the time impossible, is only disquieting and discontenting. But for a woman, her love itself, even though it be for the time detached from its object, is a sweet and precious thing. She can yield herself up to its influence, can steep her mind and soul in it, till a glow of intense happiness steals through her whole frame; and hence her patience during separation is so much greater than a man's.

And it was so to a certain extent with Helen. Those few moments of intense abstraction had their own peculiar pleasure for her, and it was only the sound of the far-off clock borne by the wind across the moor from Thurwell Court which recalled her to herself. Then she started, and in a moment more would have been on her way home.

But that lingering farewell glance toward Falcon's Nest suddenly changed into a startled fearful gaze. Her heart beat fast, and she took an involuntary step forward. There was no doubt about it. A dim moving light shone from the lower windows of the cottage.

Her first wild thought was that her lover had himself returned, and a thrill of intense joy passed through her whole being, only to die away before the cold chill of a heart-sickening dread. Was it not far more likely to be an intruder of the type of Benjamin Levy, a spy or emissary of the law, searching amongst his papers as Benjamin Levy had done, for the same hideous reason. Her heart sank with fear, and then leaped up with the fierce defensive instinct of a woman who sees her lover's enemies working for his ruin. She did not hesitate for an instant, but walked swiftly along the cliff-side towards that tremulous light.

The twilight was fast deepening, and the cold grey tint of the dull afternoon was gradually becoming blotted out into darkness. As she drew nearer to her destination, the low moaning of the sea below became mingled with the melancholy sighing of the wind amongst the thick fir trees which overhung the cottage. The misty rain blew in her face and penetrated her thick ulster. Everything around was as dreary and lonely as it could be. The only sign of any human life was that faint glimmering light now stationary, as though the searcher whoever he might be, had found what he wanted, and had settled down in one of the rooms.

As she drew nearer she saw which it was, and trembled. All the rest of the cottage was in black darkness. The light shone only from the window of that little inner study on the ground floor.

She had passed through the gate, and with beating heart approached the window. A few yards away she paused and looked in.

A candle was burning on a small bracket, and, though its light was but dim, it showed her everything. The cabinet was open, and papers were strewn about, as though thrown right and left in a desperate search; and, with his back to her, a man was seated before it, his bared head resting upon his arms, and his whole attitude full of the passionate abandonment of a great despair. She had but one thought. It was her lover returned, and he needed her consolation. With a new light in her face she turned and moved softly toward the front door. As she reached the threshold she paused and drew back. There was the sound of footsteps inside.

She stepped behind a bush and waited. In a moment the door of the cottage was thrown suddenly open, and the tall figure of a man stood in the entrance. For one moment he hesitated. Then with a sudden passionate gesture he raised his hands high above his head, and she heard a long deep moan burst from his quivering lips.

The pity which swelled up in her heart she kept back with a strong hand. A strange bewilderment was creeping over her. She had seen only the dark outline of the figure, but surely it was not the figure of her lover. And then she held her breath, and walking swiftly away, passing so close to her that she could look into his white, strained face, Sir Allan Beaumerville strode down the garden, and disappeared in the shadows of the plantation.

XXIX

The Scene Changes

The midday sun had risen into a sky of deep cloudless blue, and a silence almost as intense as the silence of night rested upon the earth. No one was abroad, no one seemed to have anything particular to do. Far away on the vine-covered slopes a few peasants were lazily bending over their work, the bright garments of their picturesque attire standing out like little specks of brilliant coloring against the dun-colored background. But in the quaint old-fashioned town itself no one was astir. One solitary Englishman made his way alone and almost unnoticed through the queer zig-zag streets, up the worn grey steps by the famous statute of Minerva, and on to the terraced walk, fronting which were the aristocratic villas of the little Italian town.

It was a solitude which was pleasing to him, for it was very evident that he was no curious tourist, or casual visitor of any sort. His eyes were full of that eager half-abstracted look which so clearly denotes the awakening of old associations, quickened into life by familiar surroundings; and, indeed, it was so. To Bernard Maddison, every stone in that quietly sleeping, picturesque old town spoke with a language of its own. The very atmosphere, laden with the sultry languorous heat of a southern sun, seemed charged with memories. Their influence was strong upon him, and he walked like a man in a dream, until he reached what seemed to be his destination, and here he paused.

He had come to the end of the terraced walk, the evening promenade of the whole town. Before him was a small orange grove, whose aromatic odor, faintly penetrating the still air, added one more to his stock of memories. On his right hand was a grey stone wall, worn and tottering with age, and overhung with green creepers and shrubs, reaching over and hanging down from the other side, and let into it, close to him, was a low nail-studded door of monastic shape, half hidden by a luxurious drooping shrub, from amongst the foliage of which peeped out star-like clusters of soft scarlet flowers.

For many moments he stood before that door, with his hand resting upon the rusty latch, lingering in a sort of apathy, as though he were unwilling to disturb some particular train of thought. Then a mellow-sounding bell from a convent in the valley below startled him, and immediately he lifted the latch before him. There was no other fastening, and the door opened. He stepped inside, and carefully reclosed it.

He was in a garden, a garden of desolation, which nature seemed to have claimed for her own and made beautiful. It was a picture of luxuriant overgrowth. The grass on the lawns had become almost a jungle. It had grown up over the base of the deep grey stone basins of exquisite shape and carving, the tiny statuettes tottering into ruin, and the worn old sun-dial, across which the slanting rays of the sun still glanced. Weeds, too, had crept up around them in picturesque toils, weeds which had started to destroy, but remained to adorn with all the sweet abandon of unrestrained growth. Some of them had put forth brilliant blossoms of many hues, little spots of exquisite coloring against the sombre hue of the stonework and the deep green of the leaves. Everywhere nature had triumphed over science and skill. Everything was changed, and nature had shown herself a more perfect gardener than man. The gravel paths were embedded with soft green moss, studded with clumps of white and purple violets, whose faint fragrance, mingled with the more exotic scent of other plants, filled the warm air with a peculiar dreamy perfume. Nowhere had the hand of man sought to restrain or to develop. Nature had had her own way, and had made for herself a fair garden.

A little overcome by the heat, and a little, too, by swiftly stirring memories, Bernard Maddison sank down upon a low iron seat, under the shade of a little clump of almond trees, and covered his face with his hands. And there came to him, as he sat there, something more vivid than an ordinary day-dream, something so real and minutely played out, that afterwards it possessed for him all the freshness and significance of a veritable trance. It seemed, indeed, as if some mysterious force had drawn aside the curtain of the past in his mind, and had bidden him look out once more upon the moving figures in a living drama.

THE WARM SUNLIGHT FADED FROM the sky, the summer heat died out of the air, the soft velvety mantle of a southern night lay upon the brooding land. Many stars were burning in the deep-blue heavens, and the horned moon, golden and luminous, hung low down in the west.

Pale, and with the fever of a great anger burning in his dry eyes, a man sat at the open window of the villa yonder, watching. Around him were scattered all the signs of arduous brain labor, books, manuscripts, classical dictionaries, and works of reference. But his pen had fallen from his hand, and he was doing nothing. He sat there idle, gazing out upon the fantastic shapes and half-veiled gloom of this fair garden. Its rich balmy odors, and the fainter perfume of rarer plants which floated languidly in through the open window, were nothing to him. He was barely conscious of the sweet delights of the voluptuous summer night. He was watching with his eyes fixed upon the east, where morning would soon be breaking.

It came at last—what he was waiting for. There was a slight click of the latch from the old postern door in the wall, and the low murmur of voices—a man's, pleading and passionate, and a woman's, half gay, half mocking. Then the door opened and shut, and a tall fair lady walked leisurely up toward the villa.

She wore no hat, but a hooded opera-cloak was thrown loosely over her shoulders, and as she strolled up the path, pausing every now and then to carelessly gather a handful of the drooping lilies, whose perfume made faint the heavy night air, its folds parted, and revealed brief glimpses of soft white drapery and flashing jewels on her bosom and in her hair. Her feet, too, were cased in tiny white satin slippers, which seemed scarcely to press the ground, so lightly and gracefully she walked. Altogether she was very fair to look upon—the fairest sight in all that lovely garden.

Not so seemed to think the man who stood back in the shadow of the window, waiting for her. His white face was ghastly with passion, and his fingers were nervously interlaced in the curtains. It was only with a supreme effort that he at last flung them from him, and moved forward as though to meet her.

She saw him standing there, pale and rigid, like a carved statue, save for the passion which burned in his eyes, and for a moment she hesitated. Then, with the resigned air of one who makes up her mind to face something disagreeable, she shrugged her shoulders, and throwing away the handful of lilies she had gathered, advanced toward him.

They neither of them spoke until they stood face to face. Then, as his motionless form prevented her stepping through the window, and barred her further progress, she came to a standstill, and addressed him lightly.

"Yours is a strange welcome home, *mon ami*," she said. "Why do you stand there looking so fierce?"

He pointed with shaking fingers away toward the east, where a faint gleam of daylight was lightening the sky.

"Where have you been?" he asked harshly. "Can you not see that it is morning? All night long I have sat here watching for you. Where have you been?"

"You know very well where I have been," she answered carelessly. "To the ball at the Leon d'Or. I told you that I was going."

"Told me! You told me! Did I not forbid it? Did I not tell you that I would not have you go?"

"Nevertheless, I have been," she answered lightly. "It was an engagement, and I never break engagements."

"An engagement? You, with no chaperon, to go to a common ball at a public room! An engagement. Yes, with your lover, I presume."

She looked at him steadily, and yawned in his face.

"You are in a bad temper, I fear," she said. "At least, you are very rude. Let me pass, will you? I am tired of standing here."

He was beside himself with passion, and for a second or two he did not speak. But when at last the words came, they were clear and distinct enough.

"Into this house you shall never pass again," he said. "You have disregarded my wishes, you have disobeyed my orders, and now you are deceiving me. You are trifling with my honor. You are bringing shame upon my name. Go and keep your assignations from another roof. Mine has sheltered your intrigues long enough!"

The hand which had kept together her opera-cloak relinquished its grasp, and it fell back upon her shoulders. The whole beauty of her sinuous figure, in its garb of dazzling white, stood revealed. The moonlight gleamed in her fair hair, bound up with one glittering gem, shone softly upon her white swelling throat and bare arms, and flashed in her dark eyes, suddenly full of passion. Her right hand was nervously clasped around a little morsel of lace handkerchief which she had drawn from the folds of her corsage, and which seemed to make the air around heavy with a sweet perfume.

"You are angry, and you do not know what you are saying," she said. "It is true that you forbade me to go to-night—but you forbid everything. I cannot live your life. It is too dull, too *triste*. It is cruel of you to expect it. Let me go in now. If you want to scold, you can do so to-morrow."

E. PHILLIPS OPPENHEIM

She stepped forward, but he laid his hands upon her dainty shoulders and pushed her roughly back.

"Never!" he cried savagely. "Go and live what life you choose. This is no home for you. Go, I say!"

She looked at him, her lovely eyes turned pleadingly upwards, and her lips trembling.

"You are mad!" she said. "Am I not your wife? You have no right to keep me here. And my boy, too. Let me pass."

He did not move, nor did he show any sign of yielding. He stood there with his hand stretched out in a threatening gesture toward her, his face pale and mute as marble, but with the blind rage still burning in his dark eyes.

"What is the boy, or what am I to you?" he cried hoarsely. "Begone, woman!"

Still she did not seem to understand.

"Where would you have me go?" she asked. "Is not this my home? What have I—"

"Go to your lover!" he interrupted fiercely. "Tell him that your husband is no longer your tool. He will take you in."

A burning color streamed into her delicate cheeks, and a sudden passion blazed in her eyes. She drew herself up to her full height and turned upon him with the dignity of an empress.

"Listen to me one moment," she said. "Ask yourself whether you have ever tried to make my life a happy one. Did I ever pretend to care for books and solitude? Before I married you I told you that I was fond of change and gaiety and life, and you promised me that I should have it. Ask yourself how you have kept that promise. You deny me every pleasure, and drive me to seek them alone. I am weary of your jealous furies, and your evil temper. As God looks down upon us at this moment, I have been a faithful wife to you; but if you will add to all your cruelties this cowardly, miserable indignity, then I will never willingly look upon your face again, and what sin I do will be on your head, not mine. Will you stand aside and let me pass?"

"Never!" he answered. "Never!"

She drew her mantle round her shoulders, and turned her back upon him with a contemptuous gesture.

"You have made me what I shall be," she said. "The sin be with you. For several weary years you have made me miserable. Now you have made me wicked."

She walked away into the perfumed darkness, and presently he heard the gate close behind her. He listened frantically, hoping to hear her returning steps. It was in vain. All was silent. Then he felt his limbs totter, and he sank back on a couch, and buried his face amongst the cushions.

XXX

Benjamin Levy Runs his Quarry to Earth

The slumberous afternoon wore slowly away. A slight breeze rustled amongst the cypresses and the olive trees, and the air grew clearer. The sun was low in the heavens, and long shadows lay across the brilliant patches of flowers, half wild, half cultivated, and on the moss-grown walks.

Still Bernard Maddison made no movement. It may have been that he shrunk from what was before him, or it may have been that he had some special purpose in thus calling up those broken visions of the past into his mind. For, as he sat there, they still thronged in upon him, disjointed and confused, yet all tinged with that peculiar sadness which seemed to have lain heavy upon his life.

Again the memory of those long lonely days of his boyhood stole in upon him. He thought of that terrible day when his father stood by his bedside, and had bidden him in an awful voice ask no more for his mother, and think of her only as dead; and he remembered well the chill of cold despair with which he had realized that that fair, sweet woman, who had called him her little son, and who had accepted his devoted boyish affection with a sort of amused pleasure, was gone from him for ever. Henceforth life would indeed be a dreary thing, alone with that cold, silent student, with whom he was almost afraid to speak, and whom he scarcely ever addressed by the name of father.

A dreary time it had indeed been. His memory glanced lightly over the long monotonous years with a sort of shuddering recoil. He thought of his father's frequent absences, and of his return from one of them in the middle of a winter's night, propped up in an invalid carriage, with a surgeon in attendance, and blood-stained bandages around his leg. And he thought of a night when he had sat up with him while the nurse rested, and one name had ceaselessly burst from those white feverish lips, laden with fierce curses and deep vindictive hate, a name which had since been written into his memory with letters of fire. Further and further on his memory dragged him, until he himself, a boy no longer, had stood upon the threshold of man-hood, and on one awful night had heard from his father's lips that story which had cast its shadow across his life. Then for the first time had sprung up of some sort of sympathy between them, sympathy which had for its foundation a common hatred, a common sense of deep, unpardonable wrong. The oath which his father had sworn with trembling lips the son had echoed, and in dread of the vengeance of these two, the man against whom they had sworn it cut himself off from his fellows, and skulked in every out-of-the-way corner of Europe, a hunted being in peril of his life. There had come a great change over their lives, and they had drifted farther apart again. He himself had gone out into the world something of a scholar and something of a pedant, and he had found that all his ideas of life had lain rusting in his country home, and that he had almost as much to unlearn as to learn. With ample means, and an eager thirst for knowledge, he had passed from one to another of the great seats of learning of the world. But his lesson was not taught him at one of them. He learned it not amongst the keen conflict of intellect at the universities, not in the toils of the great vague disquiet which was throbbing amongst all cultured and artistic society, but in the eternal silence of Mont Blanc and her snow-capped Alps, and the whisperings of the night winds which blew across the valleys. At Heidelberg he had been a philosopher, in Italy he had been a scholar, and in Switzerland he became a poet. When once again he returned to the more feverish life of cities he was a changed man. He looked out upon life now with different eyes and enlarged vision. Passion had given place to a certain studied calm, a sort of inward contemplativeness which is ever inseparable from the true artist. Life became for him almost too impersonal, too little human. Soon it threatened to become one long abstraction, accompanied necessarily with a weakened hold on all sensuous things, and a corresponding decline in taste and appreciation. One thing had saved him from relapsing into the nervous dreamer, and the weaver of bright but aimless fancies. He had loved, and he had become a man again, linked to the world and the things of the world by the pulsations of his passion and his strong deep love. Was it well for him or ill, he wondered. Well, it might have been save for the deadly peril in which he lived, and which seemed closing fast around him. Well, it surely would have been. . .

Lower and lower the sun had sunk, till now its rim touched the horizon. The evening breeze stealing down from the hills had gathered strength until now it was almost cold. The distant sound of footsteps, and the gay laughing voices of the promenaders from the awakening

E. PHILLIPS OPPENHEIM

town broke the deep stillness which had hung over the garden and recalled Bernard Maddison from thoughtland. He rose to his feet, a little stiff, and walked slowly along the path towards the villa. At that same moment, Mr. Benjamin Levy, tired and angry with his long waiting, stole into the garden by the postern-gate.

XXXI

Benjamin Levy Writes Home

June 10th.

My Dear Dad

"I wired you yesterday afternoon, immediately on our arrival at this outlandish little place, to write to me at the hotel Leon d'Or, for it seems that we have reached our destination—by we, of course, I mean Mr. Maddison and myself, though he has not the least idea of my presence here. Well, this is a queer old crib, I can tell you, and the sooner we are on the move again the better I shall be pleased. The fodder is odious, not fit for a pig, and the wine is ditto. What wouldn't I give for a pint of Bass like they draw at the Blue Boar? Old England for me is my motto!

"And now to biz! So far all's well. I'm on the right tack and no mistake. We got here middle day, yesterday—came over the hills from the railway in a regular old bone-shaker of a coach. My tourist get-up is quite the fig, and though I caught Mr. M—— eyeing me over a bit supercilious like once, he didn't recognize me if ever he did see me down at Thurwell Court, which I don't think he did. Well, directly we got here, off started Mr. M—— through the town, and after a bit I followed. Lord! it was hot and no mistake, but he didn't seem to notice it, though the perspiration was streaming down my back like anything. About a mile out of town we came to a great high wall with a door in it, and before I could say 'Jack Robinson' or get anywhere near him, in he went. Well, I hung round a bit, and soon I found a sort of opening in the wall where I could just see in, and there he was sitting down on a seat in a regular howling wilderness of a garden, as though the whole place belonged to him, if you please. All right! I thought, I'm agreeable to a rest, and I sat down too, little thinking what was in store for me. Four mortal hours passed before he stirred, and jolly stiff and tired I was, I can tell you. But it was a lucky thing for me all the same, for when he got up and made for the house it was almost dark, so without more ado I just opened the door and walked in myself. There was no end of shrubs and trees about the place, and though I followed him on another path only a few yards away, he couldn't see me, and there was no chance

E. PHILLIPS OPPENHEIM

of his hearing, for the moss had grown over the gravel like a blooming carpet, which was all lucky for me again.

"Well, we were just close to the house, when we both of us got a start, and I nearly yelled out. Round the corner of his path, thank goodness! came a tall, white-haired old lady, in a long black dress, with an ivory cross hanging down, and looking as dignified as possible. She no sooner saw him than she stopped and cried out, 'Bernard! Bernard!' and seemed as though she were going to faint. She pulled herself together, however, and things became very interesting for me, I can tell you.

"Mr. M—— he was going to take her hands and kiss her, but she drew them away and stood back. Lord! how awful her face did look! It gave me a regular turn just to look at her.

"'Bernard!' she cried out in a low, shaking voice, 'I know all—all!'

"'What do you mean, mother?' he asked.

"Then she stretched her arms up, and it was dreadful to look at her.

"'I had a dream!' she cried, 'a dream which kept me shuddering and sleepless from midnight to daybreak. I dreamed I saw him—dead—cold and dead!'

"He said nothing, but he seemed fearfully upset. I kept crouched down behind a shrub and listened.

"'In the morning I sent for a file of English newspapers,' she went on. 'One by one I searched them through till I came to August last year. There I found it. Bernard, it was at Thurwell Court. I had a letter in my pocket from you with the postmark Thurwell. Don't come near me, but speak! Is there blood upon your hands?'

"And now, dad, the most provoking things happened. It seemed just as though it were done to spite me. He had his mouth open to answer, and I had my ears open, as you may guess, to listen, and see what happens, and tell me if it wasn't a rare sell! Off the old woman goes into a faint all of a sudden. He catches hold of her and sings out for help. Down I ran to the door as hard as I could, slammed it as though I had just come in, and came running up the path. 'Anything the matter?' I called out, as though I didn't know my way. 'A lady fainted,' he shouts; 'come and help me carry her into the house;' so up I went, and together we carried her inside and laid her on a couch in one of the queerest-furnished rooms I ever saw. There was servants with lighted lamps running about, and another woman who seemed to be a relation, and such a fuss they all made, and no mistake. However, Mr. M—— cooled them all down again pretty soon, for he could see that it was only an ordinary faint, and then he began to look at me curiously. I had made up my mind to stay until the old woman came round, but he was too many for me, for he got up and took me to the door himself. Of course, he was awfully polite and all that, and was very much obliged for my help, but I twigged it in a moment. He wanted me gone, so off I skedaddled.

"Well, back I went to the inn, and began to make a few cautious inquiries about the lady of the Villa Fiorlessa, for that was the name of the house where I had left Mr. M——. I could not get on at all at first, not understanding a word of the blessed lingo, but by good luck I tumbled across an artist chap who turned out a good sort, and offered to interpret for me. So we had the landlord in, and I ordered a bottle of his best wine—nasty greasy stuff it was—and we went at it hammer and tongs. Pretty soon I had found out everything I wanted to.

"Nearly twenty years ago the lady—Mrs. Martival she was called—had come to the Villa Fiorlessa with her husband and one little boy. They were, it seems, one of the worst-matched couples that could be imagined. Mr. Martival was a gloomy, severe man, who hated going out, and worked at some sort of writing day and night. His wife, on the other hand, who was a Frenchwoman, was passionately fond of travel, and change, and gaiety. Her life was consequently very like a prison, and it is stated, too, that besides denying her every whim and forcing her to live in a manner she utterly disliked, her husband ill-treated her shamefully. Well, she made a few friends here and went to see them pretty often, and just at that time an English milord—you can guess who he was—came here to see the statue, and met Mrs. Martival, whom he seems to have known before her marriage. The exact particulars are not known, but it is supposed that Mrs. Martival would have been married to this young Englishman, Sir Geoffrey Kynaston, but for some deep scheming on the part of Mr. Martival. Anyhow, there was a desperate quarrel between Mr. and Mrs. Martival, when she charged him with duplicity before this marriage, and he forbade her to meet Sir Geoffrey Kynaston again. Quite properly she refused to obey him, and they met often, although every one seems quite sure that at that time they met only as friends. Mr. Martival, however, appears to have thought otherwise, for one night, after what they call their carnival dance here, which every one in the neighborhood had attended, Mr. Martival had the brutality to close his doors against her, and refuse to let her enter the house. It was the crowning piece of barbarism to a long course of jealous cruelties. Mrs. Martival spent that night with some friends, and seems even then

E. PHILLIPS OPPENHEIM

to have hesitated for a long time. Her married life had been one long disappointment, and this brutal action of her husband had ended it. Sir Geoffrey Kynaston was madly in love with her, and she was one of those women who must be loved. In the end she ran away with him, which seemed a very natural thing for her to do.

"The queerest part of it is to come, though. Sir Geoffrey was devoted to her, and would have married her at once if Mr. Martival would have sued for a divorce. He showed her every kindness, and he lavished his money and his love upon her. But it seems that she was a devout Roman Catholic, and the horror of what she had done preyed upon her so, that in less than a month she left Sir Geoffrey, and entered one of the lower sort of nunneries as a menial. From there she went to the wars as a nurse, and did a great deal of good. When she returned, of all places in the world she came back to the Villa Fiorlessa, partly from a curious notion of penance, that she might be continually reminded of her sin. The queerest part of it is, however, that the people round here behaved like real Christians, and jolly different to what they would have done at home. They knew all her history, and they welcomed her back as though that month in her life had never been. That's what I call charity, real charity, dad! Don't know what you think about it. Well, there she's lived ever since with her sister, who had lots of money (she died last year), and the poor people all around just worshipped them.

"Now, to go back a bit. Mr. Martival, although he had been such a brute to his wife, no sooner found out that she was with Sir Geoffrey Kynaston than he swore the most horrible oaths of vengeance, and went off after them. He was brought back in a fever, with a pistol shot in his leg, which served him d——d well right, I think. No sooner was he better than he started off again in pursuit, but Sir Geoffrey dodged him, and they never met. Meanwhile the young cub, whom you will recognize as Mr. M——, had grown up, and what must his father do when he returned but tell him as much of the story as suited him, with the result that he too swore an oath of vengeance against Sir Geoffrey Kynaston. Time goes on, and Mr. Martival and his son both leave here. Mr. Martival is reported to have died in Paris, his son goes to England, and is lost sight of. We can, however, follow the story a little further. We can follow it down to its last scene, and discover in the Mr. Brown who had taken a small cottage near Sir Geoffrey's seat, within a week of his return home, and whom soon afterwards we discover bending over Sir Geoffrey's murdered body, the boy who, fired with what his father had thundered into his ears as his mother's ruin, had sworn that oath of vengeance against Sir Geoffrey.

"All this looks very simple, doesn't it? and I dare say, my dear dad, you're wondering why I don't come straight away home, and cause a sensation at Scotland Yard by clearing up the Kynaston murder. Simply because that isn't quite my game. I didn't come over here to collect evidence against Mr. M——, for I could have laid my hand on plenty of that at home. There is something else at the back of it all, which I can only see very dimly yet, but which will come as a crasher, I can tell you, when it does come. At present I won't say anything about this, only keep your eyes open and be prepared. Ta-ta!

Your obedient son,
BEN

P.S. Don't worry about Xs. They won't come out of your pocket in the long run, I can tell you.

P.S. 2. Wednesday evening. Here's a pretty pickle! You remember the artist I told you about. I'm d——d if he isn't a regular from S.Y., and he's got his pocket-book pretty full, too. The game is serious now and no mistake. Mind you, I think we stand to win still, but I can't be quite sure while this chap's on the lay. Look out for telegrams, and don't be surprised if I turn up at any moment. It may come to a race between us. D——n, I wonder how he got on the scent!

E. PHILLIPS OPPENHEIM

XXXII

A Strange Trio of Passengers

Before the open window of her room, looking out upon the fair wilderness below, and over its high stone walls to the dim distant line of hills vanishing in an ethereal mist, lay Mrs. Martival, and by her side stood Bernard Maddison, looking down into her white suffering face.

Sorrow and time together had made strange havoc with its beauty, and yet the lines had been laid on with no harsh hand. There was a certain dignity which it had never lost, which indeed resigned and large-minded sadness only enhances, and her simple religious life had given a touch of spirituality to those thin, delicate features so exquisitely carved and moulded. The bloom had gone from her cheeks for ever, and their intense pallor was almost deathlike, matching very nearly her snow-white hair, but her eyes seemed to have retained much of their old power and sweetness, and the light which sometimes flashed in them lent her face a peculiar charm. But now they were full of a deep anxiety as she lay there, a restless disquiet which showed itself also in her nervously twitching fingers.

Far away down the valley the little convent clock struck the hour, and at its sound she looked up at him.

"You go at nine o'clock, Bernard?"

"At nine o'clock, mother, unless you wish me to stay."

She shook her head.

"No, I shall be better alone. This thing will crush me into the grave, but death will be very welcome. Oh, my son, my son, that the sin of one weak woman should have given birth to all this misery!"

He stooped over her, and held her thin fingers in his strong man's hand.

"Do not trouble about it, mother," he said. "I can bear my share. Try and forget it."

Her eyes flashed strangely, and her lips parted in a smile which was no smile.

"Forget it! That is a strange speech, Bernard. Have I the power to beckon to those hills yonder, and bid them bow their everlasting heads?

Can I put back the hand of time, and live my life over again? Even so futile is my power over memory. It is my penance, and I pray day and night for strength to bear it."

Her voice died away with a little break, and there was silence. Soon she spoke again.

"Tell me—something about her, Bernard."

His face changed, but it was only a passing glow, almost as though one of those long level rays of sunlight had glanced for a moment across his features.

"She is good and beautiful, and all that a woman should be," he whispered.

"Does she know?"

He shook his head.

"She trusts me."

"Then you will be happy?" she asked eagerly. "Happy even if the worst come! Time will wipe out the memory."

He turned away with a dull sickening pain at his heart. The worst he had not told her. How could he? How could he add another to her sorrows by telling her of the peril in which he stood? How could he tell her what he suspected to be true—that in that quiet little Italian town English detectives were watching his every movement, and that at any moment he might be arrested? With her joyless life, and with this new misery closing around her, would it not be well for her to die?

"It is farewell between us now, Bernard, then?" she said softly. "God grant that you may be going back to a new and happier life. May I, who have failed so utterly, give you just one word of advice?"

He bowed his head, for just then he could not have spoken. She raised herself a little upon her couch, and felt for his hand.

"Bernard, you are not as your father was," she said; "yet you, too, have something of the student in you. Don't think that I am going to say anything against learning and culture. It is a grand thing for a man to devote himself to; but, like everything else, in excess it has its dangers. Sometimes it makes a man gloomy and reserved, and averse to all change and society, and intolerant toward others. Bernard, it is bad for his wife then. A woman sets so much store by little things— her happiness is bound up in them. She is very, very human, and she wants to be loved, and considered, and feel herself a great part in her husband's life and thoughts. And if it is all denied to her, what is she to do? Of necessity she must be miserable. A man should never let his wife feel that she is shut out from any one of his great interests. He should never let those little mutual ties which once held them together grow weak, and fancy because he is living amongst the ghosts of great thoughts that little human responsibilities have no claim upon him. Bernard, you will remember all this!"

"Every word, mother," he answered. "Helen would thank you if she had been here."

A horn sounded from outside, and he drew out his watch hastily.

"The diligence, mother!" he exclaimed; "I must go."

He took her frail form up into his arms, and kissed her.

"If all goes well," he said in a low tone, "I will bring her to you."

"If she will come, I shall die happy," she murmured. "But not against her will or without knowing all. Farewell!"

That night three men were racing home to England as fast as express train and steamer could bear them. One was Bernard Maddison, another Mr. Benjamin Levy, and the third his artist friend.

XXXIII

Visitors for Mr. Bernard Maddison

In an ordinary case, with three men starting from a given point in North Italy at the same time, the odds seem in favor of their all reaching their destination at the same time. As it happened, however, there was another factor to be considered, which had its due result. Bernard Maddison was rather more at home on Continental railroads than he was on English ones, whereas neither of the other two had ever before left their own country save under the wing of "Cook." The consequence was that by the aid of sundry little man(oe)uvres, which completely puzzled his would-be companions, Bernard Maddison stood on the platform of Waterloo while they were still in the throes of seasickness. As a further consequence two telegrams were dispatched from Ostend, and were duly delivered in England. The first was from Benjamin Levy to his father.

"Meet all boat trains at Waterloo, and try to recognize B. M. King will do to shadow. Ascertain Miss Thurwell's address. Home early to-morrow."

The second was from his acquaintance, the artist, to Scotland Yard.

"Bernard Maddison ahead of us. Meet all trains. Tall, dark, thin, pale, brown check traveling ulster. Photograph for sale in Regent Street if can get to shop."

Both telegrams were conscientiously attended to, and when Bernard Maddison drove out of the station his hansom was followed by two others. There was nothing very suspicious about his movements. First of all he was set down at his club, which meant a wait of an hour and a half for his watchers. At the end of that time he reappeared with all the traces of his journey effaced, and in a fresh suit of clothes, carrying now a smaller portmanteau. He lit a cigarette, and sent for a hansom. This time he was set down at King's Cross, and took a ticket for a small town on the Yorkshire coast. Hereupon the employee of Messrs. Levy

& Son retired, having ascertained all that he was required to ascertain. The other myrmidon, however, having dispatched his subordinate to headquarters with particulars of his destination, took up the chase.

It was late in the afternoon before they reached their journey's end, but Bernard Maddison was quite unconscious of any fatigue, and marching straight out of the station, turned toward Mallory. The man who was following him, however, hired a carriage, and drove down to the hotel. He knew quite well where the other was going to, and as nothing could be done that night, he determined to enjoy as much as he could of his seaside trip, and, after making up for his day's fasting by a satisfactory tea, he spent the evening on the jetty listening to the town brass band.

THAT WAS A STRANGE WALK for Bernard Maddison. Two sensations were struggling within him for the mastery, fear and despair at the terrible crisis which seemed to yawn before his feet, and that sweet revolution of feeling, that intense, yearning love, which had suddenly thrown a golden halo over his cold barren life. But as he left the road and took the moorland path along the cliff, the battle suddenly came to an end. Before him stretched the open moor, brilliant with coloring, with dark flushes of purple, and bright streaks of yellow gorse, and the sunlight glancing upon the hills. There was the pleasant murmuring of the sea in his ears, a glistening, dancing, silver sea, the blue sky above, and the fresh strong breeze full of vigorous, bracing life. Something of a glad recklessness stole over him and lightened his heart. This was no scene, no hour for sad thoughts. Where was the philosophy of nursing such, of giving them a home even for a moment? Joy and sorrow, what were they but abstract states of the mind? Let him wait until the ashes were between his teeth. The future and the past no man could command, but the present was his own. He would claim it. He would drink deep of the joy which lay before him.

And as he walked on over the soft springy turf, with the tall chimneys of Thurwell Court in the valley before him, life leaped madly through his veins, and a deep joy held memory in a torpor, and filled his heart with gladness. The whole passionate side of his nature had been suddenly quickened into life by his surroundings, and by the thought that down yonder the woman whom he loved was waiting for him. Once again, come what may, he would hold her in his arms and hear her voice tremble with joy at his return. Once more he would hold her face up to his, and look into her dim, soft eyes, full of that glowing lovelight which none can fail to read. Once again he would drink deep of this delicious happiness, a long sweet draught, and if life ended after that moment he would at least have touched the limits of all earthly joys.

And suddenly he stood face to face with her. He had passed Falcon's Nest, dismantled and desolate, with scarcely a careless glance, and had entered the long pine grove which fringed the cliff side. Already he was close to the spot where they had stood once before, and with all the subtle sweetness of those memories stealing in upon him he had turned aside to look through the tree tops down into the sea, as they had done together. Thus he was standing when he heard light firm footsteps close at hand, and a little surprised cry which rang in his ears like music, for it was her voice.

They stood face to face, their hands clasped. In that first moment of tremulous joy neither of them spoke. Each was struggling for realization, for even an inward expression of the ecstasy of this meeting. For them there was a new glory in the sunny heavens, a new beauty in the glistening sea and the softly waving pine trees, even in the air they breathed. The intensity of this joy filled their hearts, their fancy, their imagination. Everything was crowned with a soft golden light; new springs of feeling leaped up within them, bringing glowing revelations of such delight as mocked expression. For them only at that moment the sun shone, and the summer winds whispered in the trees, and the birds sang. The world was theirs, or rather a new one of their own creation. The past and the future emptied their joys into the overflowing bowl of the present. Life stood still for them. There was no horizon, no background. Oh, it is a great thing, the greatest thing upon this earth, to love and be loved!

Each dreaded speech. It seemed as though a single word must drag them down from a new heaven to an old earth. Yet those murmured passionate words of his, as he drew her softly into his arms, and her head sank upon his shoulder—they were scarcely words. And then again there was silence.

It lasted long. It seemed to him that it might have lasted forever. But the sun went down behind the hills, and a dusky twilight stole down upon the earth. Then she spoke.

"My love, my love! you must listen to me. I have a confession to make."

"A confession? You!" he echoed.

Her cheeks burned with a fire which seemed to her like the fire of shame. Her tongue seemed hung with sudden weights. She had doubted him. The hideousness of it oppressed her like a nightmare; yet her voice did not falter.

"You remember those dying words of Rachel Kynaston?"

"I have never forgotten them," he answered simply.

"They laid a charge upon me. I told myself that it was a sacred charge. Listen, my love—listen, and hate me! I have been to detectives. I paid them money to hunt you down; I have done this, I who love you. No, don't draw your arms away. I have done this. It was before I knew. Oh, I have suffered! God! how I have suffered! It has been an agony to me. You will forgive me! I will not let you go unless you forgive me."

He looked down at her in silence. His cheeks were pale and his eyes were grave. Yet there was no anger.

"I will forgive you, Helen," he whispered—"nay, there is nothing to forgive. Only tell me this: you do not doubt me now?"

"Never again!" she cried passionately. "God forgive me that I have ever doubted you! It is like a horrible dream to me; but it lies far behind, and the morning has come."

He kissed her once more and opened his arms. With a low happy laugh she shook her tumbled hair straight, and hand in hand they walked slowly away.

"You have been long gone," she whispered reproachfully.

He sighed as he answered her. How long might not his next absence be!

"It has seemed as long to me as to you, sweetheart," he said. "Every moment away from you I have counted as a lost moment in my life."

"That is very pretty," she answered. "And now you are here, are you going to stay?"

"Until the end," he said solemnly. "You know, Helen, that I am in deadly peril. The means of averting it which I went abroad to seek, I could not use."

She thought of those letters, bought and safely burnt, and she pressed his fingers. She would tell him of them presently.

"They shall not take you from me, Bernard, now," she said softly. "Kiss me again, dear."

He stooped and took her happy upturned face with its crown of wavy golden hair between his hands, looking fondly down at her. The thought of all that he might so soon lose swept in upon him with a sickening agony, and he turned away with trembling lips and dim eyes.

"God grant that they may not!" he cried passionately. "If it were to come now, how could I bear it to the end?"

They walked on in silence. Then she who had, or thought she had, so much more reason to be hopeful than he, dashed the tears away from her eyes, and talked hopefully. They would not dare to lay a finger upon Bernard Maddison, whatever they might have done to poor Mr. Brown. His great name would protect him from suspicion. And as he listened to her he had not the heart to tell her of the men who had followed him abroad, that he was even then doubtless under surveillance. He let her talk on, and feigned to share her hopefulness.

The time came when they passed into the grounds of the Court, and then she thought of something else which she must say to him.

"We have a visitor, Bernard—only one; but I'm afraid you don't like him."

Something told him who it was. He stopped short in the path.

"Not Sir Allan Beaumerville?"

She nodded.

"Yes. I'm so sorry. He invited himself; and there is something I must tell you about him."

His first instinct was to refuse to go on, but it was gone in a moment, after one glance into Helen's troubled face.

"Don't look so ashamed," he said, smiling faintly. "I'm not afraid of him. What is it you were going to tell me about him?"

"He went out the other day alone, to do some botanizing," she said. "Do you know where I saw him?"

He shook his head.

"No. Where?"

"In your cottage. I saw him sitting at your table, and I saw him come out. He looked terribly troubled, just as though he had found out something."

He seemed in no wise so much disturbed as she had feared.

"It's astonishing how many people are interested in my affairs," he said with grim lightness.

"No one so much as I am," she whispered softly. "Bernard, I must tell you something about papa. I had almost forgotten."

"Yes. Has he been exercising a landlord's privilege, too?"

"Of course not, sir. But, Bernard, people have been talking, and he has heard them, and—"

Her face grew troubled, and he stood still.

"He suspects, too, does he? Then I certainly cannot force him to become my host."

She took hold of both of his hands, and looked up at him pleadingly.

"Don't be stupid, Bernard, dear, please. I didn't say that he suspected. Only people have been talking, and of course it leaves an impression. You must make friends with him, you know. Won't you have something to ask him—some day—perhaps?"

She turned away, blushing a little, and he was conquered.

"Very well, love, I will come then," he said. "Only, please, you must go and tell him directly we get there; and if he would rather not have me for a guest, you must come and let me know. I will sit at no man's table under protest," he added, with a sudden flush of pride.

"He'll be very pleased to have you," she said simply. "A few words from me will be quite enough."

"Your empire extends further than over my heart, I see," he said, laughing. "There is your father coming round from the stables. Suppose we go to him."

They met him face to face in the hall. When he saw who his daughter's companion was he looked for a moment grave. But he had all the courtly instincts of a gentleman of the old school, and though outside he might have acted differently, the man was under his own roof now, and must be treated as a guest. Besides, he had implicit faith in his daughter's judgment. So he held out his hand without hesitation.

"Glad to see you, Mr. Maddison. We began to fear that you had deserted us," he said.

"I have been away longer than I intended," Bernard Maddison answered quietly.

"Of course you dine here," Mr. Thurwell continued, moving away. "You'll find Beaumerville in the library or the smoke room. You know your way about, don't you? My gamekeeper wants to speak to me for a moment. I shan't be long."

He crossed the hall, and entered his own room. Helen slipped her arm through her lover's, and led him away in the opposite direction, down a long passage to the other end of the house.

"Consider yourself highly favored, sir," she said, pausing with her hand upon one of the furthest doors. "You are the only male being, except my father, who has ever been admitted here."

She led him into a daintily furnished morning room, full of all those trifling indications of a woman's constant presence which possesses for the man who loves her a peculiar and almost reverent interest. There was her fancy work lying where she had put it down on the little wicker table, a book with a paper knife in it, one of his own; by its side an open piano, with a little pile of songs on the stool, and a sleek dachshund blinking up at them from the hearthrug. The appointments of the room were simple enough, and yet everything seemed to speak of a culture, a refinement, and withal a dainty feminine charm which appealed to him both as an artist and a lover. She drew an easy chair to the fire, and when he was seated, came and stood over him.

"I expect you to like my room, sir," she said softly. "Do you?"

"It is like you," he answered; "it is perfect."

They were together for half an hour, and then the dressing bell sounded. She jumped up at once from her little low chair by his side.

"I must go and give orders about your room," she said. "Of course you will stop with us. I have made up my mind where to put you. Roberts shall come and take you to your room in a few moments."

"Dressing will be a farce for me," he remarked. "I have no clothes."

"Oh, we'll forgive you," she laughed. "Of course you were too anxious to get here to think about clothes. That was quite as it should be. Good-by! Don't be dull."

He was alone only for a few minutes. Then a servant knocked at the door and took him to his room. He looked around him, and saw more evidences of her care for him. In the sitting room, which opened on one side, was a great bowl of freshly cut flowers, a pile of new books, and a photograph of herself. The rooms were the finest in the house. The oak paneled walls were hung with tapestry, and every piece of furniture was an antique curiosity. It was a bedchamber for a prince, and indeed a royal prince had once slept in the quaint high four-poster with its carved oak pillars and ancient hangings.

To Bernard Maddison, as he strolled round and examined his surroundings, it all seemed like a dream—so delightful, that awakening was a thing to be dreaded indeed. The loud ringing of the second bell, however, soon brought him back to the immediate present. He hastily made such alterations in his toilet as were possible, and descended. In the hall he met Helen, who had changed her dress for a soft cream-colored dinner gown, and was waiting for him.

"Do you like your room?" she asked.

"Like it? It is perfect," he answered quietly. "I had no idea that Thurwell was so old. I like you, too," he added, glancing approvingly at her and taking her hand.

"No time for compliments, sir," she said, laughing. "We must go into the drawing-room; Sir Allan is there alone."

He followed her across the hall, and entered the room with her. Sir Allan, with his back to them, was seated at the piano, softly playing an air of Chopin's to himself. At the sound of the opening door, he turned round.

"Sir Allan, you see we have found another visitor to take pity on us," Helen said. "You know Mr. Maddison, don't you?"

The music, which Sir Allan had been continuing with his right hand, came to a sudden end, and for the space of a few seconds he remained perfectly motionless. Then he rose and bowed slightly.

"I have that pleasure," he said quietly. "Mr. Maddison is a neighbor of yours, is he not? I met him, you know, on a certain very melancholy occasion."

"Will you go on playing?" she asked, sinking down on a low settee; "we should like to listen."

He sat down again, and with half-closed eyes recommenced the air. Helen and Bernard Maddison, sitting side by side, spoke every now and then to one another in a low tone. There was no general conversation until Mr. Thurwell entered, and then dinner was announced almost immediately.

There was no lack of conversation then. At first it had lain chiefly between Mr. Thurwell and Sir Allan Beaumerville, but catching a somewhat anxious glance from Helen, her lover suddenly threw off his silence. "When Maddison talks," one of his admirers had once said, "everyone else listens"; and if that was not quite so in the present case, it was simply because he had the art of drawing whoever he chose into the conversation, and making them appear far greater sharers in it than they really were. What was in truth a monologue seemed to be a brilliantly sustained conversation, in which Maddison himself was at once the promoter and the background. On his part there was not a single faulty phrase or unmusical expression. Every idea he sprang upon them was clothed in picturesque garb, and artistically conceived. It was the outpouring of a richly stored, cultured mind—the perfect expression of perfect matter.

The talk had drifted toward Italy, and the art of the Renaissance. Mr. Thurwell had made some remark upon the picturesque beauties of some of the lesser-known towns in the north, and Bernard Maddison had taken up the theme with a new enthusiasm.

"I am but just come back from such a one," he said. "I wonder if I could describe it."

And he did describe it. He told them of the crumbling palaces, beautiful in their perfect Venetian architecture, but still more beautiful now in their slow, grand decay, in which was all the majesty of deep repose teeming with suggestions of past glories. He spoke of the still, clear air, the delicate tints of the softened landscape, the dark cool green of the olive trees, the green vineyards, and the dim blue hills. He tried to make them understand the sweet silence, the pastoral simplicity of the surrounding country, delicate and airy when the faint sunlight of early morning lay across its valleys and sloping vineyards, rich and drowsy and languorous when the full glow of midday or the scented darkness of the starlit night succeeded. Then he passed on to speak of that garden— the fairest wilderness it was possible to conceive—where the violets grew like weeds upon the moss-grown paths, and brilliant patches of wild geraniums mingled their perfume with the creamy clematis run wild, and the clustering japonica.

"She who lives there," he went on more slowly, turning from Helen toward Sir Allan, "is in perfect accord with everything that is sweet and stately and picturesque in her surroundings. I see her now as she met me in the garden, and stretched out her hands to greet me. It is the face, the form of a martyr and an angel. She is tall, and her garb is one of stately simplicity. Her hair is white as snow, and the lines of her face are wasted with sorrow and physical decay. Yet there is sweetness and softness and light in her worn features—aye, and more almost than a human being's share of that exquisite spirituality which is the reward only of those who have triumphed over pain and suffering and sin. Guido would have given the world for such a face. Little does an artist think at what cost such an expression is won. Through the fires of shame and bitter wrong, of humiliation and heart-shattering agony, the human cross has fallen away, and the gold of her nature shines pure and refined. God grant to those who have wronged her, those at whose door her sin lies, as happy a deathbed as hers will be. Sir Allan, I am boring you, I fear. We will change the subject."

"Not at all. I have been—very interested," Sir Allan answered in a low tone, pouring himself out a glass of wine, and raising it to lips as white as the camellia in his buttonhole.

"We are all interested," Helen said softly. "Did you stay with her?"

"For three days," he answered. "Then, because I could not bring myself to tell her the news which I had gone all that way to impart, I came away."

There was a moment's silence. A servant who had just entered the room whispered in Mr. Thurwell's ear.

"Two gentlemen wish to speak to you, Mr. Maddison," he said, repeating the message. "Where have you shown them, Roberts?—in the library?"

"I wished to do so, sir," the man replied, "but—"

He glanced over his shoulder. Every one looked toward the door. Just outside were two dark figures. To three people at the table the truth came like a flash.

Sir Allan sat quite still, with his eyes fixed upon Bernard Maddison, who had risen to his feet, pale as death, with rigidly compressed lips, and nervously grasping his napkin. Helen, too, had risen, with a look of horror in her white face, and her eyes fastened upon her lover. Mr. Thurwell looked from one to the other, not comprehending the situation. The whole scene, the glittering table laden with flowers and wine, the wondering servant, the attitude and faces of the four people, and the dark figures outside, would have made a marvelous tableau.

Suddenly the silence was broken by a low agonized cry. Helen had thrown her arms with a sudden impulsive gesture around her lover's neck.

"My love, my love!" she cried, "it is I who have done this thing. They shall not take you from me—they shall not!"

XXXIV

Arrested

As is often the case, the person most concerned in the culmination of this scene was apparently the least agitated, and the first to recover his self-possession. Gently loosening Helen's arms from around him, Bernard Maddison walked steadily toward the door, and confronted his visitors. One was his fellow-passenger from London, the other a tall, wiry-looking man, who was standing with his hat under his arm, and his hands in the pocket of a long traveling coat.

"I am Bernard Maddison," he said quietly. "What is your business with me?"

"I am sorry, sir, that it is rather unpleasant," the man answered, lowering his voice. "It is my duty to arrest you under this warrant, charging you with the murder of Sir Geoffrey Kynaston on the 12th of August last year. Please do not make any answer to the charge, as anything that is now said by you or anyone present, in connection with it, can be used in evidence against you."

"I am ready to go with you at once," he answered. "The sooner we get away the better. I have no luggage here, so I do not need to make any preparations."

He felt a hand on his arm, and turned round. Mr. Thurwell had recovered from his first stupefaction, and had come to his side. Close behind him, Sir Allan Beaumerville was standing, pale as death, and with a curious glitter in his eyes.

"Maddison, what is this?" Mr. Thurwell asked gravely.

"I am arrested on a charge of murdering Sir Geoffrey Kynaston at your shooting party last year," Bernard Maddison answered quietly. "I make no reply to the charge, save that I am not guilty. I am sorry that this should have occurred at your house. Had I received any intimation of it, I would not have come here. As it is, I can only express my regret."

Although in some respects a plain man, there was a certain innate dignity of carriage and deportment which always distinguished Bernard Maddison among other men. Never had it been more apparent than at that moment. There was unconscious hauteur in his manner of meeting this awful charge, in his tone, and in the perfect calm of his demeanor,

E. PHILLIPS OPPENHEIM

which was more powerful than any vehement protestations could have been. Mr. Thurwell had long had his doubts, and very uneasy doubts, concerning this matter, but at that moment he felt ashamed of them. He made up his mind on impulse, but what he said he meant and adhered to.

"I believe you, Mr. Maddison," he said cordially, holding out his hand. "I think that the charge is absurd. In any case, please reckon me amongst your friends. If there is no one else whom you would prefer to see, I will go and get Dewes down from town in the morning."

For the first time Bernard Maddison showed some slight sign of emotion. He took Mr. Thurwell's hand, but did not speak for a moment. Then, as they stood there in a little group, Helen glided up to them with a faint smile on her lips, and a strange look in her white face.

"Father," she said, "thank God for those words!"

Then she turned to her lover, and gave him both her hands, looking up at him through a mist of tears, but still with that ghostly smile upon her parted lips.

"Bernard," she said softly, "you know that I have no doubts. You must go now, but it will not be for long. You will come back to us, and we shall be glad to see you. You need not trouble about me. See, I am quite calm. It is because I have no fear."

He stooped and kissed her hands, but she held up her face.

"Kiss me, Bernard," she said softly. "Father," she added, turning half round toward him, "I love him. We should have told you everything to-morrow."

Mr. Thurwell bowed his head, and turned away to speak to the detectives, who had remained discreetly outside the door. Sir Allan returned to his seat, and poured himself out a glass of wine. For a moment they were all alone, and he held her hands tightly.

"This will all come right, love," she whispered softly; "and it will make no difference, will it? Promise me that when it is over you will come straight to me. Promise me that, and I will be brave. If you do not, I shall break my heart."

"Then I promise it," he answered, with a slight tremble in his voice.

But looking at him anxiously, she was not satisfied. His white face, firm and resolute though it was, had a certain despair in it which chilled her. The hopefulness of her words seemed to have found no echo in his heart.

"Dearest," she whispered, "it will all come right."

His expression changed, but the effort of it was visible. His smile was forced, and his words, light though they were, troubled her.

"We must hope so. Nay, it will come right, dear. Wish me good-by now, or rather, *au revoir*. My guardians will be getting impatient."

They were virtually alone, and he drew from her lips one long, passionate kiss. Then, with a few cheerful words, he turned resolutely away. Mr. Thurwell, who had been waiting outside, came to him at once.

"The brougham is at the door," he said, with an anxious glance at Helen, who was leaning back against a chair, her hands locked in one another, ghastly pale, and evidently on the point of fainting. "These men have only an open trap, and it is a cold drive across the moor. To-morrow you go to York to be brought before the magistrates. I shall be there."

"You are very good," Bernard Maddison said earnestly; "but, so far as defence is concerned, I will have no lawyer's aid. What little there is to be said, I will say myself."

Mr. Thurwell shook his head.

"It does not do," he said. "But there will be time to consider that. The magistrates will be sure to commit you for trial. They must have evidence enough for that, or Mr. Malcolm would never have signed the warrant against anyone in your position."

"I am quite prepared for that," he answered. "Let us go."

They left the room at once. Helen had fainted in her chair. Sir Allan Beaumerville had apparently disappeared.

They stood on the doorstep for a moment while the carriage, which had been driven a little way down the avenue to quiet the mettlesome horses, returned, and Mr. Thurwell spoke a few more encouraging words.

"Jenkins has packed some things of mine, which may be useful to you, in a portmanteau," he said. "You will find it in the carriage, and also an ulster. Keep up your spirits, Maddison. All will be well."

"At any rate, I shall never forget your kindness," Bernard Maddison answered, grasping his hand. "Good-by, Mr. Thurwell!"

"Good night, Maddison, good night! I shall see you to-morrow."

The impatient horses leaped forward, and Mr. Thurwell turned back into the hall, and made his way back into the dining room. Helen had recovered sufficiently to be able to go to her room, he was told. Sir Allan was still sitting at the table, quietly sipping a cup of coffee. His legs were crossed, and he was smoking one of his favorite Egyptian cigarettes.

"Has he gone?" he said, looking round languidly.

Mr. Thurwell frowned. He was a man of somewhat imperturbable manners himself, but he was far from being unfeeling, and Sir Allan's silence and non-expression of any sympathy toward Bernard Maddison annoyed him not a little.

"Yes, he's gone," he answered shortly. "I can't believe that there's the slightest vestige of truth in that ridiculous charge. The man is innocent; I'm sure of it."

Sir Allan shrugged his shoulders.

"I don't believe he's guilty myself," he answered; "but one never knows."

XXXV

COMMITTED FOR TRIAL

Early on the following morning Mr. Thurwell ordered his dog cart, and drove into Mallory. The arrest of Bernard Maddison had been kept quite secret, and nothing was known as yet of the news which was soon to throw the little town into a state of great excitement. But in the immediate vicinity of the courthouse there was already some stir. The lord lieutenant's carriage was drawn up outside, and there was an unusual muster of magistrates. As a rule the cases brought before their jurisdiction were trivial in the extreme, consisting chiefly of drunkenness, varied by an occasional petty assault. There was scarcely one of them who remembered having sat upon so serious a charge. Lord Lathon came over to Mr. Thurwell directly he entered the retiring room.

"You have heard of this matter, I suppose?" he inquired, as they shook hands.

"Yes," Mr. Thurwell answered gravely. "He was arrested at my house last night."

"I can't believe the thing possible," Lord Lathon continued. "Still, from what I hear, we shall certainly have to send it for trial."

"I am afraid you will," Mr. Thurwell answered. "I shall not sit myself; I am prejudiced."

"In his favor or the reverse?" his lordship inquired.

"In his favor, decidedly," Mr. Thurwell answered, passing out behind the others, and taking a seat in the body of the room.

The general impatience was doomed to be aggravated. The first prisoner was an old man charged with assaulting his wife. The bench listened for a few minutes to her garrulous tale, and managed to gather from it that a caution from their worships was what she chiefly desired. Having arrived at this point, Lord Lathon ruthlessly stopped her, and dismissed the case, with a few stern words to the elderly reprobate, who departed muttering threats against his better half which, for her bodily comfort, it is to be hoped that he did not put into execution.

Then there was a few minutes' expectation, at the conclusion of which Bernard Maddison was brought in between two policemen, very calm and self-possessed, but very pale. Directly he appeared

Mr. Thurwell rose and shook hands with him, a friendly demonstration which brought a faint glow into his cheeks.

He was offered a chair, and the services of the solicitor of the place, the latter of which he declined. Then the chief constable, a little flurried and nervous at the unwonted importance of his office, rose, and addressed the bench.

The case against the prisoner was, he said, still altogether incomplete, and he had only one witness, whose evidence, however, he felt sure, would be such as to justify their sending the matter to be decided before a judicial tribunal. No doubt they all remembered the painful circumstances of Sir Geoffrey Kynaston's death, and the mystery with which it was surrounded. That death took place within a stone's throw of the cottage where the prisoner was then living, under an assumed name, and more than three miles away from any other dwelling place or refuge of any sort. He reminded them of the speedy search that had been made, and its extraordinary non-success. Under those circumstances a certain amount of suspicion naturally attached itself to the prisoner, and a search warrant was duly applied for, and duly carried out. At that time nothing suspicious was discovered, owing in some measure, he was bound to say, to the scrupulous delicacy with which the magistrate who had signed it—looking toward Mr. Thurwell—had insisted upon its being carried out. Subsequently, however, and acting upon later information, Detective Robson of Scotland Yard was appointed to look into the case, and the result of his investigation was the issuing of the warrant under which the prisoner stood charged with the murder of Sir Geoffrey Kynaston. Their worships would hear the evidence of Detective Robson, who was now present.

Detective Robson stepped forward, and was sworn. On the 15th of June last, he said, he searched the prisoner's cottage on the Thurwell Court estate. He there found in the secret recess of a cabinet, which had apparently not been opened for some time, a dagger, produced, in a case evidently intended to hold two, and which was an exact facsimile of the one, also produced, with which the murder was committed. He found also a towel, produced, which was stained with blood, and several letters. With regard to the towel, he here added, that in one corner of the room was fixed a small basin, and on the floor just beneath, covered over by a carpet, and bearing several signs of attempted obliteration, was a large blood stain. The woman who had cleaned the cottage prior to Mr. Maddison's occupation, was in court, and would swear that the stain in question was not there at that time. He mentioned these details first, he went on to say, but the more important part of his evidence had reference to these letters, and his subsequent action with regard to them. He would call attention to one of them, he remarked, producing it, and allow the bench to draw their own conclusions. He would read it to them, and they could then examine it for themselves.

The thin rustling sheet of foreign notepaper, which he held in his hand, was covered closely with delicate feminine handwriting, and emitted a faint sweet perfume. For the first time during the hearing of the case Bernard Maddison showed some slight emotion as the letters were handed about. But he restrained it immediately.

The sentence which Detective Robson read out was as follows:—

"Bernard, those who have sinned against their fellow creatures, and against their God, may surely be left to His judgment. The vengeance which seeks to take life is a cruel bloodthirsty passion which no wrong can excuse, no suffering justify. Forgive me if I seem to dwell so much upon this. That terrible oath which, at his bidding, I heard you swear against Sir Geoffrey Kynaston rings ever in my ears!"

There were other sentences of a somewhat similar nature. As Mr. Thurwell listened to them he felt his heart sink. What could avail against such evidence as this?

There was no hesitation at all on the part of the magistrates. Bernard Maddison had pleaded "not guilty," but had declined to say another word. "Anything there is to be said on my behalf," he remarked quietly, in answer to a question from the bench, "I will say myself to the jury before whom I presume you will send me."

While the committal was being made out, Mr. Thurwell leaned over and whispered to him.

"Helen sends her love. I will arrange about the defence, and will try and see you myself before the trial."

"You need send no lawyer to me," he answered. "I shall defend myself."

Mr. Thurwell said no more. He was a little dazed by those letters, but he was not going to allow himself to be influenced by them, for his daughter's sake, as well as his own. He did not like to admit himself in the wrong, and he had made up his mind that this man was innocent. Innocent he must therefore be proved. As to his defending himself, that was all nonsense. He would see to that. Dewes should be instructed.

The committal was read out, and Bernard Maddison was removed from the court. On the following day he was to be taken to York, there to be tried at the forthcoming assizes. Mr. Thurwell bade him keep up his courage in a tone which, though it was intended to be cheerful, was not particularly sanguine. There was but one opinion in the court, and despite all his efforts its influence had a certain effect upon him. But Bernard Maddison never carried himself more proudly than when he bowed to Lord Lathon, and left the court that morning.

At home Helen was eagerly waiting for the news. She had no need to ask, for her father's face was eloquent.

"Is it—very bad?" she whispered.

He looked away from her with a queer feeling in his throat. To see his daughter, who had always been so quiet, and self-contained, and dignified—his princess, he had been used to call her—to see her trembling with nervous fear, was a new and terrible thing to him, and to be able to offer her no comfort was worse still. But what could he say?

"The evidence was rather bad," he admitted, "and only a portion of it was produced. Still, we must hope for the best."

"Please tell me all about it," she begged, very quietly, but with a look in her white face which made him turn away from her with a groan. But he obeyed, and told her everything. And then there was a long silence.

"How did he look?" she asked, after a while.

"Very pale; but he behaved in a most dignified manner throughout," he told her. "He must be well born. I wonder what or where his people are? I never heard of any of them. Did you?"

She shook her head.

"He told me once that he had no friends, and no relations, and no name save the one which he had made for himself," she said. "I don't know whether he meant that Maddison was not his real name, or whether he meant simply his reputation."

"There must be people in London who know all about him," Mr. Thurwell remarked. "A man of his celebrity can scarcely conceal his family history."

Helen had walked a little away, and was standing before the window, looking out with listless eyes.

"Father, I wonder whether Sir Allan Beaumerville has anything to do with this?" she said. "Has he ever hinted to you that he suspected Mr. Maddison?"

"Certainly not," he answered. "Why do you ask?"

"Because one afternoon last week I saw him come out of Falcon's Nest. It was the afternoon he went botanizing."

Mr. Thurwell shook his head.

"The detective mentioned the date of his visit and search," he said. "It was a month ago."

She wrung her hands, and turned away in despair.

"It must have been through those dreadful people I went to," she sobbed. "Oh, I was mad—mad!"

"I scarcely think that," Mr. Thurwell said thoughtfully. "They would not have kept altogether in the background and let Scotland Yard take the lead, if it had been so. What is it, Roberts?"

The servant had entered bearing an orange-colored envelope on a salver, which he carried towards Helen.

"A telegram for Miss Thurwell, sir," he said.

She took it and tore it open. It was from the Strand, London, and the color streamed into her cheeks as she read it aloud.

"We must see you at once in the interests of B. M. Can you call on us to-morrow morning? Levy & Son."

"When are the assizes at York, father?" she asked quickly.

"In ten days."

"And you are going to London to-day, are you not, to see Dewes?"

"Yes."

"Then I will go with you," she said, crumpling up the telegram in her hand.

XXXVI

Mr. Levy Promises to do his Best

Once more Mr. Benjamin Levy trod the pavement of Piccadilly and the Strand, and was welcomed back again amongst his set with acclamations and many noisy greetings. One more unit was added to the vast army of London youth who pass their time in the fascinating but ignominious occupation of aping the "man about town" in a very small way. And Benjamin Levy, strange to say, was happy, for the life suited him exactly. He had brains and money enough to be regarded, in a certain measure, as one of their leaders, and to be looked up to as a power amongst them, and it was a weakness of his disposition that he preferred this to being a nonentity of a higher type.

Certain of his particular cronies had organized a small supper at a middle-class restaurant on the previous night in honor of his return, and as a natural consequence Mr. Benjamin Levy walked down the Strand at about half-past ten on the following morning, on his way to the office, a little paler than usual, and with a suspicion of a "head." It would have suited him very much better to have remained in bed for an hour or two, and risen towards afternoon; but business was business, and it must be attended to. So he tried to banish the effects of the bad champagne imbibed on the previous night with a stiff glass of brandy and soda, and lighting a fresh cigarette, turned off the Strand and made his way to the office.

"Guv'nor in?" he inquired of the solitary clerk, a sharp-featured, Jewish-looking young man, who was sitting on a high stool with his hands in his pockets, apparently unburdened with stress of work.

The youth nodded, and jerked his head backwards.

"Something's up!" he remarked laconically; "he's on the rampage."

Mr. Benjamin passed on without remark, and entered the inner office. It was easy indeed to see that something had gone wrong. Mr. Levy was walking restlessly up and down, with a newspaper in his hand, and muttering to himself in a disturbed manner. At his son's entrance he stopped short, and looked at him angrily.

"Benjamin, my boy," he said, rustling the paper before his face, "you've been made a fool of. Scotland Yard have licked us!"

Mr. Benjamin yawned, and tilted his hat on the back of his head.

"What's up now, guv'nor?" he inquired.

His father laid the paper flat on the desk before him, and pointed to one of the paragraphs with trembling fingers.

"Read that! Read that!" he exclaimed.

His obedient son glanced at it, and pushed the paper away in contempt.

"Stale news," he remarked shortly.

Mr. Levy looked at him amazed.

"Maybe you knew all about it," he remarked a little sarcastically.

"May be I did," was the cool reply.

"And yet you have let them be beforehand with us!" Mr. Levy exclaimed angrily. "If this was to be done, why did we not do it?"

"Because we've got a better game to play," answered the junior partner of the firm, with a hardly restrained air of triumph.

Mr. Levy regarded his son with a look of astonishment, which speedily changed into one of admiration.

"Is this true, Benjamin?" he asked. "But—but—"

"But you don't understand," Benjamin interrupted impatiently. "Of course you don't. And you'll have to wait a bit for an explanation, too, for here's the very person I was expecting," he added, raising himself on his stool, and looking out of the window. "Now, father, just you sit quiet, and don't say a word," he went on quickly. "Leave it all to me; I'll pull the thing through."

Mr. Levy had only time to express by a pantomimic sign his entire confidence in his son's diplomacy before Miss Thurwell was announced. She was shown in at once.

"I had your telegram," she began hurriedly. "What does it mean? Can you do anything?"

Mr. Benjamin placed a chair for her, and took up his favorite position on the hearthrug.

"I hope so, Miss Thurwell," he said quietly. "First of all, of course you are aware that Mr. Maddison's arrest was as much of a surprise to us as to any one. We neither had any hand in it, nor should we have dreamed of taking any step of the sort."

"I thought it could not be you," she answered. "How do you think it came about?"

Mr. Levy, junior, shrugged his shoulders.

"Quite in the ordinary course," he answered. "So I should think. The police have never let the matter really drop, and I should imagine that he had been watched for some time. How it came to pass, however, it is not worth while discussing now. The question with you, I presume, is—can he be saved?"

"Yes, that is it," Helen answered quietly, but with deep intensity. "Can he be saved? Do you know anything? Can you help?"

Mr. Benjamin Levy cleared his throat, and appeared to reflect for a moment or two. Then he turned towards Helen, and commenced speaking earnestly.

"Look here, Miss Thurwell," he said, "your interest in this matter is, of course, a personal one. Mine, on the other hand, is naturally a business one. You understand that?"

She nodded.

"Yes, I understand that," she said.

"Let us put it on a business basis, then," he went on. "The question is, what will you give us to get Mr. Maddison off? That's putting it baldly; but we've no time to waste mincing matters."

"I will give you one—two thousand pounds, if you can do it," she said, her voice trembling with eagerness. "Will that be enough?"

"Two thousand five hundred—the five hundred for expenses," Mr. Benjamin said firmly. "Father, make out a paper, and Miss Thurwell will sign it."

"At once," she answered, drawing off her glove. "Mr. Levy, you have some hope! You know something. Tell me about it, please," she begged.

"Miss Thurwell," he said, "at present I can tell you no more than this. I really think that I shall be able in a short time to upset the whole case against Mr. Maddison. I can't tell you more at present. Let me have your address, and you shall hear from me."

She had signed her name to the document which Mr. Levy had drawn up, and she now wrote her address. Mr. Benjamin copied the latter into his pocket-book, and prepared to show his visitor out.

"I really don't think that you need be very anxious, Miss Thurwell," he said hopefully. "At present things look bad enough, but I think that when the time comes, I shall be able to throw a different light upon them."

"Thank you," she answered, dropping her veil. "You will let me know immediately you have definite news?"

"Immediately, Miss Thurwell. You may rely upon that. Good-morning!"

He closed the door after her, and, returning to his seat, scribbled something on a piece of paper. Then he rang the bell.

"Is Morrison about?" he asked the boy.

"Been in and gone. Round at the Golden Sun, if wanted."

"Take him this slip of paper," ordered Benjamin, "and tell him to keep a keen watch on the person whose name and address are there. Understand?"

The boy nodded, and withdrew. Then Mr. Benjamin looked across at his father.

"Well, guv'nor?" he remarked laconically.

"Benjamin," his fond parent replied with enthusiasm, "you are indeed a jewel of a son."

"I think I am," Benjamin replied modestly. "Come out and have a drink."

XXXVII

BERNARD A PRISONER

The arrest and committal of Bernard Maddison on a charge of murder created the most profound sensation in every circle of English society. His work, abstruse and scholarly though some of it was, had appealed to a great reading public, and had made his name like a household word. That long deep cry for a larger and sweeter culture which had been amongst the signs of this troubled generation, had found its most perfect and adequate expression in his works. He had been at once its interpreter and its guide. There were thoughtful men and women, a great mixed class, who, in their own minds, reckoned themselves as his apostles, and acknowledged no other intellectual master. Some were of the highest rank of society, others of the very lowest. It was a literary republic of which he had been the unacknowledged dictator, containing all those whose eyes had been in any way opened, who had felt stirring even faintly within them that instinct of mind-development and expansion to which his work seemed peculiarly fitted to minister. And so, although his career as an apostle of culture had been but a short one, he was already the leader of a school whose tenets it would have been a heresy to modern taste to doubt or question.

The news of this tragical event, therefore, fell like a thunderbolt upon society, eclipsing every other topic in the newspapers, in conversation, and general interest. The first instinct of every one appeared to be to look upon the whole affair as a ludicrous piece of mismanagement on the part of the police, and Scotland Yard came in for a good deal of scathing criticism, as is usual in such cases. But when the evidence before the magistrates was carefully read, and sundry other little matters discussed, men's tongues began to run less glibly. Of course it was impossible that it could be true; and yet the evidence was certainly strong. In the country generally the first impulse of generous disbelief was followed by a period of pained and reserved expectancy. In clubdom, where neither fear of the devil nor love of God had yet been able to keep the modern man of the world from discussing freely any subject interesting to him, a gradual but sure reaction against the possibilities of his innocence set in.

There were plenty of men about still who remembered Sir Geoffrey Kynaston, and the peculiar manner of his life. During his long absence from England there had been many rumors about, concerning its reason, and now these were all suddenly revived. The breach of a certain commandment, a duel at Boulogne, and many other similar adventures were freely spoken of. After all, this story, improbable though it sounded, was far from impossible. It had always been reckoned a little mysterious that nothing whatever had been known of Bernard Maddison's antecedents, great though had been his fame, and assiduous his interviewers. As all these things began slowly to fit themselves together, men commenced to look grave, and to avoid the subject in the presence of their woman-kind, who were one and all unswerving in their loyalty to that dear, delightful Bernard Maddison, who had written those exquisite books. But in the smoking-room and among themselves views were gradually adopted which it would have been heresy to avow in the drawing-room.

No man appeared to take less interest in the event and the discussion of it than Sir Allan Beaumerville. Known generally amongst his acquaintances as a cynic and pessimist, men were pretty sure what his opinion would be. But he never expressed it. Whenever he strolled up to any group in the smoking-room or library of the club, and found them discussing the Maddison murder case, he turned on his heel and walked another way. If it were broached in his presence it was the signal for his retirement, and any question concerning it he refused point-blank to answer. Gradually the idea sprang up, and began to circulate, that Sir Allan Beaumerville had formed an idea of his own concerning the Maddison murder, and that it was one which he intended to keep to himself. Every one was curious about it, but in the face of his reticence, no one cared to ask him what it was.

A PLAIN WHITEWASHED CELL, WITH high bare walls and tiny window, through which the sunlight could only struggle faintly. Only one article of furniture which could justly be called such, a rude wooden bedstead, and seated on its end with folded arms and bent head, like a man in some sort of stupor, sat Bernard Maddison.

He was in that most pitiable of all states, when merciless realization had driven before it all apathy, all lingering hope, all save that deadly cold sea of absolute, unutterable despair. There had been moments on his first arrival here, when he had fallen into a dozing sleep, and had leaped up from his hard bed, and had stretched up his hands above his head, and had called out in agony that it must be a dream, a hideous nightmare from which he would awaken only to look back upon it with horror. And then his glazed, fearful eyes had slowly taken in his surroundings—the stone walls, the cold floor, the barred window—and pitiless memory had dragged back his thoughts amongst the vivid horrors of the last forty-eight hours. It was all there, written in letters of fire. He shrunk back upon his mattress and buried his face in his hands, whilst every instinct of manliness fought against the sobs which seemed as though they would rend to pieces his very frame.

Once more the morning light had come, and the burning agony of the hours of darkness was exchanged for the cold, crushing despair of the weary day. They had brought his breakfast, which he had loathed and left untasted. And then, as he sat there, so worn out with physical and mental exhaustion, something of a dull miserable apathy acted like opium on his wearied nerves and brain. He sat there thinking.

The great passions of the world are either our sweetest happiness or our most utter misery. Not unfrequently the one becomes the other. Circumstances may change, but the force remains, sometimes, after yielding us the most exquisite pleasure, to lash us with scorpion-like whips. The love of Bernard Maddison had thrilled through heart and soul—it had become not a thing of his life, but his whole life. Every impulse and passion of his being had yielded itself up to it. Ambition, intellectual visions, imaginative fancies, all these had been not indeed driven out by this passion, but more fatal still, they had opened their arms to receive it, they had bidden it welcome, and heart and brain and imagination had glowed with a new significance and a new-born power. A lesser love would have had a lesser effect; it would have made rivals of these other parts of himself. Not so the love of Bernard Maddison. Every fiber of his deep, strong nature was strengthened and beautified by this new-kindled fire. At that moment, had he been free to write, he would have been conscious of a capacity beyond any which he had ever before possessed. For a great nature is perfected by a great love, as the blossoms of spring by the April showers and May sun. The dry dust of scholarship sometimes chokes up the well of fancy. The perfect humanity of love acts like a sweet, quickening impulse upon it, breathing sweet soft life into dry images, and rich coloring into pallid visions. Such love, which is at once spiritual and passionate, of heaven and of the earth, absorbing and concentrative, widening and narrowing, is to a man's nature, if he be strong enough to conceive and appreciate it, the very food, the essence of sublimated life.

To Bernard Maddison it had been so. To its very depths he realized it as he sat in his prison cell with something of the deep passive resignation of the man who stands with one foot in the grave. The latter part of his life—nay, the whole of it—had been full of noble dreams and pure thoughts. His genius had never run riot over the whole face of nature, to yield its fruits in a sickly sweet realism with only faint flashes of his deeper power. Always subordinated by the innate and cultured healthiness of his mind, he had sent it forth a living power for good. Great joy had been his as he had watched his message to the world listened to, and understood, and appreciated. Another age might witness its fruits, it was sufficient for him that the seed was rightly planted.

Oh, the horror of it—the burning, unspeakable horror! In his ears there seemed to come ringing from the world without the great hum of gossip and lies which were dragging his name down into hell. A murderer! The time might come when she too would think thus of him, when the tragedy of her first love might fade away, and the lovelight might flash again in her eyes, but not for him. He shook his head wildly, stretched out his hands as though to hide something from his quivering face, and barely suppressed the groan of deep agony which trembled on his lips. God in His mercy keep him from such thoughts! Death, disgrace, surpassing humiliation, let them float in their ghostly garments before his shuddering gaze, but keep that thought from him, for with it madness moved hand in hand. As Michael Angelo had stifled his grief at Vittoria Colonna's death, in the sweet hope of rejoining her as soon as the last lingering breath should leave his mortal body, and as Dante had hoped for his Beatrice, so let him think of the woman without whom no human life was possible for him, almost, he cried out in his agony, no spiritual hope or longing.

The sound of the key in the lock of his door, and the tramp of footsteps on the stone floor outside, awoke him with a start from his half-dreaming state. The thought of visitors being permitted to come had never occurred to him, nor did it even then. The footsteps had paused outside his door, but he felt no interest in them, nor ever the vaguest stirrings of curiosity. Then the harsh lock was turned with a grating sound, and two figures, followed by the prison warder, entered the room.

XXXVIII

"There is My Hand. Dare You Take It?"

There is nothing which can transport one so quickly from thoughtland to acute and comprehensive realization, as the sound of a human voice or the consciousness of a human presence. Like a flash it all came back to the lonely occupant of the prison cell—the personal degradation of his position, his surroundings, and everything connected with them. And with it, too, came a strong, keen desire to bear himself like a man before her father.

He rose to his feet, and the pitiful bareness of the place seemed to become suddenly enhanced by the quiet dignity of his demeanor. Out of the gloom Mr. Thurwell came forward with outstretched hand, followed by another gentleman—a stranger. Between the two men, that one long ray of sunlight lay across the stone floor, and as Bernard Maddison stepped forward to meet his visitor, it gleamed for a moment upon his white, haggard face, worn and stricken, yet retaining all that quiet force and delicacy of expression which seemed like the index of his inward life. It was the face of a poet, of a dreamer, a visionary perhaps—but a criminal! the thing seemed impossible.

"This is very good of you, Mr. Thurwell," he said in a low but clear tone. "I scarcely expected that I should be permitted to see visitors."

Mr. Thurwell grasped his hand, and held it for a moment without speaking. He had all an Englishman's reticence of speech in times of great emotion, and it seemed to him that there was nothing that he could say. But silence was very eloquent.

"I have brought Mr. Dewes with me," he said at last. "He wants to see you about the defence, you know. The high sheriff's a friend of mine, so I got him to pass me in at the same time; but if you'd rather see Dewes alone, you'll say so, won't you?"

There had been an acute nervous force working in Bernard Maddison's face during that brief silence. At Mr. Thurwell's words, a change came. He dropped his visitor's hand, and his features were still and cold as marble, and almost as expressionless, save for the lightly drawn lips, and lowered eyebrows, which gave to his expression a fixed look of power.

"That is very kind and thoughtful of you, Mr. Thurwell, and I am sorry that you should have had the trouble to no purpose. I have nothing to add to my previous decision. I will not be represented by either lawyer or counsel."

Mr. Dewes moved forward out of the background, and bowed. He was a handsome, middle-aged man, looking more like a cavalry officer than a solicitor. But, as everyone knew, so far as criminal cases were concerned, he was the cleverest lawyer in London.

"You are relying upon your innocence, of course, Mr. Maddison," he said; "but it is a very great mistake to suppose that it will establish itself without extraneous aid. You will have the Attorney-General against you, and you must have some one of the same caliber on your side. The old saying, 'Truth will out,' does not apply in an assize court. It requires to be dragged out. I think you will do well to accept my services. Roberts holds himself open to take the brief for your defence, if I wire him before midday."

"I seldom change my mind," Bernard Maddison said quietly. "In the present case I shall not do so. If it seems to me that there is anything which should be said on my behalf, I shall say it myself."

There was a short silence. Mr. Dewes looked at Mr. Thurwell, and Mr. Thurwell looked both perplexed and worried.

"Maddison, you must admit that yours is an extraordinary decision," he said at last. "You must forgive me if I ask you in plain words what your reason is for it. I ask as one who is willing to be your friend in this matter; and I ask you as Helen's father."

A sudden spasm of pain passed across Bernard Maddison's face. He shrunk back a little, and when he spoke his voice sounded hollow and strained.

"I do not deny you the right to ask—but I cannot tell you. Simply it is my will. It is best so. It must be so."

"Can you not see, Mr. Maddison," the lawyer said quietly, "that to some people this will seem almost like a tacit admission of guilt?"

"I shall plead 'not guilty,'" he answered in a low tone.

"That will be looked upon only as a matter of form," Mr. Dewes remarked. "Mr. Maddison, I should not be doing my duty if I did not point out to you that the evidence against you is terribly strong. Just consider it yourself, only for a moment. Sir Geoffrey Kynaston is known to have seriously wronged a member of your family. You are known to have sworn an oath of vengeance against him. There are witnesses coming from abroad to prove that. Immediately on his return to his home you take a cottage, under an assumed name, close to his estate. He is found murdered close to that cottage, of which it seems that at that time you were the only occupant. You are the only person known to have been near the spot. The dagger is proved to be yours. Letters are found in your cabinet urging you to desist from your threatened vengeance. There is the stain of blood on the floor of your study, near the place where you would have washed your hands, and a blood-stained towel is found hidden in the room. All this and more can be proved, and unless you can throw a fresh light upon these things, there is no jury in the world that would not find you guilty. You hold your fate in your own hands."

"I have considered all this," Bernard Maddison answered in a low tone. "I know that my case is almost hopeless, and I am prepared for the worst."

Mr. Thurwell turned away, and walked to the furthermost corner of the apartment. For his daughter's sake, and for the sake of his own strong liking for this man, he had resolutely shut his eyes upon the damning chain of evidence against him. Now he felt that that he could do so no longer. Nothing but guilt could account for this strange reticence. He was forced to admit it at last. His compassion was still strong, but it was mingled with a great horror. He felt that he must get away as soon as possible.

Mr. Dewes, who had all along had the most profound conviction of the guilt of the accused man seized his opportunity, and stepping close up to him, whispered in his ear:

"Mr. Maddison, I should like to save you if I can. There have been cases—forgive me for suggesting it—in which, by knowing every circumstance and trifling detail connected with a crime, we have been able to build up a def—"

Bernard Maddison drew himself up with a sudden hauteur, and raised his hand.

"Stop, Mr. Dewes!" he said firmly. "I do not blame you for assuming what you do, but you are mistaken. I am not guilty. I do not ask you to believe it. I only ask you to bring this painful interview to an end."

"We will go," said Mr. Thurwell, suddenly advancing from the other end of the cell. "I am not your judge, Bernard Maddison, and it is not for me to hold you guilty. God shall pass His own judgment upon you. There is my hand. Dare you take it?"

For answer, Bernard Maddison stepped forward and clasped it in his own. Once more he had moved from out of the darkness, and a soft stream of sunshine fell upon his pallid face. White though it was, even to ghastliness, it betrayed no sign of blanching or fear, and his dark eyes, from their hollow depths, shone with a clear, steadfast light. Once more its calm spirituality, the effortless force which seemed to lurk in every line and feature of the pale wasted countenance, had its effect upon Mr. Thurwell. He wrung the hand which it had cost him a suppressed effort to take, and for the moment his doubts faded away.

"God help you, Maddison!" he said fervently. "Shall I tell her anything from you?"

A faint smile parted his tremulous lips. At that moment he was beyond earthly suffering. A sweet, strong power had filled his heart with peace.

"Tell her not to grieve, and that I am innocent," he said softly. "Farewell!"

XXXIX

Mr. Benjamin Levy is Busy

A woman stood on the little stone piazza of that Italian villa, with her face raised in agony to the blue sky, and her thin white hands wrung together with frantic nervous strength. Her whole attitude was full of the hopeless abandonment of a great tearless grief; and slowly dawning passion, long a stranger to her calm face, was creeping into her features. On the ground, spurned beneath her feet, was a long official-looking letter and envelope. A thunderbolt had flashed down upon the sweet stillness of her serene life.

She was quite alone, and she looked out upon an unbroken solitude— that fair neglected garden with its high walls which seemed to give it an air of peculiar exclusiveness.

"I will not go," she said, speaking quickly to herself in an odd, uneven tone. "The law of England shall not make me. I am an old woman. If they do, they cannot open my lips. I! to stand up in one of their courts, and tell the story of my shame, that they may listen and condemn my son. Oh, Bernard, Bernard, Bernard! The Lord have mercy upon you for this your crime! Mine was the sin. Mine should be the guilt. Oh, my God, my God! Is this just, in my old age, to pour down this fire of punishment upon my bowed head? Have I not suffered and done penance—ay, until I had even thought that I had won for myself peace and rest and forgiveness? Was it a sin to think so? Is this my punishment? Oh, Bernard, my son, my son! Let not the sin be his, O Lord. It is mine—mine only!"

Sweet perfumes were floating upon the soft still air, and away on the hill sides the morning mists were rolling away. The sun's warmth fell upon the earth and the flowers, and birds and humming insects were glad. And in the midst of it all she stood there, a silent, stony figure, grief and anguish and despair written in her worn face. God was dealing very hardly with her, she cried in her agony. Truly sin was everlasting.

"Signorina!"

She turned round with a start. A servant girl stood by her side with a card on a salver.

"A gentleman to see the signorina," she announced; "an English gentleman."

The woman turned pale with fear, and her fingers trembled. She would not even glance at the name on the card.

"Tell him that I see no one. I am ill. I will not see him, be his business what it may. Do you hear, child? Go and send him away."

The girl curtsied and disappeared. Her mistress stepped back into the room, and listened fearfully. Soon there came what she had dreaded, the sound of an altercation. She could hear Nicolette protesting in her shrill *patois*, and a rather vulgar, but very determined English voice, vigorously asserting itself. Then there came the sound of something almost like a scuffle, and Nicolette came running in with red eyes.

"Signorina, the brute, the brute!" she cried; "he will come in. He dared to lay his hands upon me. See, he is here! Oh, that Marco had been in the house! He should have beaten him, the dog, the coward, to oppose a woman's will by force!"

While she had been sobbing out her complaint, her assailant had followed up his advantage, and Mr. Benjamin Levy, in a rather loud check suit, and with a cringing air, but with a certain dogged determination in his manner, appeared. Mrs. Martival turned to him with quiet dignity, but with flashing eyes.

"Sir, by what right do you dare to enter my house by force, and against my command? I will not speak with you or know your business. I will have no communication with you."

"Then your son will be hanged!" Mr. Benjamin said, with unaccustomed bluntness.

Mrs. Martival trembled, and sank into a chair. Mr. Benjamin followed up his advantage.

"I am not from the police. I have no connection with them. On the other hand, I am considerably interested in saving your son, and I tell you that I can put into your hands the means of doing so. Now, will you listen to me?"

Something in Mrs. Martival's face checked him. The features had suddenly become rigid, and an ashy pallor had stolen over them. Nicolette, who had been lingering in the room, suddenly threw herself on her knees beside her mistress's side, and caught hold of her hands.

"Oh, the wretch!" she cried, "the miserable wretch; he has killed my mistress!"

He stood helplessly by while she ran backwards and forwards with cold water, smelling salts, and other restoratives, keeping up all the while a running fire of scathing comments upon his heartless conduct, of which, needless to say, he understood not a single word. Beneath his breath he cursed this unlucky fainting fit. He had already lost a day on the way, and the time was short. What if she were to be ill—too ill to be moved! The very thought made him restless and uneasy.

In the midst of the confusion Mrs. Martival's housekeeper returned from her marketing in the little town, and to his relief he found that she understood English. He interrupted Nicolette's shrill torrents of abuse against him, and briefly explained the situation.

"I do not wish to force myself upon her," he said. "I do not wish to be troublesome in any way. But when she is conscious, I want you just to show her half a dozen words which I will write on the back of a card. If, when she has read them, she still wishes me to go, I will do so without attempting to see her again."

The woman nodded.

"Very well," she said; "wait outside."

He left the room and walked softly up and down the passage, eyeing with some contempt the rich faded curtains and quaint artistic furniture about the place, so unlike the gilded glories of his own taste. In about half an hour the housekeeper came out to him.

"She is conscious now," she said; "give me your message."

He gave her a card on which he had already penciled a few words, and waited, terribly anxious, for the result. The woman withdrew, and closed the door. For a moment there was silence. Then a wild, fierce cry rang out from the room and echoed through the house. Before it had died away the door was flung open, and she stood on the threshold, her white hair streaming down her back, and every vestige of color gone from her face. Her eyes, too, shone with a feverish glow which fascinated him.

"Is it you who wrote this?" she cried, holding up the card clenched in her trembling fingers. "If you are a man, tell me, is it true?"

"I believe it is," he answered. "In my own mind, I am certain that it is. You are the only person who can prove it. I want you to come to England with me."

"I am ready," she said. "When can we start?"

He looked at his watch.

"I will be here in half an hour with a carriage," he said. "If we can get over the hills by midday, we shall catch the express."

"Go, then," she said calmly; "I shall be waiting for you."

He hurried away, and soon returned with a carriage from the inn. In less than an hour they had commenced their journey to England.

IT WAS AN EARLY SUMMER evening in Mayfair, and Sir Allan Beaumerville stood on the balcony of his bijou little house, for which he had lately deserted the more stately family mansion in Grosvenor Square. There was a soft pleasant stillness in the air, and a gentle rustling of green leaves among the trees. The streets below were almost blocked with streams of carriages and hansoms, for the season was not yet over, and it was fast approaching the fashionable dinner hour. Overhead, in somewhat curious contrast, the stars were shining in a deep cloudless sky, and a golden-horned moon hung down in the west.

Sir Allan was himself dressed for the evening, with an orchid in his buttonhole, and a light overcoat on his arm. In the street, his night brougham, with its pair of great thoroughbred horses, stood waiting. Yet he made no movement toward it. He did not appear to be waiting for anyone, nor was he watching the brilliant throng passing westward. His eyes were fixed upon vacancy, and there was a certain steadfast, rapt look in them which altered his expression curiously. Sir Allan Beaumerville seldom used his powers of reflection save for practical purposes. Just then, however, he was departing from his usual custom. Strange ghosts of a strange past were flitting through his mind. Old passions, which had long lain undisturbed, were sweeping through him, old dreams were revived, old memories kindled once more smoldering fires, and aided at the resurrection of a former self. The cold man-of-the-world philosophy, which had ruled his life for many years, seemed suddenly conquered by this upheaval of a stormy past. Under the influence of the serene night, the starlit sky, and the force of these old memories, he seemed to realize more than he had ever done before the littleness of his life, its colorless egotism, the barrenness of its routine. Like a flash it stood glaringly out before him. Stripped of all its intellectual furbishing, the chill selfishness of the creed he had adopted struck home to his heart. A finite life, with a finite goal—annihilation! Had it really ever satisfied him? Could it satisfy anyone? A great weariness crept in upon him. Epicureanism could have been carried no further than he had carried it. He had steeped his senses in the most refined and voluptuous pleasures civilization had to offer him. Where was the afterglow? Was this all that remained? A palled appetite, a hungry heart, and a cold, chill despair!

E. PHILLIPS OPPENHEIM

What comfort could his much-studied philosophy afford him? It had satisfied the brain; had it nothing to offer the heart? Something within him seemed to repeat the word with a grim echo. Nothing! nothing! nothing!

What was it that caused his eyes to droop till they rested upon two figures on the opposite pavement? He could not tell whence the power, and yet he obeyed the impulse. They glanced over the man with indifference and met the woman's upturned gaize. And Sir Allan Beaumerville stood like a figure of stone, with a deathlike pallor in his marble face.

The stream of carriages swept on, and the motley crowds of men and women passed on their way unnoticing. Little they knew that a tragedy was being played out before their very eyes. A few noticed that stately white-haired lady gazing strangely at the house across the way, and a few too saw the figure of the man on whom her eyes were bent. But no one could read what passed between them. That lay in their own hearts.

Interruption came at last. Mr. Benjamin Levy's excitement mastered his patience. He asked the question which had been trembling on his lips.

"Is it he?"

She started, and laid her hand upon his shoulder for support. She was very much shaken.

"Yes. See, he is beckoning. He wants me. I shall go to him. May God give me strength!"

She moved forward to cross the road. He caught hold of her arm in sudden fear.

"You mustn't think of it," he exclaimed. "You will spoil everything. I want you to come with me to—D—n! Come back, I say; come back! Curse the woman!"

He stood on the pavement, fuming. She had glided from his grasp, and his words had fallen upon deaf ears. Already she was half across the road. The door of Sir Allan's house stood open, and a servant was hurrying down to meet her. At that moment Mr. Benjamin Levy felt distinctly ill-used.

"D—d old fool!" he muttered to himself angrily. "Hi, hansom, Scotland Yard, and drive like blazes! The game's getting exciting, at any rate," he added. "It was mine easy before that last move; now it's a blessed toss up which way it goes. Well, I'll back my luck. I rather reckon I stand to win still, if Miss Thurwell acts on the square."

XL

A Strange Birthday Party

I t was close upon midnight, and one of the oldest and most exclusive of West-end clubs was in a state of great bustle and excitement. Sir Allan Beaumerville was giving a supper party to his friends to celebrate his sixtieth birthday, and the guests were all assembled.

Sir Allan himself was the last to arrive. The final touches had been given to the brilliantly decorated supper table, and the *chef*, who had done his best for the greatest connoisseur and the most liberal member in the club, had twice looked at his watch. As midnight struck, however, Sir Allan's great black horses turned into Pall Mall, and a few minutes later he was quietly welcoming his guests, and leading the way into the room which had been reserved for the occasion.

As a rule men are not quick at noticing one another's looks, but to-night more than one person remarked upon a certain change in their host's appearance.

"Beaumerville's getting quite the old man," remarked Lord Lathon, as he helped himself to an ortolan. "Looks jolly white about the gills to-night, doesn't he?"

His neighbor, a barrister and wearer of the silk, adjusted his eyeglass and looked down the table.

"Gad, he does!" he answered. "Looks as though he's had a shock."

"Not at all in his usual form, at any rate," put in Mr. Thurwell, *sotto voce*, from the other side of the table.

"Queer thing, but he seems to remind me of some one to-night," Lord Lathon remarked to the Home Secretary, who was on the other side. "Can't remember who it is, though. It's some fellow who's in a devil of a scrape, I know. Who the mischief is it?"

"You mean Maddison, don't you?" Sir Philip Roden answered. "Plenty of people have noticed that. There is a likeness, certainly."

"By Jove, there is, though!" Lord Lathon assented; "I never noticed it before. I'm devilish sorry for Maddison, Roden, and I hope you won't let them hang him."

The conversation turned upon the Maddison case and became general. Everybody had something to say about it except Sir Allan. He himself, it was noticed, forbore to pass any opinion at all, and at the first opportunity he diverted the talk into another channel.

The quality of his guests spoke volumes for the social position and popularity of their entertainer. Probably there were not half a dozen men in London who could have got together so brilliant and select an assembly. There were only twenty, but every man was a man of note. Politics were represented by the Home Secretary, Sir Philip Roden, and the First Lord of the Treasury; the peerage by the Duke of Leicester and the Earl of Lathon. There were two judges, and a half a dozen Q.C.'s, the most popular novelist of the day, and the most renowned physician. A prince might have entertained such a company with honor.

It had been arranged that the advent of cigars should be the signal for the Duke of Leicester to rise and propose their host's health. But to the surprise of every one, whilst his grace was preparing for the ordeal, and was on the point of rising, Sir Allan himself slowly rose to his feet, with a look in his still, cold face so different from anything that might be expected of a man who rises at two o'clock in the morning after a capital supper to make a speech to his guests, that every one's attention was at once arrested.

"I am given to understand, gentlemen," he said slowly, "that his grace the Duke of Leicester was about to propose my health on your behalf. I rise to prevent this for two reasons. First, because to a dying man such a toast could only be a mockery; the second reason will be sufficiently apparent when I have said what I have to say to you."

Every one was stupefied. Had their host suddenly gone mad, or had those empty bottles of Heidseck which had just been removed from his end of the table anything to do with it? Several murmurs for an explanation arose.

"I had forgotten for the moment," Sir Allan continued, "that none of you are yet aware of what I have only known myself during the last few days. I am suffering from acute heart disease, which may terminate fatally at any moment."

A sudden awed gloom fell upon the party. Cigars were put down, and shocked glances exchanged. A murmur of condolence arose, but Sir Allan checked it with a little gesture.

"I need scarcely say that I did not ask you to meet me here this evening to tell you this," he continued. "My object is a different one. I have a confession to make."

The general bewilderment increased. The air of festivity was replaced by a dull restrained silence. Could it be that their host's illness had affected his brain? A painful impression to that effect had passed into the minds of more than one of them.

"You will say, perhaps," Sir Allan continued, speaking very slowly, and with a certain difficulty in his articulation, which did not, however, prevent every word from being distinctly audible, "that I am choosing a strange time and place for making a personal statement. But I see amongst those who have done me the honor of becoming my guests to-night, men whom I should wish to know the whole truth from my own lips—I refer more particularly to you, Sir Philip Roden— and to-night is my last opportunity, for to-morrow all London will know my story, and I shall be banned forever from all converse and intercourse with my fellow-men.

"Very few words will tell my story. Most of you will remember that I came into my title and fortune late in life. My youth was spent in comparative poverty abroad, sometimes practicing my profession, sometimes living merely as a student and an experimenting scientist. In my thirtieth year I married a woman of good family, with whom I was very much in love, so much so that in order to win her I forged a letter from the man whom she would otherwise have married, and obtained her consent in a fit of indignation at his supposed infidelity. That man, gentleman, was Sir Geoffrey Kynaston."

There was a subdued murmur of astonishment. Every one's interest was suddenly redoubled. Sir Allan proceeded, standing at the head of the table, motionless as a statue, but with a strange look in his white face.

"In every possible way I failed in my duty as a husband toward my wife. She was light-hearted, fond of change, gayety, travel. I shut her up in a quiet, old-fashioned town while I pursued my studies, and expected her to content herself with absolute solitude. For years I crushed the life out of her by withdrawing every interest and every amusement from her life. We had one child only, a son.

"From bad, things grew to worse. What I had dreaded came to pass. She discovered my treachery. Still, she was faithful to me, but we were husband and wife in name only.

"Time passed on, and she made a few friends, and went out occasionally. Then, who should come by accident to the little town where we lived but Sir Geoffrey Kynaston. I was madly, insanely jealous, and I forbade my wife to meet him. She declined to obey me, and she was quite right to do so. At that time she was as faithful to me as any woman could be, and she treated my suspicions, as they deserved to be treated, with contempt. Sir Geoffrey and she met as friends, and if it had not been for my brutality they would never have met in any other way.

"One night there was a fête and dance in our little town. My wife went, against my orders, and Sir Geoffrey escorted her home. A demon of jealousy entered into my soul that night. Although all the time I knew that my wife was faithful to me, the worse half of my nature whispered to me that she was not, and, wretch that I was, I stooped to listen to it. When she returned I was mad with a fit of ungovernable rage. I shut my doors against her, and refused to allow her to enter my house. I taunted her with her infidelity. I bade her go to her lover. She went to some friends, and for two days she waited for a message from me. I sent none, and on the third day she left the place with Sir Geoffrey Kynaston. In less than a month she was in a convent, and from that day to this she has lived the life of a holy woman."

There was a slight tremor in his voice for the first time, and he paused. The silence was profound. Everyone sat motionless. Everyone's eyes were fixed upon him. In a moment he continued.

"Although by sheer brutality, by coarse insults and undeviating cruelty, I had driven my wife to the edge of the precipice, my rage against the man, whom I knew she had always loved, burned as fiercely as though he had won her from me by the cruelest means. I followed them to Vienna, and insulted him publicly. My wife left him on that very night, and he has never seen her since; but Sir Geoffrey and I fought on the sands near Boulogne, and I strove my utmost to kill him. Fortune was against me, however, and I was wounded. I returned to my home with my thirst for vengeance unabated. I taught my son to curse the name of Sir Geoffrey Kynaston, and as soon as I had recovered from my wounds I hunted him all over Europe. Where he spent those years I cannot tell, but he eluded me. Often I reached a town only to learn that he had left it but a few days; once, I remember, at Belgrade, I was only a few hours behind him. But meet him face to face I could not.

"When at last I saw my son again, I found him grown up, and in his first words he told me boldly that he had espoused his mother's cause, and that he withdrew altogether from his vow of vengeance against Sir Geoffrey Kynaston. I left him in a fury, and almost immediately afterwards came the unexpected news of my accession to the baronetcy of Beaumerville. I made up my mind then to turn over the past chapter of my life, and start the world afresh. I had always been known by the family name of Martival, and my wife was unaware of my connection with the Beaumerville family. Taking advantage of this, I sent her false news of my death at Paris, and started life afresh as Sir Allan Beaumerville.

"The past, however, soon began to cast its shadows into the future. A new author, calling himself Bernard Maddison, was one night introduced to me at a crowded assembly. I held out my hand, which he did not take, and recognized my son."

There was a general start. The first gleam of light struggled into the minds of the little group of listeners. They began to see whither this thing was tending, and everyone looked very grave.

"I had nothing to fear," Sir Allan continued. "My son showed by his looks the contempt in which he held me. We met frequently after that, but we never exchanged a single word. He kept my secret, too, from his mother—not for my sake, but for her own.

"Six months after our first meeting Sir Geoffrey Kynaston returned to England. It may seem strange to you, gentlemen, but my hate for this man had never lessened, never decreased. The moment I heard the news I began to lay my plans.

"Then, for the first time, my son sought me. He had come, he said, to make one request, and if I granted it, he would leave me in peace forever. Would I tell him that my oath had been buried with the old life, and that I would seek no harm to my old enemy? I simply declined to discuss the matter with him, and he went away.

"From that time he commenced to watch me. I laid my plans deeply, but somehow he got to hear of them. When I went down on a visit to you, Lord Lathon, that I might be near Sir Geoffrey, he took a small cottage in the neighborhood, intending to do his best to counteract my schemes. But I was too cunning for him.

"On the morning of Sir Geoffrey's murder I was on the cliffs, under the pretence of botanizing. While there I heard the guns of a shooting party, and through a field-glass I saw Mr. Thurwell and Sir Geoffrey Kynaston. At that time I scarcely thought that chance would bring Sir Geoffrey within my power, but I made up my mind to watch them.

"Accordingly I descended from the cliffs, and, on my way, passed close to my son's cottage. I looked in at his sitting-room through the open windows, and it seemed as though the devil must have guided my eyes. His cabinet was open, and right opposite my eyes was a pair of long Turkish daggers carelessly thrown down with a heap of other curios. I listened. There was no one about. I stepped through the window, seized one of them, and hurried away. About a hundred yards from the cottage was a long narrow belt of plantation running from a considerable distance inland almost to the cliff side. Here I concealed myself, and looked out at the shooting party. I could see them all hurrying across the moor except Sir Geoffrey Kynaston. While I was wondering what had become of him, I heard footsteps on the other side of the plantation. I stole back to the edge and looked out. Coming slowly down by the side of the ditch was Sir Geoffrey, with his gun under his arm, and whistling softly to himself. He was alone. There was no one within sight. Gentlemen, it is an awful confession which I am making to you. I stole out upon him as he passed, and stabbed him to the heart, so that he died without a groan."

Rembrandt might have found a worthy study in the faces of the men seated round that brilliant supper table. Blank horror seemed to hold them all speechless. Sir Allan, too, was trembling, and his hand, which rested upon the table, was as white as the damask cloth.

Suddenly there was a knock at the door, and a waiter entered.

"A gentleman wishes to speak with Sir Allan Beaumerville," he announced.

Sir Philip Roden rose to his feet, and pointed to the door.

"The gentleman must wait, Nillson," he answered. "Leave the room now, and see that we are not interrupted until I ring the bell."

The servant bowed and withdrew, after a wondering glance at the faces of the little party. Sir Philip Roden left his seat and, crossing the room, locked the door.

"Sir Allan Beaumerville," he said quietly, "there can be only one course to take with regard to the painful disclosures which you have laid before us to-night. If you have anything to add, please let us hear it quickly."

Sir Allan continued at once.

"I went back to my son's cottage. I washed my hands in his room, and the towel I concealed in his cabinet. Just as I was leaving he entered. What passed between us I need not mention. I took up my botanizing case and hurried away along the cliffs, and afterward was met by Mr. Thurwell's servant, with whom I returned once more to look upon my work. Then came the time when suspicion commenced to fall upon my son. I implored him to leave the country. He refused. At last he was arrested. For the father whom he can only despise he has been willing to die. To-night I had made up my mind to leave a confession of my guilt and fly. My plans are changed. Only a few hours ago I looked into the face of one whom I had never thought to see again in this world. Her advice I am now following. To her care I entrusted my confession, and to your ears I have detailed it. My story is done, gentlemen. Sir Philip Roden, I place myself in your hands."

His last words had been almost drowned by a clamorous knocking at the closed door. When he had ceased, Sir Philip Roden rose and opened it. Two men entered at once, followed by Mr. Benjamin Levy. The men recognized Sir Philip, and saluted.

"What is your business?" he asked.

"We hold a warrant for the arrest of Sir Allan Beaumerville, sir," was the respectful answer, "granted on the sworn information of Mr. Benjamin Levy there, by Mr. Pulsford, half an hour ago. Which is he, sir?"

Sir Philip pointed to where his late host was standing a little away from the others, his hand resting on the carved knob of his high-backed chair, and his eyes fixed wildly upon them. The man advanced to him at once.

"You are my prisoner, Sir Allan Beaumerville," he said quietly. "I hold a warrant here for your arrest on the charge of having murdered Sir Geoffrey Kynaston on the 12th of August of last year."

Those who were watching Sir Allan's face closely saw only a slight change. Its deep pallor grew only a shade more livid, and there was a faint twitching of the features. Then with an awful light flashing into his burning eyes, and a cry which rang through the whole building, he threw up his arms and fell like a log across the hearth rug. Every one sprang up and crowded round him, but the physician pushed his way through the group and fell on his knees. He was up again in a moment, looking very pale and awed.

"Keep back, gentlemen; keep back, please," he said in a low tone. "Never mind about the brandy, Sir Philip. Every one had better go away. These people from Scotland Yard need not wait. Sir Allan will answer for his crime at a higher court than ours."

And so it indeed was. Tragical justice had herself added the last and final scene to the drama. Sir Allan Beaumerville's lips were closed for ever in this world.

XLI

INNOCENT

An hour or two before the *dénouement* of Sir Allan Beaumerville's supper party, his brougham had driven up to Mr. Thurwell's town house, and had set down a lady there. She had rung the bell and inquired for Miss Thurwell.

The footman who answered the door looked dubious.

"Miss Thurwell was in, certainly, but she was unwell and saw no visitors, and it was late. Could he take her name?"

The lady handed him a note.

"If you will take this to Miss Thurwell, and tell her that I am waiting, I think that she will see me," she said quietly.

The man took it, and, somewhat impressed by the bearing and manner of speech of the unknown lady, he showed her into the morning-room, and ringing for Miss Thurwell's maid, handed her the note and awaited the decision. It was speedily given. The lady was to be shown to her room at once.

The agonizing suspense in which Helen had been living for the last few days had laid a heavy hand upon her. Her cheeks were thin, and had been woefully pale until the sudden excitement of this visit had called up a faint hectic flush which had no kindred with the color of health. Her form, too, seemed to have shrunken, and the loose tea-gown which she wore enhanced the fragility of her appearance. She had been sitting in a low chair before the fire, with her head buried in her hands, but when her visitor was announced she was standing up with her dry, bright eyes eagerly fixed upon the woman who stood on the threshold. The door was closed, and they looked at one another for a moment in silence.

To an artist, the figures of these two women, each so intensely interested in the other, and each possessed of a distinctive and impressive personality, would have been full of striking suggestions. Helen, in her loose gown of a soft dusky orange hue, and with no harsher light thrown upon her features than the subdued glow of a shaded lamp, and occasional flashes of the firelight which gleamed in her too-brilliant eyes, seemed to have lost none of her beauty. All her surroundings, too, went to enhance it: the delicately-toned richness of the coloring around, the faintly perfumed air, the indefinable suggestion of feminine daintiness, so apparent in all the appointments of the little chamber. From the semi-darkness of her position near the door Helen's visitor brought her eager scrutiny to an end. She advanced a little into the room and spoke.

"You are Helen Thurwell?" she said softly. "Sir Allan Beaumerville has bidden me come to you. You have read his note?"

"Yes, yes, I have read it," she answered quickly. "He tells me that you have news—news that concerns Bernard Maddison. Is it anything that will prove his innocence?"

"It is already proved."

Helen gave a great cry and sank into a low chair. She had no doubts; her visitor's tone and manner forbade them. But the tension of her feelings, strung to such a pitch of nervousness, gave way all at once. Her whole frame was shaken with passionate sobs. The burning agony of her grief was dissolved in melting tears.

And the woman whose glad tidings had brought this change stood all the while patient and motionless. Once, when Helen had first yielded to her emotion, she had made a sudden movement forward, and a sweet, sympathetic light had flashed for a moment over her pale features. But something had seemed to restrain her, some chilling memory which had checked her first impulse, and made her resume her former attitude of quiet reserve. She stood there and waited. By and by Helen looked up and started to her feet.

"I had almost forgotten; I am so sorry," she said. "Do sit down, please, and tell me everything, and who you are. You have brought me the best news I ever had in my life," she added with a little burst of gratitude.

Her visitor remained standing—remained grave, silent, and unresponsive; yet there was nothing forbidding about her appearance. Looking into her soft gray eyes and face still beautiful, though wrinkled and colorless, Helen was conscious of a strange feeling of attraction toward her, a sort of unexplained affinity which women in trouble or distress often feel for one another, but which the sterner fiber of man's nature rarely admits of. She moved impulsively forward, and stretched out her hands in mute invitation, but there was no response. If anything, indeed, her visitor seemed to shrink a little away from her.

"You ask me who I am," she said softly. "I am Sir Allan Beaumerville's wife; I am Bernard Maddison's mother."

Helen sank back upon her chair, perfectly helpless. This thing was too much for her to grasp. She looked up at the woman who had spoken these marvelous words, half frightened, altogether bewildered.

"You are Sir Allan Beaumerville's wife," she repeated slowly. "I do not understand; I never knew that he was married. And Bernard Maddison his son!"

Helen sat quite still for a moment. Then light began to stream in upon her darkened understanding. Suddenly she sprang to her feet.

"Who was it? then, who killed—Oh, my God, I see it all now. It was—"

She ceased, and looked at her visitor with blanched cheeks. A low, tremulous cry of horror broke from Lady Beaumerville's white lips. Her calmness seemed gone. She was trembling from head to foot.

"God help him! it was my husband who killed Sir Geoffrey Kynaston," she cried; "and the sin is on my head."

Helen was scarcely less agitated. She caught hold of the edge of the table to steady herself. Her voice seemed to come from a great distance.

"Sir Allan! I do not understand. Why did he do that horrible thing?"

"Sir Geoffrey Kynaston and my husband were mortal enemies," answered Lady Beaumerville, her voice scarcely raised above a whisper. "Mine was the fault, mine the guilt. Alas! alas!"

The stately head with its wealth of silvery white hair was buried in her hands. Her attitude, the agony which quivered in her tone dying away in her final expression of despair like chords of wild, sad music, and above all her likeness to the man she loved, appealed irresistibly to Helen. A great pity filled her heart. She passed her arm round Lady Beaumerville, and drew her on to the sofa.

There were no words between them then. Only, after a while, Helen asked quietly:

"Sir Allan—must he confess?"

"It is already done," her visitor answered. "To-morrow the world will know his guilt and my shame. Ah," she cried, her voice suddenly changing, "I had forgotten. Turn your face away from me, Helen Thurwell, and listen."

In the silence of the half-darkened chamber she told her story—told it in the low, humbled tone of saintly penitence, rising sometimes into passion and at others falling into an agonized whisper. She spoke of her girlhood, of the falsehood by which she had been cheated into a loveless marriage, and the utter misery which it had brought. Then she told her of her sin, committed in a moment of madness after her husband's brutal treatment, and so soon repented of. Lightly she touched upon her many years of solitary penance, her whole lifetime dedicated willingly and earnestly to the expiation of that dark stain, and of the coming to her quiet home of the awful news of Sir Geoffrey's murder. In her old age her sin had risen up against her, remorseless and unsatiated. Almost she had counted herself forgiven. Almost she had dared to hope that she might die in peace. But sin is everlasting, its punishment eternal.

Here her voice died away in a sudden fit of weakness, as though the fierce consuming passion of her grief had eaten away all her strength. But in a moment or two she continued.

"I thought my husband dead, and the sin my son's," she whispered. "They sent to me to come to his trial, that they might hear from my lips what they thought evidence against him. I would have died first. Then came a young man who told me all, and I came with him to England. I have seen and spoken with my husband. On his table he showed me signed papers. His confession was ready. 'This night,' he said, 'I take my leave of the world.' Thank God, he forgave me, and I him. We have stood hand-in-hand together, and the past between us is no more. He bade me come here, and I have come. I have seen the woman my son loves, and I am satisfied. Now I will go."

Her eyes rested for a moment upon Helen, full of an inexpressible yearning, and there had been a faint, sad wistfulness in her tone. But when she had finished, she drew her cloak around her, and turned toward the door.

Helen let her take a few steps, scarcely conscious of her intention. Then she sprang up, and laid her hand upon Lady Beaumerville's shoulder.

"You are his mother," she said softly. "May I not be your daughter?"

"Helen, Helen, I have strange news for you!"

The room was in semi-darkness, for the fire had burnt low and the heavily shaded lamp gave out but little light. Side by side on the low sofa, two women, hand-in-hand, had been sobbing out their grief to one another. On the threshold, peering with strained eyes through the gloom, was Mr. Thurwell, his light overcoat, hastily thrown over his evening clothes, still unremoved.

She rose to her feet, and he saw the dim outline of her graceful figure, even a vision of her white, tear-stained face.

"The truth has come out," he said gravely. "To-morrow Bernard will be free. The man who killed Sir Geoffrey Kynaston has confessed."

"Confessed!" Helen repeated. "Where? To whom?"

"To the Home Secretary, to a party of us as we sat at supper, his guests at the club. Helen, be prepared for a great surprise. The murderer was Sir Allan Beaumerville."

"I know it," Helen whispered hoarsely across the room. "Have they arrested Sir Allan?"

Mr. Thurwell's surprise at his daughter's knowledge was forgotten in the horror of the scene which her words had called up. Across the darkened air of the little chamber it seemed to float again before his shuddering memory, and he stretched out his hands for a moment before his face.

"Arrested him—no!" he answered in an agitated tone. "I have seen nothing so awful in all my life. He made his confession at the head of his table, the police were clamoring outside with a warrant, and while we all sat dazed and stupefied, he fell backward—dead."

A cry rang through the little chamber, a sudden wail, half of relief, half of anguish. Helen fell upon her knees by the side of the sofa. Mr. Thurwell started, and moved forward.

"Who is that?" he asked quickly. "I thought you were alone."

"It is his wife," Helen answered, not without some fear. "See, she has fainted."

Mr. Thurwell hesitated only for a moment. Then his face filled with compassion.

"God help her," he said solemnly. "I will send the women up to you, and a doctor. God help her!"

XLII

At Last

The morning sunlight lay upon that wonderful fair garden of the villa. The tall white lilies, the scarlet poppies, the clustering japonica, the purple hyacinths, and the untrimmed brilliantly-flowering shrubs, lifted their heads before its sweet, quickening warmth, and yielded up their perfume to the still clear air. The languorous hour of noon was still far off. It was the birth of a southern summer day, and everything was fresh and pure, untainted by the burning, enervating heat which was soon to dry up the sweetness from the earth, and the freshness from the slightly moving breeze. Away on the brown hills, fading into a transparent veil of blue, the bright dresses of the peasant women stooping at their toil, the purple glory of the vineyards, and the deep, quiet green of the olive groves—all these simple characteristics of the pastoral landscape were like brilliant patches of coloring upon a fitting background. Soon the haze of the noonday heat would hang upon the earth, deadening the purity of its color, and making the air heavy and oppressive with faint overladen perfumes. But as yet the sun lay low in the heavens, and the earth beneath was like a fair still picture.

The heavy lumbering coach which connected the little town with the outside world was drawn up at the gate of the villa, and twice the quaintly sounding horn had broken the morning stillness. It was a moment of farewell, a farewell not for days or for years, but forever.

Their words denied it, yet in their hearts was that certain conviction, and much of that peculiar sadness which it could not fail to bring. Yet she would not have them stay for the end. She had bidden them go, and the hour had come.

Too weak to walk, or even sit upright, they had laid her upon a sofa in front of the open windows, through which the perfume from the garden below stole sweetly in on the bosom of the slowly stirring south wind. On one side of her stood a tall mild-faced priest from the brotherhood who had made their home in the valley below, on the other were Bernard and his wife, her son and daughter.

There was no doubt that she was dying, that she was indeed very near death. Yet she was sending them away from her. The brief while they three had lived there together had been like a late autumn to her life, which had blossomed forth with sweet moments of happiness such as she had never dreamed of. And now her summons had come, and she was ready. In her last moments she must return once more to that absolute detachment from all save spiritual things in which for many years she had lived, a saintly, blessed woman. So she had bidden them go, even her son, even that fair sweet English girl who had been more than a daughter to her. She had bidden them go. The last words had been spoken, for the last time her trembling lips had been pressed to her son's. Yet they lingered.

And there came of a sudden, floating through the window, the sweet slow chiming of the matins bell from the monastery below. Almost it seemed as though the soft delicate air through which it passed, the exquisite beauty of the sloping landscape and old garden over which it traveled, had had a rarefying influence upon the sound itself, and had mellowed its tones into a strain of the most perfect music throbbing with harmony and dying away in faint, delicious murmurs. They stood and listened to it, and a sudden light swept into the pale face upon the couch. They all looked at her in a sudden awe. The priest sank upon his knees by her side, and prayed. Long desired, it had come at last at this most fitting moment. The glory of death shone in her face, and the light of a coming release flashed across her features. She died as few can die, as one who sees descending from the clouds a long-promised happiness, and whose heart and soul go forth to meet it with joy.

They stayed and buried her under a cypress tree, in a sunny corner of the monastery churchyard, where a plain black cross marked her grave. Then they turned their faces toward England.

AND IN ENGLAND THEY WERE happy. For the first few years they chose to live almost in retirement at their stately home, for with no desire for notoriety, Sir Bernard Beaumerville found himself on his return from abroad the most famous man in London. To escape from the lionizing that threatened him, Helen and he shut themselves up at Beaumerville Court, and steadfastly refused all invitations. Of their life there little need be said, save that to each it was the perfect realization of dreams which had once seemed too sweet to be possible.

And in the midst of it all he found time to write. From the quaint oak library, where he had gone back into the old realms of thoughtland, he sent out into the world a great work. Once more the columns of the daily papers and the reviews were busy with his name, and for once all were unanimous. All bowed down before his genius, and his name was written into the history of his generation. Through a burning sea of trouble, of intellectual disquiet and mental agony, he had emerged strengthened at every point. Love had fulfilled upon him its great office. He was humanized. The impersonality, which is the student's bane, which deepens into misanthropy, cynicism, and pessimism, yielded before it. The voices of his own children became dearer to him than the written thoughts of dead men. It was the reassertion of nature, and it was well for him. So was he saved, so was his genius unfettered from the cloying weight of too much abstract thought, which at one time, save for his artistic instincts, would have plunged him into the morass of pedantry and turned his genius into a pillar of salt. A woman had saved him, and through the long years of their life together he never forgot it.

THE END

A Note About the Author

E. Phillips Oppenheim (1866–1946) was a British writer who rose to prominence in the late nineteenth century. He was born in London to a leather merchant and began working at an early age. Oppenheim spent nearly 20 years in the family business, while juggling a freelance writing career. He composed short stories and eventually novels with more than 100 titles to his credit. His first novel, *Expiation* was published in 1886 followed by *The Mystery of Mr. Bernard Brown* (1896) and *The Long Arm of Mannister* (1910). Oppenheim is best known for his signature tales full of action and espionage.

A Note from the Publisher

Spanning many genres, from non-fiction essays to literature classics to children's books and lyric poetry, Mint Edition books showcase the master works of our time in a modern new package. The text is freshly typeset, is clean and easy to read, and features a new note about the author in each volume. Many books also include exclusive new introductory material. Every book boasts a striking new cover, which makes it as appropriate for collecting as it is for gift giving. Mint Edition books are only printed when a reader orders them, so natural resources are not wasted. We're proud that our books are never manufactured in excess and exist only in the exact quantity they need to be read and enjoyed.

bookfinity™

Discover more of your favorite classics with Bookfinity™.

- Track your reading with custom book lists.
- Get great book recommendations for your personalized Reader Type.
- Add reviews for your favorite books.
- AND MUCH MORE!

Visit **bookfinity.com** and take the fun Reader Type quiz to get started.

Enjoy our classic and modern companion pairings!

Classic & Modern